RAGGED
LAKE

RAGGED LAKE

RON CORBETT

A FRANK YAKABUSKI MYSTERY

Published by ECW Press
665 Gerrard Street East
Toronto, Ontario, Canada M4M 1Y2
416-694-3348 / info@ecwpress.com

RECYCLED
Paper made from
recycled material
FSC® C103567
www.fsc.org

LIBRARY AND ARCHIVES CANADA
CATALOGUING IN PUBLICATION

Corbett, Ron, 1959–, author
Ragged Lake / Ron Corbett.

(A Frank Yakabuski mystery)
Issued in print and electronic formats.
ISBN 978-1-77041-394-8 (softcover)
ALSO ISSUED AS: 978-1-77305-094-2 (PDF),
978-1-77305-095-9 (EPUB)

I. TITLE.

PS8605.07155R33 2017   C813'.6
C2017-902413-2   C2017-902992-4

Cover design: Michel Vrana
Cover photo: cabin in the woods © Thomas_
Zsebok_Images/iStockPhoto; stormy winter
sky © dimitris_k/iStockPhoto

The publication of *Ragged Lake* has been generously supported by the Canada Council for
the Arts, which last year invested $153 million to bring the arts to Canadians throughout the
country, and by the Government of Canada through the Canada Book Fund. *Nous remercions le
Conseil des arts du Canada de son soutien. L'an dernier, le Conseil a investi 153 millions de dollars pour
mettre de l'art dans la vie des Canadiennes et des Canadiens de tout le pays. Ce livre est financé en partie
par le gouvernement du Canada.* We also acknowledge the support of the Ontario Arts Council
(OAC), an agency of the Government of Ontario, which last year funded 1,737 individual artists
and 1,095 organizations in 223 communities across Ontario for a total of $52.1 million, and the
contribution of the Government of Ontario through the Ontario Book Publishing Tax Credit
and the Ontario Media Development Corporation.

Ontario
Ontario Media Development
Corporation

ONTARIO ARTS COUNCIL
CONSEIL DES ARTS DE L'ONTARIO
an Ontario government agency
un organisme du gouvernement de l'Ontario

Canada Council
for the Arts

Conseil des Arts
du Canada

Canadä

For Frank Kuiack

AUTHOR'S NOTE

This is a work of fiction. All places and characters are imagined. While the story takes place somewhere on the Northern Divide, there are no literal depictions of any city or town on the Divide.

A. A violent order is a disorder; and
B. great disorder is an order. These
two things are one. (Pages of illustrations.)

      "Connoisseur of Chaos,"
      Wallace Stevens

CHAPTER ONE

The cabin had been built by the headwaters of the Springfield River, not far from Five Mile Camp where the Cree who worked for O'Hearn Forest Products once lived. This was on the Northern Divide, where rivers ran north and south and all the trees were coniferous, a land of lush, green forests and running water — so much running water there was a low hum in the air for much of the year.

The cabin was built by a family: a man, woman, and young girl who arrived at the headwaters one spring and started hauling lumber from the abandoned work camp. When O'Hearn learned of the theft, it sent a bull rigger to investigate; but when the man came back to Springfield, he told the company to forget about it. The family was coco. The trusses and frames had been put together without the aid of a mitre, he explained, so there was a demented-playhouse slant to the roofline. The door was rough-hewn planks. The windows were mismatched sizes. The strangest part of all was perhaps the roof, which was made of beer and pop cans flattened to resemble tin shingles. From a distance, the rigger said, laughing at the memory, the cabin looked like a Christmas tree about to keel over.

"They will be gone in a year," he promised. "Don't waste your time and money on lawyers. Forget about them."

The family rarely left the cabin, or the land near the cabin, going only occasionally to the nearby village of Ragged Lake to cash a cheque the man had mailed to him care of the Mattamy Fishing Lodge. There, they would buy provisions from the kitchen. Except for these two interactions — cashing a cheque with a bartender, buying food from a cook — the family seemed to have no other dealings with people.

"Want anything else this month?" the cook would sometimes ask the man. "I can give you a deal on some eggs. Or whisky. Would you like whisky? I can talk to the bartender about getting you some."

"The eggs won't make it," the man would answer, "and I don't need whisky."

"What man up here doesn't need whisky?"

"Bad for you —" and here the squatter would point to his head and make a sound like a gun going off "— blows off your head."

"But you put it back on with more whisky," the cook would answer. "That's how whisky works."

But the squatter never bought whisky. Just dried milk, Red River cereal, coffee, sugar, flour, and other non-perishables that he packaged carefully into a Woods rucksack. He'd lift it onto his back and walk five miles back to his cabin. He was a middle-aged man with long, blond hair matted and unwashed — black flies and sumac buds mashed into the strands of his hair in summer, ice and snow in winter. Tall and thin, he usually wore mechanic bibs and flannel shirts, and his skin was that of an old man, weather-scarred and burnished. The woman was tall and beautiful. The young girl looked like her mother.

No one in Ragged Lake ever visited the family, and, with Five Mile Camp long abandoned, people rarely even came close. The cabin was not on a snowmobile trail. The fishing on the Springfield was generally considered poor until the river widened five miles to the south. The cabin was as cut off from people and the daily activities of people as an archaeological ruin waiting to be discovered.

It was for this reason no one in Ragged Lake could say with certainty when the family was murdered.

It was a tree-marker working for O'Hearn near the head-waters, marking pine to be cut, who found them, surprised when he saw the cabin, because it was on none of his maps. When the boy approached, he caught the scent of something warm and tart, a broad, sweet scent on a day that had until then carried only the sharp, thin smells of winter. Pine gum and frozen water. Spruce and falling snow.

The boy never went inside the cabin. Peered through a window and then took off for Ragged Lake, making good time on his snowshoes, then telling the bartender at the Mattamy something bad had happened by the headwaters of the Springfield. Something that shouldn't have happened, because no cabin should have been out there on O'Hearn timber rights, on O'Hearn land. Something evil-bad had happened.

They needed to phone someone.

CHAPTER TWO

The call was logged in at the Cork's Town detachment of the Springfield Regional Police at 6:17 p.m. on a Tuesday evening, the first week of February. An elderly dispatcher took the call, asked a few questions, then reached for an incident-report form and repeated most of his questions. The call was logged out at 6:29. After that, the dispatcher hit a key on his computer and a list of names and phone numbers appeared on his screen. He dialed the third on the list.

When the phone was answered, the dispatcher said, "Yak, I know you're gone for the day, but I just took a call from some bartender at a fishing lodge up in Ragged Lake. Guy says there's been some people killed up there."

Frank Yakabuski rubbed his eyes and looked around the small apartment where he was sitting. His father had gone to the kitchen when his cellphone rang and was now running water for a kettle. Yakabuski held up one finger and his father nodded.

"People killed? What are you talking about, Donnie?"

"It was all a jumble, Yak. You need to talk to the guy. The Mattamy Fishing Lodge. That's where he said he was phoning from. I've got the number."

"The Mattamy? Up in Ragged Lake? Since when do we take calls for Ragged Lake?"

"The past four years, Yak. You didn't get the memo? Oh, right, major crimes. Excuse me, Senior Detective Frank Yaka-freakin'-buski."

"Just asking, Donnie. Is that because of the detachment closing in High River?"

"You got it. You must be one hell of a detective."

"All right, all right. Give me the number."

"Got it right here. How's Billy, by the way?"

Yakabuski stared at his father. His dad was looking out his kitchen window, waiting for the kettle to boil, a Hudson's Bay blanket on his knees and an open paperback on his lap. Three years ago, his father had walked into the Stedman's department store in High River looking for mosquito netting for his hunt cabin only to be followed a minute later by a stickup crew from Springfield. Yakabuski's father saw them come in. One man stationing himself by the front door. The other two heading toward a back office. His father followed the two heading toward the office before shouting: "Cops! Put your hands where I can see 'em!"

He was old-school. From a generation that thought if a cop told you to put your hands where he could see them, that's what you did. Instead, the two men turned, craned their necks to see if they were missing something, then raised the sawed-off shotguns they had hidden beneath their coats and fired. It was only the tremendous bulk of Yakabuski's dad that saved him. He took the blast in his hips and stomach instead of his chest. He still ended up face down in the toy aisle of the Stedman's with Teenage Mutant Ninja Turtle figurines raining down on him. But he didn't die.

"He's good. Thanks for asking."

"Never gets any easier, does it? If there's anything Linda or I can do, all you have to do is ask, Yak. You know that, right?"

"I know that, Donnie. Thanks."

"You can't do it all yourself. There are plenty of people down here who think the world of your dad. You could get all the help you needed if you just—"

"Still got that number, Donnie?"

"Right. Here it is."

• • •

Yakabuski walked into the kitchen to find his dad still staring out the window. The kettle had boiled and then clicked off.

"You have to make a call?"

"I do."

"You can make it here if you want."

"I can make it in the car, too."

"It won't matter?"

"I don't see how."

His dad nodded and the trace of a smile slipped across his face. He turned his wheelchair to look at his son.

"When did you start taking calls for Ragged Lake?"

6

"Four years ago, Donnie says. After the feds closed down their detachment in High River. Any major crime comes to us, apparently. There's a bartender at the Mattamy says some people have been killed up there."

Ragged Lake was high in the North Country, right on the Northern Divide, about four hundred miles from Springfield.

"Killed how?"

"Donnie didn't know."

"How many?"

"He didn't know."

"Fuckin' Donnie. How would you even get to Ragged Lake this time of year? You can't drive any of the logging roads."

"If the lodge is open, maybe there's a plane."

"Maybe."

The sun was about to sink below a line of low-rise apartments on a bluff the other side of the river. For the past thirty minutes its trajectory had cast an oblong shadow across the city, moving over the highways and subdivisions, the rail line and glass office towers downtown. The towers refracted the last of the rays and looked for a second like the flames you sometimes see shooting from a spent fire. Then the sun slipped below the bluff and the city was covered in a shadow that turned in seconds from grey to cobalt to black.

"I better go make that call."

CHAPTER THREE

Yakabuski started his Jeep, put it in gear, and headed toward the on-ramp for Highway 7. He was going to his ice-fishing hut before heading home. The ling had been running well and if there was anything to this call, he wouldn't be back for a few days.

When he was on the highway, he punched the number Donnie had given him.

The phone was answered on the first ring. "Mattamy Fishing Lodge."

"This is Detective Frank Yakabuski with the Springfield Regional Police. Someone up there phoned and reported—"

"You want the kid."

And the line went quiet. A few seconds later, another voice came on. A younger voice. Yakabuski repeated his introduction, then said, "What's happening up there, son?"

"There's people dead, sir. That's what's happening up here."

"At the Mattamy?"

"No sir, by some old Indian camp out by the headwaters of the Springfield. Where there ain't supposed to be no cabin and there ain't supposed to be no people."

"What were you doing out there, son?"

"Marking pine for O'Hearn. It's got to be some sort of squatters' cabin. That's why I checked it out. I was thinking maybe the company should know about it. I was just marking pine and then . . . man . . . oh man . . ."

"Take another drink, son."

"Sorry?"

"Take another drink of whatever you have in front of you. Then tell me what you've seen."

"Thank you, sir."

The boy's voice was a little steadier when he came back. He said, "I was out marking trees for O'Hearn, the bush around Ragged Lake. I'm by some old bush camp late in the afternoon when I see a cabin. It's a strange-looking cabin. You gotta see it. I go check it out. I knock on the door but no one answers, so I look through a window — curious, you know, I've always been that way, gets me into all sorts of trouble. Once, in Elmira, I was driving a logging truck and I went past—"

"Take another drink, son."

"Thank you, sir."

Back on the phone, the tree-marker said at first he couldn't make out what was inside the cabin, but then his eyes adjusted and he could make out a couch, an airtight, some floor-to-ceiling curtains he guessed were room dividers. Then he saw a man lying on the floor. A man without a chest.

"No, that ain't right. Maybe he had a chest. I can't say for sure. It's just that he was . . . he was . . ."

"There were two parts to him."

"That's right, sir. There were two freakin' parts to him."

"You said dead *people*. What else did you see?"

"I saw a woman. Lying behind a couch. A naked woman. Oh, I don't know if she was *naked* naked, like, but she didn't have any pants on. I could see her legs. There was blood everywhere."

"Did you go inside?"

"Hell, no. I didn't know what was going on. I headed off to Ragged Lake as fast as I could. Got the bartender here to call you."

Yakabuski didn't say anything for a minute. He had been to Ragged Lake only once before, fishing with his father when he was a boy. He remembered taking days to get there. Then he remembered they had gone fishing at the Goyette Reservoir first, so it wouldn't have taken days.

"Let me speak to the bartender."

"Yes, sir."

The first voice came back and Yakabuski said, "Do you know this kid?"

"No. He's a tree-marker for O'Hearn. He don't live 'round here."

"Do you know who lives in that cabin he's talking about?"

"Squatters. A man and a woman. You'd see 'em in town sometimes."

"Know their names?"

"No."

"Anyone in town know their names?"

"Doubt it. They're squatters."

"How do you get to Ragged Lake this time of year?"

"There's no road in the winter. You can take a bush plane, or there's a train runs out of High River every second day."

"What if you don't have a bush plane and you're not in High River?"

"Then you're taking a snowmobile down the old S and P Line. From where you are, I'd say it's about ten hours."

CHAPTER FOUR

Yakabuski took the Cork's Town exit from Highway 7 and began driving down narrow streets. Cork's Town was where Springfield began, where the first settlers came — also the place everyone left as soon as they had the chance. Which didn't make a lot of sense to Yakabuski when he looked at where they went. The suburbs, built around Cork's Town — on the lowest land in the Valley, so homes were flooded every spring and some of them never smelled quite right when you went inside. Or the Nosoto housing projects the other side of the river. Or the high-rise condominium towers, gated and beached like dead fish twenty miles downriver.

He drove past the abandoned warehouses and steerage-forward buildings, down a street of lumbermen's cottages that never got torn down, for some reason. Within a few minutes, he was clear of Cork's Town and driving beside the Springfield, at one of the widest points on the river, a big sweeping curve of snow-filled river that cut through the night like a plume of smoke. Yakabuski followed the river and five miles on took a hard left. He stopped to open the gate to a closed-for-the-season trailer park and cut through, out onto an ice road. There was a small colony of ice-fishing huts on Entrance Bay, and Yakabuski, as he did every year, had the last hut on the road.

Likely a domestic. That's what he was telling himself when he parked. If you were going to live in a squatter's cabin five miles outside a ghost town — which is what Ragged Lake was these days, ever since they closed the pulp and paper mill more than a decade ago — well, you never wanted to be too cynical about certain things in this world, but if you were going to do a thing like that, plus keep a gun around, you were just asking for trouble. Like anyone wouldn't go mad-trapper crazy after two winters.

He unlocked the door to his hut, threw some kindling into the airtight, lit the wood, and took the wooden board off the hole augered in the ice. He took his rig down, and, when the fire was burning nicely, he slid the tail of a whitefish over a number-six hook. He counted out line and stopped at twenty feet. Took a handful of tails from the bait bucket and threw them into the hole. The scales were silver, with a sheen, and, as they sank through the black water, Yakabuski thought for a moment they looked like a splash of shooting stars.

Yakabuski had been with the Springfield Regional Police twelve years, the last eight in major crimes. He was from High River, where he was related to half the town — High River being the oldest Polish settlement in Canada, a thing you would never deduce from the name. The town was in the Upper Springfield Valley, near the western arm of the Northern Divide, and already named when the Poles arrived.

Yakabuski was big for a Polish kid. Six-foot-four, more than 230 pounds by the time he was sixteen. He towered over his schoolmates, his cousins — everyone in High River, pretty much. It was assumed by most that he would join the High River police force after high school, like his father, or take on with O'Hearn, like his uncles, where his size and last name alone would pretty much assure he would be running a bush camp before he turned thirty.

He did neither. Not many Poles from the Upper Springfield Valley had wanderlust, but Frank Yakabuski was the rare exception. He wanted to see the world, and so he enlisted in the army the day after graduating high school, a light infantry battalion garrisoned out west, about as far from the Northern Divide as possible. There are officers yet serving in the Third Battalion who claim he was the best light infantry soldier they'd ever seen. An utter natural. His stamina was legendary, winning him every Ironman contest he entered at the garrison. In the field, he could go days without food or water, track anything, predict what the weather was going to do almost to the minute. In hand-to-hand combat, he had no peers. He was the first one in his battalion chosen for tours in Bosnia and Afghanistan, was seconded to a United Nations quick response team, and got written up in dispatches because of it. For "Heroism" in the Pashwan Valley, which is as good as it gets for Dispatches, although the specifics were left vague.

It seemed Yakabuski could go anywhere he wanted in the army. Yet he mustered out after eleven years. No good reason ever given to his family. A year later, he was living in Springfield, working for the regional police. He was quickly seconded again, this time to a federal task force set up during the biker wars in Quebec. Yakabuski was a star recruit, as no one knew him in Montreal or Buffalo, and when he grew out his hair, put on a leather jacket, and stopped smiling, he looked the part. One big, mean mother biker.

Yakabuski kept jigging the hook and tail, looked around his ice hut, and began to laugh, imagining Papa Paquette sitting there beside him, fishing for ling. Papa hated everything about the outdoors. Like most bikers. He used to call Yakabuski a bush-boy, and Yakabuski called him a Crescent Street dandy. Until Yakabuski testified against him. Then the head of the Popeyes motorcycle gang had other words to describe his former friend. Yakabuski had been undercover nearly three years. When he returned to Springfield, he was transferred to major crimes and made a senior detective.

Springfield would never be home to him. It was a northern city of nearly a million people, built where three rivers came together in a low, meandering valley that collected, because it was the low point in the valley, all the flotsam, stray logs, and lost souls within five hundred miles. Springfield was the ultimate catch basin. A hopped-up, biker-torqued, mills-running-all-night, jingle-jangled crossroads on the edge of North America's great boreal forest. Yakabuski had grown to both love and fear the city.

He pulled up his line shortly before midnight and put the board over the hole. Nothing. Not so much as a bite. Two nights earlier, the ling had been running so well he had thrown back more than a dozen. He thought about that a minute, then scolded himself for being silly. That was just

15

old bush-camp nonsense, believing that a bad fishing trip, if it happened right before a journey, was the sign of bad travelling ahead. Superstitious nonsense. Besides, even if it had been true once, no one believed in portents or signs anymore.

. . .

The call came in to a throwaway cellphone almost three thousand miles from Springfield. The man who answered sat on a lounge chair beside an infinity pool with a view of the Gulf of Mexico. He was middle-aged, in good shape, with thick, bulbous arms covered in tattoos, legs the size of fence posts. He went by many names, but the most common was Cambio. He waited, and after a while he heard a voice say: "We may have a problem."

Cambio didn't speak. Kept staring at a cruise ship as it dropped anchor in a small bay, the foredeck speckled with tourists in their brightly coloured vacation clothes. When he was a boy, there had not been a single hotel in this village. He didn't consider himself an old man, but he was starting to think like one, already missing the way things had once been.

The man on the other end cleared his throat and said, "Some people have been killed outside town. Squatters. The cops are on their way."

Cambio shifted his weight on the lounge chair and watched a tender bringing the first of the tourists to shore.

"Was it you?" he asked.

"What? No. Fuck no. We had nothing to do with it." A longer pause this time, the man who'd placed the call clearing his throat and taking several deep breaths before continuing. "It wasn't us. I swear. We don't know what happened. They were just squatters. No one fuckin' knew 'em. We're just hearing about it. The cops are coming tomorrow."

The tender pulled up to the wharf. Cambio fantasized briefly about an RPG round hitting the bow, could see in his mind's eye the explosion, the fire, the plumes of smoke afterward. No more tourists. As simple as that.

"Squatters?"

"That's right. They were living by an abandoned bush camp about five miles outside town."

"It wasn't you?"

"No. I swear."

"Does our friend in Springfield know what's happened?"

"Yes. I've already told him. I wanted to make sure you knew, too."

"You do not think he would tell me?"

"I'm not sure. That's not what I'm saying. I just thought you should know."

"All right. Don't do anything. Stay indoors. Tell me what the police are doing when they get there." Cambio hung up and scratched the underside of his chin with the phone for several minutes, wondering if he was being lied to. He wondered about it most of the day.

Just before dusk, he punched a pre-set number on his phone. When the ringing stopped, he heard the sounds of a bar. The clicking of pool balls. The laughter of drunken men. But no one spoke.

"I may need you to go to Ragged Lake," said Cambio. "You should get a crew ready."

In a nightclub in Springfield, a man put his cellphone back into the pocket of his winter parka, smiled, pushed back his hair, and ordered another quart of beer.

CHAPTER FIVE

The traffic snaking into Springfield that morning was what you would expect to find in any northern city in mid-February. Late-model sedans with salt stains etched around the tire wells. Minivans and pickup trucks. Cube vans with a metallic tradesman sign stuck to a panel somewhere. Occasionally a long-haul lumber truck, with logs stacked eight high, so tall the sun was momentarily blocked, casting the small knot of cops by the side of the highway into shadows.

The two cops with Yakabuski were young, maybe the youngest in the Ident department, which made sense to him. Heading to the Northern Divide in the dead of winter — that was an assignment senior Ident cops got out of by not answering their phones late at night. The two constables were called Buckham and Downey. Local boys — Donnie Buckham so local that the town they were setting out from that morning was named after his family. Buckham's Bay.

The Springfield Regional Police had four Polaris snowmobiles, and they were going to be using the three of them being unloaded from a cargo trailer parked nearby. There wouldn't be much patrolling on the snowmobile trails for a few days. But that happened from time to time. There were many places in the Springfield policing district that weren't easy to get to during the winter, and the sleds were moved around.

"I got to tell you, Yak, this doesn't make a lot of sense to me."

Yak looked at the young constable and tried to remember his first name. He was the taller of the two. Maybe a year older. "What doesn't make sense?"

"Heading up to Ragged Lake because of a phone call. We don't even know if a crime has been committed, is that right? We get a phone call from some bar, and we're on our way to the Northern Divide?"

Matt. The shorter one was Donnie. Both spoke in Valley accents, with clipped consonants and downward inflections at the end of their sentences, rarely registering surprise, rarely lilting. Yakabuski imagined them growing up in mill towns along the Springfield, the sons of mill hands, the grandsons of mill hands, young men who would be working at a mill right now if mill jobs still existed. But they didn't. So they became paramedics. Firefighters. Cops. Both had hair cut so short it reminded Yakabuski of the hard fuzz you find on kiwis.

"Ragged Lake is our jurisdiction for major crime, Matt. Been that way, I'm told, since the High River police detachment was shut down. It's a pain in the ass, I know."

"It's more than a pain in the ass. We're going to be gone two days, at least. Can't someone check it out before we go all the way up there? At least confirm there's been a crime?"

"There's no one to send."

"Yeah, come on, Matt, lighten up," said Buckham. "Look at these machines. They're prit' near brand-new. This is going to be a blast."

"I don't mind a sled trip," said Downey. "I just don't like wasting my time. Does this make sense to you? We're the guys checking out a call from Ragged Lake? Why don't we check out the dark side of the fuckin' moon on our way back?"

"It's our call," repeated Yakabuski. "Let's quit wasting our time and get going."

"Fuck. Can't that tree-marker send us a photo or something? I bet you it's all a fuckin' joke."

"Why don't we get him to fill out the police report, too?"

"That's not what I'm saying."

"You don't know what you're saying, Matt." And with that, Yakabuski gave the cop an angry look. "We can't ask that tree-marker to investigate. Even a little. This could be a homicide case with no one in custody. Do you know what you'd be asking that kid to do?"

The men unloading the snowmobiles had stopped talking and were now staring into the forest, as though they had just seen an animal. Downey was staring at his feet. Buckham was looking around, trying to find something to stare at. None of them knew Yakabuski well. Only by reputation. The man who brought down Papa Paquette. He was a big cop. He was annoyed. They kept staring.

Taking advantage of the unease, Yakabuski said, "Come on, let's go. I'd like to be at that cabin by mid-afternoon."

• • •

The Springfield to Portsmouth Line had been built in the early twentieth century by lumber baron James Rundle Bath, who'd wanted a railway line running through the Springfield Valley and then down the Northern Divide all the way to Lake Superior. His plan was to bring timber and newsprint to market in the American Midwest. At the time the rail line began construction, in 1903, Bath was the third richest man in British North America. The rail line became a testament to hard work and the folly that can ensue when one man accrues a king's riches.

"I've never been on the S and P in the winter," said Buckham, settling himself on the seat of the Polaris and turning over the engine. "My dad used to fish Lac Claire from time to time and we'd take a truck up. Never was on the train."

"You weren't missing much," said Yakabuski. "The truck was probably quicker."

Originally slated to be finished in three years, the S and P took more than a decade to complete. Not a foot of track along the Northern Divide was laid without blasting. Not a mile of laid track made sense when you looked at a map, if you simply wanted to go as quickly as possible from Town A to Town B. The route was dictated by what Bath owned, a meandering path through unsettled land, from bush camp to bush camp, timber right to timber right, until almost surprisingly the train rounded a corner, cleared the forest, and pulled out onto the shores of Lake Superior.

The day after the rail line was finished, Minnesota, Michigan, and North Dakota slapped a twenty-five percent duty on imported softwood, and Bath never brought a board foot of wood to the American Midwest. It is said the lumber baron never complained, never tried to fight the duty, and never seemed particularly vexed by what had happened. By then, Bath was the second richest man in British North America.

"When did you have to use the train?" asked Buckham.

"My dad liked to fish Lac Claire as well. He was a cop and he had a special rail pass. I was on the train quite a few times when I was a boy."

"Can't imagine it was ever busy."

"It was in the spring. You'd get the Sports coming up from the States on their way to the lodges. Some hunters in the fall."

The fishing lodges were the first to close. One by one, although it took only a decade before they were all gone. Little Joe Lodge. Arrowhead. The Northern Inn, which was owned by Bath himself and had dinnerware made by Royal Doulton, using a pattern only slightly different from one used by Queen Elizabeth II during formal state dinners. The lodges could not compete with the auto parks, motels, campgrounds, and good highways that arrived in the North Country in the mid-sixties. Could not compete with the wave of working-class families that could suddenly pitch a tent right next to a lodge and be out on the lake fishing next to some industrialist from Pittsburgh.

The mills shut down next, the sawmills closing first, no longer able to make money shipping cut wood from the Northern Divide when softwood forests were being planted and replenished by the tens of thousands of hectares down south, and long-haul trucks could get timber to market within hours. After that, the pulp and paper mills shut down. After that, the folly was also shut down, following more than a decade of what was little more than on-call service. O'Hearn was the last company still using the rail line to ship newsprint from its Ragged Lake mill, when it had enough orders.

The rail line sat there for a long time while people waited to see if the mills would reopen. Then, five years ago, the ties were pulled and the bed was turned into a recreational path, one used by hikers and cyclists in summer, cross-country skiers and snowmobilers in winter. Thanks to Bath's circuitous route, by setting out from Buckham's Bay, the cops would cut more than two hours from their journey, although it was less than a thirty-minute car ride from Cork's Town. By going off trail and bushwhacking from Kowalski Lake to Palmer's Junction, they might save another two. But they were still looking at a six- to seven-hour snowmobile journey.

There had been a storm the day before, and nearly eight inches of fresh snow was on the old rail bed. The world had that talcum powder freshness to it you get sometimes after a winter storm. All three cops took deep breaths of cold air before Yakabuski turned his snowmobile toward the first trail marker, a triangular piece of tin painted red and nailed to the trunk of a cedar around two hundred yards north.

CHAPTER SIX

The cops drove past the second-growth cedar and scrub pine surrounding Buckham's Bay, then a string of old homesteader farms, travelling beside stone fences that had been protecting bad land for nearly two centuries. When the sun had inched above the treeline, they branched away from the Springfield to follow the Matagami, a tributary that ran true north. Before long, the cedar gave way to hardwood, a few leaves still clinging to the trees, waving in the wind like badly faded flags. The cops drove past Cobden and Grimsly, then the ghost town of All Bright, settled by Mormon missionaries in the late 1890s, come all the way from Salt Lake City to build an agrarian commune on the backside of the Northern Divide. They'd left ten years later, destitute and faithless, having suffered the fate of most who tried to farm this land or were afflicted with blind faith. The missionaries caught the train finally to Springfield, where the women found employment in brothels and the men were killed on sight because of the clothes they wore. All that remained of All Bright when the cops passed that morning was the skeleton frame of an old wooden silo and some stone windrows.

They left the rail line to travel the backcountry of Wilco, hooking up with the Highland Hiking Trail and running beside that for more than an hour, climbing until they reached the top of an escarpment so high and so steep there were only bushes and small shrubs growing. Lakes appeared far below them as if in some distant land. Whispery patches of mist made it seem as though they were travelling above the clouds, and all three cops were grateful when they got off the escarpment and started the descent into a valley of white pine, a dense old-growth forest with tree trunks as large as the hulls of wooden sailing ships. They travelled in shadows cast by the giant trees, shivering in the sudden cold. When they reached the shore of Kowalski Lake, they cut across an ice road to reach the tiny hamlet of Palmer's Junction.

Palmer's Junction had been a fur trading post, then a Bath work camp during construction of the S and P. It crossed the Buffalo-Montreal Railway line on the northern shore of Kowalski Lake and was still a functioning railway yard. There were a half-dozen permanent homes in the hamlet, along with some mobile trailers for work crews, three large metal garages, and a gas pump. The gas was intended for only BMR work vehicles but was sold to anyone who drove up and asked for it. It was an understanding people had when living this far north. The men who pumped the gas at Palmer's Junction were a quickly moving secession of soon-to-be-pensioned brakemen, crippled up engineers, and bad drunks.

"Don't get many cops here," said the old man working

the pump that morning, and it didn't sound like a complaint. "Where you boys heading?"

"Ragged Lake," said Yakabuski.

"Why you have to go all the way up there?"

"I'll tell you on the way back."

The old man shrugged and didn't bother asking another question. There was smoke coming from two of the homes in the hamlet. In one house, a drape moved back and forth while the cops got gas. Nothing moved in the other. When it came time to pay, the man brought out an old credit card machine and etched the back of Yakabuski's card with a finger that looked as black and hardened as a chisel.

"They're calling for snow," said the old man when he handed Yakabuski the receipt.

"Not till tomorrow. Isn't that right?"

"That's right."

They drove on. The land around Palmer's Junction was flat, much of it clear-cut by logging companies in the seventies and eighties, the second-growth pine still short enough to allow a big clear sky to hang over them as they travelled. There were no clouds, except high in the stratosphere, where you could barely make out some wispy tails. They reached Lac Claire, the headwaters of the Matagami, but followed the shoreline because it was a large lake and looked open in the middle. Then they started to climb again, this time not the high ridges left by retreating glaciers but the tectonic plates of the Northern Divide. There were now so many frozen rivers and creeks around them, it was difficult to follow a trail, the frozen water bleeding out through the forest like ruptured veins. They drove past lakes with tributaries flowing in and out from the four major compass points.

Rivers that ran in circles. When they reached the Old Duck River, they stopped.

While the sun was bright and clear, it was a cold day and Yakabuski took a Thermos of coffee from the cargo bin of his snowmobile and passed it to Buckham. When they had all poured a cup, they knelt to drink, huddling together to try and block the wind.

"Fuck, it's cold," said Downey.

"We won't be stopped long," said Yakabuski, who had taken off his left mitt and was punching in a number on a satellite phone. The bartender answered on the second ring.

"Mattamy Fishing Lodge."

"So, how do I get to this cabin?"

"Did you get maps?"

"Yes."

"You're on the Old Duck right now, where it hooks up with the S and P?"

"Yes. Where I said we'd stop."

"All right, you want to go west from where you are, follow the river, don't follow the track into town. The old work camp is on the south shore of Old Duck. You're about fifteen miles away. The cabin is a mile west of that, on Cap Lake. There's an Indian name for that lake that's probably on your maps but everyone around here just calls it Cap Lake."

"Capimitchigama."

"That's it. The cabin is on the north shore."

"We'll be coming to the Mattamy after we're done."

"We already got your rooms."

"Good."

Before he hung up, Yakabuski heard a muffled conversation. The bartender talking to someone. He couldn't make out what was being said. Then he heard: "Tree-marker says you won't be able to miss the cabin."

. . .

Yakabuski could see the cabin a mile away. The roof was red, blue, and green, and, coming through the forest, it looked to him like a navigational buoy.

"You ever seen something like that, Yak?" asked Buckham when the three cops were standing in front of the cabin and could see that the roof had been made of old pop and beer cans — Coke, Export, Laker — the colours faded some, but not much.

"Never."

"The whole thing looks jerry-rigged to me," said Downey.

"It does," agreed Yakabuski. "I have a few uncles who would admire workmanship like this."

They took in not only the cabin but the land around it — the small frozen lake, the thick stand of spruce, surely dark most of the year, a strange place to build a cabin when the south shore was already cleared. They walked the three steps to the front door. Paused for a moment before entering. Perhaps waiting for a sign, figuring if they were truly about to enter a murder scene, then a rational, determinate world would offer some sort of portent. An animal scurrying away. A foul stench coming from the cabin. But it was a cold, clear day and there was nothing. So after a respectful pause, Yakabuski gave the door a shove.

They saw the dead man right away. He was sprawled on the floor in front of a couch, blood pooled around his body. The blood was frozen, so it was tricky walking inside the cabin, and Yakabuski entered carefully, skating around the floor as though it were an ice rink, sliding on his boots before motioning for the other cops to be careful when they came in.

The man wasn't cut in two, although Yakabuski had always doubted that part of the story. He was just twisted at a weird angle, the top of him going forty-five degrees to the right, the bottom forty-five degrees to the left, the way a body isn't meant to twist. It wasn't natural, so the kid's mind had broken it down as two separate things. Yakabuski had guessed that as soon as the tree-marker had said the man had been cut in half. He didn't need an Ident cop to confirm it, although Downey offered it up anyway.

"He's been shotgunned, Yak. Close range. Took the bulk of the spread right in the chest."

Yakabuski walked behind the couch to see the woman.

"Same thing here," said Buckham, looking down at a woman easily fifteen years younger than the man, mid-twenties maybe, long black hair, attractive face, pants rolled to her ankles, a sheet of blood where everything in the middle of her should have been.

"She's Cree," said Buckham.

The three cops knew they would have to come back the next morning to start processing the room, so they didn't bother getting bags from the cargo sled. Any work started and then stopped could be tainted evidence at a trial. Instead, they skated around the room surveying its contents. An airtight stove. A country-style hutch with cereal bowls and dinner plates. A sink below the window looking onto the lake, a bucket of frozen water beside it. A work bench against the back wall, made from an old door. A bedroom with a curtain divider and, inside the bedroom, a hardwood wardrobe and steel-posted bed. Yakabuski was looking at the bed, at the way it was made, the sheets taut and stiff-angled, the way a maid would have done it, when Downey called out.

"Yak, you better come over here."

He could tell something had just changed from the tone alone. He walked to the opposite side of the cabin, where the two cops had pushed back another curtain. Yakabuski stood at the foot of another bed. There was blood everywhere. You could hardly tell there were sheets on the bed for all the blood. Just a frozen, dull-red layer of ice where sheets should have been.

Staring up through the ice was the face of a young girl.

. . .

They stayed another half-hour, getting on their hands and knees, shining flashlight beams under the coach, the hutch, the kitchen table, the two beds, the air inside the cabin getting colder, the cops' breath becoming thicker as they worked, little white clouds that spun around their heads and then disappeared. Yakabuski had investigated cases like this before. He suspected the Ident cops had as well. These were the cases that made you go home and hug your children, your girl, your next-door neighbour, whomever you could grab, make vows to whatever god you knelt before, swear to all that was holy that you would never let your life fall apart so badly you think your best option is get off this lousy planet and take everyone you love with you.

When they were finished, the three cops stood in the

darkening gloom, saying nothing until Buckham finally said what all three were thinking.

"Yak, there's no gun here."

CHAPTER
SEVEN

They drove to Ragged Lake in darkness, down an old logging road that, according to Yakabuski's maps, was a more direct route to the village than backtracking to the S and P. With Yakabuski in the lead, they crossed frozen rivers and thick stands of spruce, Downey with his head huddled from the wind, Buckham, shorter and not seeming as bothered by the cold, travelling erect, looking around. They climbed a high ridge with old-growth pine and a view of the Northern Divide beneath the stars, a ragged, twisting spine of rock that cut through the night, throwing shadows to both sides. In the distance, sat the massive body of water that was Ragged Lake, stretching north like an inland sea.

They passed an abandoned O'Hearn bush camp, the whitewashed boards of a cookhouse showing bleached and skeletal through the trees. Then the silhouettes of rusted machinery. A busted timber dam. A small cemetery. After that, they were driving beside miles of chain-link fence that seemed without purpose, coming finally to a shuttered, Cold War–era radar station. Its massive satellite dish lay rusting, fallen to one side. The fence by the front gate was knocked down. The government must have simply walked away. Left everything behind. The bush was convenient for making quick retreats like that.

As they neared Ragged Lake, the forest grew thick and they lost the stars, were forced to travel slowly around the trees, headlights stabbing a path while they tried not to be diverted too far from a straight line. Yakabuski craned to hear the wind above the roar of the snowmobiles, for the slight change in pitch and keel that would let him know the wind was travelling over open ground, that cleared land or a lake lay in that direction. For nighttime bushwhacking they did fairly well, clearing the forest by the southwest arm of the lake, more or less where they were aiming.

They saw the abandoned pulp and paper mill first, a red-brick monolithic building that in the darkness was sensed before seen. The length of two football fields. The breadth of one more. Something so out of scale with its surroundings it seemed to have more presence than a fixed location. When their eyes adjusted, they saw wooden cottages surrounding the mill and what looked like an old school or community centre, a long, rectangular building with a heavy cap of snow, the roof collapsed on the northeast corner. There was an old railway siding. Two-storey homes squatted next to the siding, with verandas leaning or shucked off like useless appendages that had been cut away. The only light was to the west of them, on the tip of a peninsula that jutted far into the lake.

Turning toward the light, the cops reached the Mattamy

Fishing Lodge within a few moments. They parked their snowmobiles at the end of a line of other snowmobiles, took off their helmets, and swatted snow from their parkas. Voices came from inside the lodge.

"I'd say we were the first ones to have been on the S and P since the storm," said Yakabuski. "You agree, Donnie?"

"Sure thing, Yak," Buckham said. "We were cutting our own track all the way from Springfield."

"First ones on that logging road, too. You agree, Matt?"

"Absolutely." Downey nodded.

Yakabuski looked up at the building in front of him. The Mattamy Fishing Lodge was made of split-rail pine, quartered and notched, with a long front porch that could hold fifty people.

"I saw one set of snowshoe tracks heading away from that cabin. That would have been the tree-marker. And one set of snowmobile tracks. Did either of you see any others?"

"No," the young cops said in unison, and then Downey finished for them: "There was just that one track, Yak."

"And that track was heading to the S and P. Whoever made it couldn't have turned south or we would have passed the track on our way up. You agree?"

"That's right. That sled was going to Ragged Lake."

"The storm was three days ago. How long do you figure?"

Both of the Ident cops hesitated before answering. It was the question that mattered.

"It wouldn't be three days," said Buckham.

"You agree, Matt?"

"I think two would be stretching it. They were probably killed the day before yesterday."

It didn't need to be said, and so it wasn't. Still, it was hard for the younger cops not to look around as they climbed the steps to the lodge. Not nervous, they would have told anyone who asked. And certainly not scared. Just wondering. If the killer they sought was hiding in the shadows right then. Or sitting inside the Mattamy waiting for them.

. . .

The lobby of the Mattamy was the way Yakabuski remembered from that one boyhood fishing trip with his father. The floor and walls of the lobby were wide-planked pine stained chocolate brown. Dark red paint framed the windows and door. There was a hardwood reception desk running nearly the length of the lobby, and wings that ran in three directions from the desk. The east and west wings were guest rooms; the north went to a bar and restaurant with a view of the lake.

Gaming trophies decorated the walls of the lobby: a twenty-eight-point bull moose; the head of a mature black bear; a muskie with its mouth open so you could see its two-inch-long teeth, larger than the shards of a bush-camp chainsaw, the snout angled so it looked like the fish was about to strike a foot-long metal spinner mounted to the plaque. Yakabuski knew, from having read the plaque as a boy, that the fish had been caught in 1954 and was once a North American record for muskie caught on eight-pound light tackle. He peered at the bronze plaque as he walked past the front desk, but it was burnished and unreadable now. The scales of the fish had turned colour as well, so it looked now like wax paper left in a kitchen drawer too long.

The cops walked around the reception desk and made their way down the north wing, following the sound of voices.

This hallway was covered with more mammal heads, more unreadable plaques, more fish with scales turned translucent. When they entered the bar, nine people turned to look at them. Nine expectant sets of eyes — a few with the unfocused look of people who had been sitting there too long.

One was obviously the tree-marker, a teenager sitting on a bar stool with a rock glass in front of him, a sherpa's toque on his head. At a round table near a stone fireplace sat an elderly couple, the woman with the high cheekbones and long black hair of the Cree, the man short, wizened, and white, dressed in dark-green work pants and a plaid shirt, with a John Deere cap on his head.

At another table, as far away from the elderly couple as the room would allow, sat a tall, lanky man in his mid-thirties. He wore fleece-lined guide pants, a heavy flannel shirt, and winter Sorels, that Yakabuski knew from having looked at a pair last autumn, cost four hundred dollars. Some sort of Sport. At a time of year when you shouldn't get Sports. Another Sport, a pudgy man about ten years younger but wearing almost identical clothing, sat at the table with him.

Behind the bar was the man Yakabuski assumed he'd spoken to on the phone. The bartender stood a little over six feet, with arms that stretched the fabric of his denim shirt, his hair tied back in a ponytail. Beside the bartender was a fat man dressed in white pants and a chef's jacket, drying a rock glass with a wet towel. Next to him stood a girl probably no older than the tree-marker, in a white uniform with yellow piping and a nametag. The last person in the room, at the bar next to the tree-marker, was a heavyset man in snow pants and a bulky cable-knit sweater. His clipped grey beard made him look a bit like Hemingway in his later years.

The bartender spoke first. "You been to the cabin?"

"Yes."

"Was it the way the kid said it was?"

"No."

There was a palpable easing of tension in the room. Bodies went slack. Eyes closed and reopened, anticipation replacing the long-distance stare of foreboding that had been there previously.

"No," Yakabuski continued. "He missed the little girl."

CHAPTER
EIGHT

Yakabuski had nine uncles — five on his dad's side, four on his mother's. Including his dad, there was a time when all ten men were working in the timber trade. It was the only reason you lived in the Upper Springfield Valley or along the Northern Divide. His dad worked bush camps for nearly eight years before becoming a cop. One of his uncles, Jacko Yakabuski, still worked the camps, nearly seventy now, and so the family considered him crazy, which was probably true, although it was going to take more than that to keep him from going to the camps every autumn. Two other uncles worked for a timber company in High River that made hydro poles, which was about as close to government work as you could get without actually having to get government work. Every other Yakabuski was now doing something else. Or nothing at all.

Several of his uncles had been tree-markers when they

were young, and Yakabuski remembered them coming in from the bush on Friday afternoons, to his father's house because they had running water, wearing their red underwear and leather suspenders, crazy beaver hats, and winter boots caked with so much snow they were the size of field boulders. The tree-marker who sat across from him now reminded Yakabuski of those uncles. It was a young man's game, and the ones who did it best were quiet and resourceful, not given to flights of fancy or abandon. Except on Saturday nights.

When Yakabuski said a young girl had been murdered as well, the foreboding and tension that had been in the room returned. There were a few gasps, a few sad faces turned downward quickly, the shuffling sound of rock glasses being moved atop the counter of the bar. No one spoke. Yakabuski unzipped his parka, and the other two cops followed suit.

"I'm Detective Yakabuski," he said, "and these are constables Downey and Buckham. We're going to need statements from everyone in the room. You're the tree-marker, right?" and he pointed to the boy. He would start the interviews with the tree-marker, as he had found the bodies. If it had been anyone else, the boy would have been the second one to give a statement.

The tree-marker followed Yakabuski into the kitchen, and there they sat on stools brought in from the bar and placed before a metal cutting table. It was a large kitchen, with a walk-in cooler and dry-goods pantry, windows looking out on Ragged Lake, three large industrial fans that twirled noiselessly above them.

"I thought you guys normally worked in pairs," said Yakabuski when he had taken off his parka and sat down.

"We do, sir. My partner got sick a couple weeks back.

Pneumonia or something. Had to put him on the train to High River."

"So you're out there by yourself?"

"It ain't a big deal. The company was all right with it."

Working the bush alone, where you didn't even have a base camp, was beyond crazy. Break your leg and you'd be as good as dead. Yakabuski wasn't surprised. O'Hearn Forestry Products had made its fortune more than a century ago, when Thomas O'Hearn, a recently arrived stonemason from Aberdeen, Scotland, bought timber rights to half the forests on the Northern Divide. Bought them cheap because no one thought you could get timber to market from the Divide without building costly dams and chutes along the Springfield River. So O'Hearn bought the timber rights for a song and then surprised everyone by not trying to build a thing.

Instead, he sent timber cribs down the Springfield and shot every set of rapids. Lots of men drowned on O'Hearn timber runs, but there were always other men willing to take their place, men who couldn't make a living on the hundred acres of rock the government had given them as a land grant, men with children walking beside them all day with stomachs howling and bones getting so thin and frail they made small creaking sounds on windy days. To Thomas O'Hearn, desperate men dying on the river was simply the cost of doing business in a tough country. A tree-marker working the bush alone? Yes, Yakabuski could see the company being all right with that.

"You told me on the phone you were marking pine for the mill here in Ragged Lake. That doesn't make any sense to me," he said.

"Me either. That's what Jimmy and I said all the time."

"That mill has been closed for a decade. Maybe longer."

"I know, sir."

"You sure you're supposed to be here? There's no other reason you'd be out at that old work camp?"

"Check with O'Hearn, sir. I'm exactly where I'm supposed to be. Marking the pine around Ragged Lake."

"So, what made you check out that cabin?"

"It was odd-looking, right? You've seen it. Wouldn't you say it was odd?"

"I guess I would."

"And it wasn't supposed to be there. So, what the hell. I had to check it out."

Yakabuski didn't say anything. The boy took another drink of rye, a big gulp, although careful to leave a thin line of liquid at the bottom so he wouldn't be empty and sad. Yakabuski pegged the boy at eighteen or nineteen. He stayed silent, knowing if he said nothing, the silence would soon become uncomfortable for the boy, almost painful, and he would end it by saying something. And that something would tell Yakabuski more about this boy than any answer to the smartest question he had to ask him.

After more time had passed than Yakabuski would have expected from a young, unworldly tree-marker, the boy finally spoke.

"I had a dream last night. One of the strangest dreams I ever had. I saw that squatter cabin at night, all dark and no sound 'cept the ice on the lake snappin' and creaking. Then I saw a flash of light, and the whole cabin lit up. Then I saw another flash. And another. It was strange light because it didn't belong there. It weren't right. Like watching headlights where you know there ain't no road. Or fireflies out in a snowstorm. I seen that once. Swear to God. Fireflies in the snow."

The boy paused a moment, as though collecting the memory. Then he said, "When I woke up this morning, my sheets were so wet you'd have thought I'd pissed in 'em. You ever have a thing like that happen to you?"

The boy stared right at Yakabuski when he asked the question, a do-you-believe-it look on his face so earnest and guileless it was uncomfortable to gaze upon, and so the cop turned away, after first telling the boy, sure, stuff like that happens all the time.

· · ·

The first thing the bartender did was take his hair out of its ponytail and brush it with his fingers, turning his arms sideways in the process, biceps rippling.

"What's your name, please?" said Yakabuski, opening the steno pad he had placed on the metal countertop but hadn't yet bothered to open.

"William Forest."

"What are you doing open this time of year, Mr. Forest? There's no fishing. Can't see there being enough business to make it worth your while."

"We get some sleds. We're on the Northern-Gateway loop, farthest point if you're doing the complete trail. Ragged Lake is where you're turning around. We used to get a lot of business when the loop first opened. Not so much these days. Price of gas and everything."

"So why stay open?"

"Probably won't after this season. The owner has been

talking about shutting it down in winter for a few years now. Just hasn't got around to doing it."

"How long have you been working here?"

"Three years."

"You a Springfield boy?"

"That's right."

"Who's sitting in the bar tonight?"

Forest looked over his shoulder, as though he could see through walls, and said, "The old couple are the Tremblays. Roselyn and Gaetan. She's from Kes'. He used to work at the mill. The big guy sitting by himself is John Holly. He's a guide. He has a cottage down by the lake. There's me and Charley, the cook. There's Marie, she's the waitress and maid, and also does the front desk in winter."

Forest stopped to run his hands through his hair one more time. Took a sip from the bottle of beer he had brought in from the bar.

"And the Sports? Who are they?"

"Good question. They checked in four nights ago. Came in on the train from High River. They had reservations. Marie checked 'em in."

"What have they been doing?"

"They rented a couple of sleds. They stay out most of the day. I think they have something do with the mill. I saw their sleds parked there earlier this week."

"You don't know why they would be parked there?"

"No idea."

"Who else lives in the village?"

"Well, hardly anyone. In the winter this place is pretty much a ghost town. There's an old Indian woman who lives on a bluff just outside town. And there's some sort of outdoor survival school in one of the bunkhouses. That's the other edge of town."

"What do they do?"

"Run survival courses, backcountry expeditions, shit like that. It's called Northern Divide Expeditions."

"They open this time of year?"

"I'm not really sure. You hardly ever see them. I think summer and fall is their busy time."

"And that's it? The entire village?"

"The entire village."

The fan blades in the kitchen dissected the light so the room was cast in quick-cut shadows and the bartender's muscles appeared jerky and disjointed. Yakabuski looked at his arms and knew somewhere in the Mattamy was a decent set of free weights. What he was not sure of was why a Springfield boy with skin the shade of tea candles was here pumping them.

. . .

"Did you know people were living at the old camp?"

The cook took a large kitchen knife and sliced through the ham and cheese sandwich he had just made.

"Sure, they came into town from time to time. Bought provisions here. The guy cashed a cheque."

"Cashed a cheque?"

"Yeah, a government cheque. Came in every month and we cashed it for him. The guy was here just three or four days ago."

"What were they like?"

"Barely saw the woman. And a little girl, swear to God, I didn't even *know* there was a little girl. She never came to town."

"So the guy, then, what was he like?"

"He was coco. That's what he was like."

"What makes you say he was crazy?"

"He never took any whisky, for one. I offered to sell him whisky plenty of times." The cook took a bite of his sandwich. Bread crumbs rolled down a circuitous route of three double chins to fall on the floor. "And you saw his cabin," he said. "You'd have to be fuckin' coco to build a place like that."

"Do you have one of those cheques?"

"It would be in the office. Marie could get it for you."

The cook took another bite of his sandwich. Reached for a bottle of beer. Stood there for a minute eating and drinking, Yakabuski waiting for him to speak and break the silence.

"Yeah, a real fuckin' coco," the cook finally said.

· · ·

John Holly could have been one of Yakabuski's uncles. A tree-marker grown old. A barrel-chested, burnish-skinned bushman who had been making his way through life as a fishing guide, bush-camp labourer, general contractor, any occupation around Ragged Lake except mill hand. Which surprised Yakabuski.

"You never worked at the mill?"

"I never liked even getting close to that place. It killed two of my brothers."

"In-the-ground killed?"

"One of 'em. He got drunk and fell into a bleaching vat. The other one you can find down in Springfield. He drinks at the Montcalm Tavern. You know the place?"

Yakabuski knew the place. One of the lowest, rankest dives in all of Springfield, a tavern for men barred from other taverns, for men travelling through life with neither friend nor kin. It was generous to even call the Montcalm a tavern, because it was more sporting pit than anything else — a ring for the deranged, desperate, and soon-to-check-out-of-this-world to congregate, compete, and run cheap hustles on each other.

"I know the place."

"Then you can understand why I prefer Ragged Lake."

"If those were your only choices in life, I suppose. The Montcalm Tavern or a ghost town on the Northern Divide. Not an easy life, I would think."

"It works for me."

"How much guiding business you get these days?"

"It's steady. I have regular clients."

"In the winter?"

"I hunker down. I like to read."

"Read in the bar much?"

"You trying to be a politician, Detective Yakabuski? No, I do not spend my nights getting drunk at the Mattamy. These are rather exceptional days. The reason I am here. "

"Did you know there was a squatter family living out by the headwaters?"

"We all knew. They came into town. And the guy built his cabin right on Cap. Some people say there's good pickerel fishing on that lake. I never thought there was, but some people say that."

46

"What did you think of them?"

"I didn't spend any time thinking about 'em at all."

"Good-looking wife."

Holly threw back his head and let out a loud, carefree laugh, his chest heaving like a blacksmith's billow.

"Detective Yakabuski, if I were a man given to chasing pussy, do you think I'd be living in Ragged fuckin' Lake?"

· · ·

Roselyn and Gaetan Tremblay were more Yakabuski kin. One of the old couples he'd see at the back of any large family gathering. There might not have been a person in the entire room who could tell you the exact family connection. The couple was too old. There were too many missing pieces. But there they'd be at the significant weddings. The saddest funerals. The kind that never strayed from each other's sides, ate silent meals with heads bowed, seemed more one person than two.

He asked the woman the first question, although it was done out of politeness more than genuine inquiry. Yakabuski was sure enough of the answer to have already started writing it in his steno pad before she started talking.

"I'm from Kesagami," she said. "I came to Five Mile Camp after my husband died. I had a sister here. That would have been almost thirty years ago."

"It was mostly Cree that lived at the camp, is that right?"

"All Cree. Occasionally you would get some Algonquin, a gang of boys that had driven up from Springfield, but they never stayed. I don't know if they never felt welcome or they never liked working at the mill, but they never stayed."

"The woman who was killed looks Cree to me."

"She was. I saw her in town a few times. I spoke to her once behind the Mattamy."

"Just the once?"

"Just the once. And we didn't talk long. I got the impression I was bothering her. If I had a different impression, I would have gone to visit her. But I didn't. So it was just the once."

"Why did you think you were bothering her?"

"Maybe that's not the right word. She wasn't rude. It's just she didn't follow up on stuff, the way you would expect people to follow up on stuff. She's Cree, right? I'm Cree. I tell her she's living next to Five Mile Camp. She acts like she never heard of the place."

"You didn't believe her?"

"How could it be true? Then I tell her I'm from Kes' and I used to live at Five Mile. You know what she says?"

"Nothing."

"That's right. How did you know that?"

"You never went to her cabin?"

"Never."

"And you, sir?"

Gaetan roused himself to stare at Yakabuski. He was a slight man, still dressed in the dark-green work clothes of a mill hand although it was twelve years at least since he had last worked a shift. A roll-your-own cigarette dangled from his thin, chapped lips. A John Deere cap sat on a head that was starting to dry out with age, like an old apple.

"I never went there," he said. "The fishin' ain't no good on the Springfield till you get miles south of Cap."

"Never went to that cabin on an ATV or anything like that? Maybe a sled in the winter?"

"It ain't on any trail system. No reason to ever go out there."

"So you've never seen that cabin?"

"I didn't say that. I seen it once. John Holly told me the guy made his roof out of beer cans, so I went out to see that. Didn't stop, though. And it was just that once."

Yakabuski stopped writing and took a sip of his coffee. After a few seconds of silence, Gaetan said, "Like I said, the pickerel ain't no good till you're miles south of that place."

· · ·

Yakabuski brought the Sports in together. Well past midnight and time to finish the interviews, move on to next steps. Downey and Buckham were getting restless, pacing in the bar, not on sentry duty exactly, but with a purposeful gait that was not dissimilar. Whenever Yakabuski came out of the kitchen to get a new interview subject, they cast expectant glances in his direction, but he had yet to speak to them. To inquiries from anyone in the bar, they shrugged their shoulders and said they would have to be patient.

"You gentlemen get a question I haven't had the chance to ask yet," said Yakabuski, when the Sports were seated. "Why are you here in Ragged Lake?"

The two men looked at each other and it was the older of the two who answered. He was a tall man, with elongated features and no facial hair, fit and able-looking, like dozens of other lanky old Sports Yakabuski had known through the years from helping his uncles with their overflow guiding business. The tall, lanky Sports were the ones you hoped were never in charge of the tip for the fishing party because they never made good tippers. You always hoped for the fat, slovenly ones that smelled vaguely of distilled liquor.

"We are here on business, Detective," he said. "We haven't told anyone this yet, but we work for O'Hearn. The company is thinking of reopening the mill. We're on a bit of an inspection tour."

"Reopening a pulp and paper mill on the Northern Divide? O'Hearn in a hurry to go bankrupt?"

"It wouldn't be a pulp mill, Detective," said the Sport, talking in a languid, sleepy way that made Yakabuski wonder for a moment if he were drunk but hiding it well. "We wouldn't bother with pulp at all. Or newsprint. We believe the mill can be refitted to make fine gloss paper."

"There's enough of a market for that?"

"Magazines are doing very well right now. Nothing like newspapers. The Asian market in particular is just exploding. We have good wood here in Ragged Lake, good pine, not the junk you use to make newsprint. It always seemed a waste to us, using that wood for newsprint. Just recently it occurred to us that there was an opportunity here."

"So, why the secrecy?"

"We would dearly like to get the jump on our competitors, Detective. We think this has the potential to reopen a lot of old mills, not just this one. The retrofit we're looking at is new and quite ingenious. We've patented the design."

"That's why the tree-marker is here."

"That's right."

"And you can get the transportation numbers to work?"

"Well, yes, we believe we can," said the Sport, not able to

hide his surprise that the cop had asked the one question that mattered. The question that needed an affirmative answer or they were all wasting their time. "We will need a better deal from BMR than what they are offering us at the moment, but they are receptive to the idea. They need the business as badly as everyone these days. It looks quite promising."

"You'll bring this old town back to life."

"I would imagine. We'll start with one shift, but we plan on running two within a year, a full rotation within eighteen months. That's the business model."

Reopening a shuttered pulp and paper mill, people going back to work at what they had been doing in the first place. Getting a second chance like that. Yakabuski had never heard of such a thing.

"All right, gentlemen, let's have your names, please."

With a deferential nod and an odd smile that managed to seem friendly but smug at the same time, the older of the two said, "I am Tobias O'Keefe. This is my assistant, David Garrett."

The younger Sport, who had yet to say a word, extended a pudgy white hand for Yakabuski to shake but let it drop in a few seconds when he saw the cop was making no attempt to grab it. Just then, the maid appeared at the doorway of the kitchen.

"Thank you, gentlemen," said Yakabuski, closing up his steno pad. "That will be all for tonight."

. . .

Yakabuski held the government cheque in his hand. He looked at the name one more time. "Four days ago?"

"That's right."

"Just him?"

"No, she was here as well. The little girl, too."

"Most people don't remember the little girl. Or her."

"They didn't come into town all that often. Hardly ever during the winter. I was surprised to see them."

Yakabuski wondered why the cook had not mentioned this.

"Do you know their names?"

"No. Well, his. It's on the cheque."

The waitress pushed back a strand of hair that had fallen from her ponytail and looked at Yakabuski. The nametag pinned to her bright yellow shirt, next to the white piping, said Marie Picard.

"They're all dead?" she said.

"Yes."

She gave a long exhale of breath and pushed another strand of hair from her face then reached back with her left hand to straighten the ponytail. She would have been the same age as the tree-marker and seemed to have little awareness of her body, how her breasts stretched the stiff polyurethane fabric of the uniform when she moved, how her eyes looked when framed by a strand of hair, where to position herself when leaning in to whisper to a stranger.

"Who would kill a little girl?" she asked.

"I'm not sure. We're going to find out, though."

"It's someone here at the lodge, isn't it?"

"We don't know that."

"It could be that."

"Could be many things."

"It's likely that."

"Miss, we don't—"

"Are we safe?"

Yakabuski had finished a complete round of interviews and she was the first one to ask. The question he was sure they all had. Everyone except one, perhaps. "You're safe," he said. "We're here and we'll stay here until we've completed our investigation. You won't ever be alone."

"How will that work?"

"I'll explain in the bar. You live in the bunkie next door, is that right?"

He had seen an old O'Hearn bunkhouse next to the lodge, two storeys, plank-wood exterior, windows frosted from the inside. Unless you burned one of them down, there was never enough heat in a lumber company bunkhouse.

"That's right."

"You'll be staying in the lodge tonight. Try to get a good night's sleep. Is there a fax machine in the office?"

CHAPTER NINE

"So what do we have, Yak?"

"It looks like murder."

Springfield police chief Bernard O'Toole was as big, fit, and combative as Yakabuski. He was a legendary figure in the city, sixth generation on the force. His great-great grandfather had been the one to arrest Patrick Aylin, king of the Shiners, an Irish street gang. Aylin was executed after the arrest, found guilty of throwing a business competitor over Kettle Falls, the competitor being a Frenchman from Val des Monts who didn't like Aylin burning down his lumberyards. The O'Tooles had been treated like royalty along the French Line ever since the execution. In certain other parts of the city — Cork's Town, the Nosoto Projects — the family was still reviled for what was seen as its betrayal of an Irish patriot.

"A man and a woman?"

"Little girl, too. Just a toddler."

"Gawdamm."

"Yep."

"I don't want to insult you, Yak, but—"

"No gun. New tracks in the snow leading to Ragged Lake. No other tracks."

"I see. So, what do we have in the village?"

"It's a ghost town. I have nine people in the Lodge and that's about the entire town. I've done a first round of interviews. Nothing obvious. There's some sort of survival school that's probably closed for the season. It's called Northern Divide Expeditions. We need to have someone run that."

"Will do. So, what's your plan?"

"We'll lock down the lodge and stay here for the night. We'll check out the survival school in the morning. There's one other person we'll bring in, an old Cree woman living outside town. We'll start the workup on the cabin. We're going to need some more bodies."

"What do you figure?"

"Another Ident team. A couple of detectives. I don't think you need to send anyone from George's office unless he wants to. We can photograph everything. Bring the bodies to him."

"You're thinking the train?"

"We can send them to High River. Transport them back to Springfield from there."

"The train will be there day after tomorrow. You're good until then?"

"We're good."

"Glad to hear that. We're down to one sled. Anything else?"

"We have a name for the man who was killed. He was getting a government cheque mailed to him at the Mattamy."

"You can do that?"

"They've been doing it for years. I think I have an uncle who still gets mail here."

"So we have a name."

"We do. It's a bit odd, though. You'll need to contact the Department of National Defence."

"National Defence? I was expecting some social agency."

"I know. And it isn't a veteran's cheque. It's the sort of cheque you send to someone still serving."

"In Ragged Lake?"

"That's what it seems to be. I'm faxing it to you right now. National Defence has public affairs people working 'round the clock. We should put in a request tonight."

"Will do. How's your satphone working?"

"Hit and miss. If you have trouble reaching me, try the landline at the Mattamy. Here's the number." Yakabuski read the number on the faceplate of the rotary phone. He picked up the cheque lying in the out-tray of the fax machine.

"You have it?" he asked.

"Guillaume Roy."

"That's our man. I need to know everything about him. His wife's name would probably help. I think she's from here."

. . .

When Yakabuski returned to the bar, he saw no one had moved. Not so much as a degree, it seemed. They sat exactly as they had been when he left to make his phone call. He rolled up the sleeve of his sweater and looked at his watch: 1:34 a.m.

"It's been a long day, so I'll keep this short," he said. "Everyone is staying at the Mattamy tonight. No one is going home or going to the bunkie. Does anyone here take prescription medication?"

John Holly and the Tremblays put up their hands.

"Is this medication you need tonight, or can it wait until the morning?"

Almost silently, the Tremblays mouthed the word morning. Holly reached into his parka and held up a pill container.

"Good. We're going to put you up in the east wing tonight. I'm going to ask each of you to stay in your room once you are there. A police officer will come for you in the morning. Any questions?" Yakabuski stared around the room. They would have a hundred questions. Once again, no one said a word. He nodded and said, "Constables Downey and Buckham will start bringing you to your rooms."

CHAPTER TEN

The one time Yakabuski had been in Ragged Lake, he was a boy and it was late spring with every river and creek running high — so much water on the Northern Divide he could hear it wherever he went. Water running north. Water running south. Water turning back on itself and running in circles, not sure which watershed to head for. It had been disorienting, the sound of all that water, as though he was always walking past a running shower.

In the winter, all that water was frozen. Yakabuski stood in his room looking out over the lake and could hear the ice expanding and contracting in the cold. It made him think of a cell-block prisoner just brought in, handcuffed and twisting on the ground, not understanding yet that he was caught and no amount of physical exertion was going to change anything. It was the natural order of things.

Who worried him most? Yakabuski stared out over the

lake and considered it. An old military police officer told him once that was how he started every investigation. By clearing his mind and asking himself who worried him most. Who didn't seem quite right? Who had he noticed? Didn't matter the reason. Forget about evidence right then. Just be honest with yourself and ask: Who am I thinking about?

The Sports? They definitely worried him. The one unknown variable. The Sports show up. People get killed. People like that always worried him. And most times there was a connection between the two events; a stranger arrives on the scene and someone is killed? You'd better find that stranger right quick. Even though, and here was evidence entering his thoughts when he was trying to think it away, it was difficult to envision either of those men being a triple murderer.

The bartender? There was something vain and foolish about William Forest, some sort of entitlement a bartender at a fishing lodge on the Northern Divide shouldn't rightly possess. The dead woman in that cabin had been a good-looking woman. There probably weren't a lot of good-looking women around Ragged Lake, even during the height of muskie season. Did the bartender think he had some sort of right?

The cook? Yakabuski didn't know what to think of the cook. He stared out over the lake and almost laughed. The man's kitchen was a mess. He didn't have the wit to use a dry towel. Maybe he was just a sloppy man. A poor cook. Although, there was something about him that didn't seem right, that didn't add up, that left you thinking he was somewhere he didn't belong.

The Tremblays and John Holly? Nothing struck Yakabuski as out of place about the old couple and the guide, although he wondered why anyone would stay in a place like Ragged Lake if they had options in life, if they were free to do as they pleased. People who lacked free will, even when they managed to keep it well hidden, always worried Yakabuski.

But he was being dishonest with himself, and he knew the old soldier's trick would not work this time out. The tree-marker was the one that worried him most. And not because the boy was a suspect. Everything about the tree-marker told Yakabuski he didn't do it, right down to the dream the boy was having, thinking that squatter family was killed at night, because he was a boy from Buckham's Bay who couldn't imagine anything that hateful and evil happening at any other time of day.

Yakabuski had told the tree-marker his dream would go away soon enough, and until it did there was nothing wrong with drinking himself stupid. He should do that. It would help. He didn't bother telling the boy there was a good chance the dreams would return years later, fifty-fifty maybe; they'd come when he wasn't expecting it, because being party to some poor soul's last painful moments on earth, people shot down and butchered like that family had been, imagining them screaming in terror, the pain and surprise — those were memories life bestowed upon you sometimes for no good or obvious reason. Like a bad inheritance. So go ahead and drink when it was easy. This omission — for reasons unknown to Yakabuski just then — worried him most.

CHAPTER ELEVEN

Cambio did not have a home. He tried not to be anywhere for three nights running. His grandfather, a trench fighter from the first Great War, had taught him that trick, told his grandson slow-witted men were routinely killed in the trenches for being third on a match. The flash of a match would be seen by an enemy sniper. The sniper would take sight as the match was passed to the second smoker. The sniper would shoot and kill the third man.

"Avoid threes of all kind," the old man told his grandson. "Never give a man three steps. Never give a man a third chance. Family members and some others you must give a second chance, but no man should be given a third.

"Three is bad luck. In the trenches you could pluck cigarettes from the mouths of every third man and smoke for free. All you needed were matches."

Now Cambio was in a hotel room in Panama City. His IT man had been working on the phones for nearly an hour and now stood back from the coffee table and nodded. Cambio looked at the array of cellular phones.

"*¿Se han creado con los viejos códigos?*"

"*Sí.*"

"*¿Los mismos números?*"

"*Sí.*"

Cambio waved the IT man out of the room and reached for a phone. There were several clicking sounds after he punched in a number, and nearly ten seconds passed before the phone started to ring. Several seconds more passed until it was answered.

"Hello, my friend," he heard a man say.

"*Buenas noches*. You are well, I hope?"

"Always."

"Good. I wanted to talk to you about the situation in Ragged Lake. I have put a crew on standby, in case we need to go there."

"That is wise."

"It is in your backyard, so I wanted to call."

"There was no need. You are right to get a crew ready. The man you have contacted is the best man for the job."

"He works for you."

"He works for all of us."

"*Sí.* You have a good man there. You are lucky to have him. We may need the full op. Depending on what happens tomorrow. Again, it is your parish. Do you have any problem with *that*?"

"No."

They fell silent. A woman had come to the hotel room door, and after being frisked she had been taken to a glassed solarium on the terrace. She sat between rows of geraniums, twirling her hair and looking at Cambio. One of his security men sat with her.

"It may be nothing," he said. "It sounds like a family matter."

"I think so, too."

"It would not be easy, living in a place like Ragged Lake. They were squatters?"

"That's what I'm told."

"Well, I thought I should call."

"Again, there was no need. Have a good night, my friend."

The line went dead, neither man quite sure who had hung up first.

CHAPTER TWELVE

When Yakabuski was in Ragged Lake fishing with his father, he would have been a boy of around ten. There had been just the two of them, and they had taken his dad's Ford Galaxy up to the Goyette Reservoir then over to Ragged, travelling beside rail lines for most of the trip because there were no roads after you passed the Goyette. They put their boat in at a municipal dock swarming with guide boats and logging tugs. Smoke belched from all six stacks of a nearby pulp and paper mill, and men in dark-green factory clothes seemed everywhere.

It was a big lake and they were gone more than an hour before starting to troll. Cliffs of gneiss and granite covered by great swaths of coniferous trees lined the shores. Only once was the shoreline any different, shortly after leaving the dock, when they passed a clear-cut valley of blackened stumps and glacier-deposited rocks.

"Shame they have to cut so close to town," his father had said, one hand on the tiller of the outboard motor, the other rolling a cigarette. "They never used to come in this close before."

"Where did they get the trees before?"

"The main camp was on the north shore." His father spit tobacco flakes into the wake of the boat. "In the spring, when they started hauling logs out of the bush, there were probably more people in the camp than there were in town. They ran the logs in booms. That's how big this lake is."

"Will we see the bush camp?"

"Maybe what's left of her. They abandoned that camp years ago."

They caught no muskie that day but spincast for pickerel before setting up camp and quickly caught their supper. His dad cooked the fish over a good bed of embers made from split maple they'd brought, a heavy weight they would not normally have bothered with, but there were no hardwood trees this far north, and they were not portaging. They made camp on an island, and from their fire Yakabuski could see the remains of the bush camp his father had been talking about. Several large bunkhouses. Some outbuildings. A wooden wharf, sagging and slipping into the lake on the starboard side.

After supper he had sat in his father's lap and stared out at the abandoned camp. Before long darkness fell and he could no longer see the camp, although he kept staring. That night was the bush-dark you get sometimes when you are miles from any town or village and the sky is clouded over, the wind still. It is a darkness as complete as God ever put upon this earth.

"How long has the camp been abandoned?" he remembered asking his father.

"A lot of years," his dad had answered. "There's another camp the other side of town that's still running. It's all Cree, that one, most of 'em mill hands."

"Where did the people go when they left?"

"Wherever people go when they have to leave a place, Frankie."

"Where is that?"

"Around here, it's probably Springfield."

"They all went to Springfield?"

"I'm not sure, Frankie. I'm just saying. They went somewhere and started over again. People have to do that sometimes."

"Will they come back?"

"I doubt it. When something is gone, it's gone. I've never seen anything come back in this world, Frankie."

. . .

Yakabuski lay in bed looking at the thin red line that had appeared over the trees on the eastern shore of Ragged Lake. Nothing more than an eyeliner sweep of colour. Not moving. Not growing. Not rising and becoming a sun. He knew the sky was filled that morning with heavy, low-hanging clouds.

He sat upright in the bed and stretched his back. Rolled it from the first vertebra to the last and counted the popping sounds. Four. That was something he wished would go away and never come back — although, for three hours' sleep in a strange bed, four pops wasn't bad. He stretched his legs and stood. More creaking and popping sounds. There were advantages to being a big man. Later in life, the disadvantages tried to catch up.

Yakabuski got dressed, took his service revolver from the nightstand, put it in his holster, and headed to the bar to relieve Buckham. It was 5:55 a.m. He had figured on two-hour rotations, with each cop getting four hours' sleep and the day starting at eight. But when he reached the bar, he found Buckham having coffee with Roselyn and Gaetan Tremblay. John Holly was sitting at the bar with Downey. The waitress was sitting at a service table next to the doorway leading to the kitchen.

"Hope you don't mind, Yak," said Buckham. "They came out and asked if they could have some coffee. Said they couldn't sleep. I figured I could watch 'em here as easily as I could down a hallway."

Yakabuski nodded. There would be time to talk to Buckham later.

"The coffee has only been on a few minutes, Mr. Yakabuski," said the waitress, walking over to him. "It should be good and fresh. I haven't seen Charley yet to get breakfast started. Are you hungry?"

"No."

"I can probably get something started."

"I'm fine. Thank you, Marie."

She walked with him to the coffee urn on the service table and stood beside him. She wore the uniform she'd had on the day before. The name tag was still pinned above her left breast.

"Did you get any sleep?" asked Yakabuski.

"No, not really."

"Not even in a good bed in a warm room?"

"I'm afraid not."

"What is it you want to ask me, Marie?"

She looked startled. "How did you know?"

"I didn't. But I suspected. What's on your mind this morning?"

"Well, it sounds silly, but I'm not sure who else to ask. Am I working today?"

. . .

Yakabuski sent Downey and Buckham to get everyone else from the rooms, and then he sat at the table with the Tremblays. He had given the waitress the answer she wanted. Yes, you should work today. Stay busy. I think we need another pot of coffee.

He had interviewed her briefly last night and knew she came from Buckham's Bay and had been working at the Mattamy less than two years, a job she got because an aunt once worked in the kitchen. She moved around the restaurant setting down cutlery and coffee cups. She considered this a good job. A lot of girls she grew up with were doing nothing at all, she told him. Queuing just for jobs at corner stores.

He wasn't sure if there was a mill still running in Buckham's Bay. Maybe some small saw mills, but that would be it. He wondered what the main industry in the town was these days. As he sipped his coffee, Holly moved over from the bar to sit with him. For more than a minute, the two men took sips of coffee but did not speak, their cups rising and falling like the pegs of a piano.

Finally, Holly smacked his lips and said, "So what *are* we doing today?"

"You'll be staying at the lodge. There'll be some more police officers arriving on the train tomorrow. We'll get everything settled away after that."

"We just sit here for the whole day?"

"That's right."

"Who do you think killed that squatter family?" Holly said it quickly. As though trying to surprise Yakabuski. Get him to reveal some truth about the crime or the investigation he wanted to keep hidden, before he had the presence of mind to conceal it. A trick that would never fool Yakabuski and only worked to frighten the Tremblays, both of whom gasped in choir-like unison.

"I have no idea, Mr. Holly."

"You think it's one of us?"

"Again, I have no idea."

Yakabuski took another sip of coffee. If it had just been Holly, he would have left it at that, but the Tremblays were so pale and scared-looking it was cause for concern. So he added, "I'm not even a hundred percent sure this is a homicide case, Mr. Holly. It was getting dark when we were at that cabin last night. We could have missed something. We may go back today, find a gun, and then what we have is a sad story of a family that headed into the woods thinking they would start a new life, go back to Walden Pond or something, but it didn't turn out like that, not near like that, and when they realized they weren't going to make it, they sat down and for whatever reason decided they had no place left to travel. We may have a sad story like that. In which case we'll all be gone on the train tomorrow, and your lives can get back to normal. But you need to sit tight today, Mr. Holly."

The old woman was nodding her head. "We will need our medications this morning, Mr. Yakabuski."

"I will have a police officer take you to your home right now, Madame. Get what you need. Clothing as well. The officer will help you."

"*Merci.*"

When the old couple left, Holly started to chuckle.

"There were three of you in a one-room cabin, and you may have missed a gun?"

"Stranger things have happened, Mr. Holly."

"I suppose."

CHAPTER THIRTEEN

Downey brought down the cook, and in a few minutes the smell of bacon came from the kitchen. Buckham brought down the Sports, the bartender, and the tree-marker. The waitress went back and forth between the tables, refilling coffee cups and taking breakfast orders. While they waited, the Sports read newspapers that had come in on the train earlier in the week. Holly started a fire in the large stone fireplace. The tree-marker kept his head turned to the table, only occasionally looking up to glance at either Yakabuski or the waitress.

Downey and Buckham sat at their own table. Downey's resentment about coming to the Northern Divide had disappeared as soon as they entered the squatter's cabin, and it was hard for him not to show his excitement right then. Buckham was having the same problem. This had not been a hoax. This had not been a waste of time. This was a legitimate crime scene with persons of interest all around them; the cops kept glancing around the room, not even bothering after a while to come up with a pretence — Is the coffee ready? Has the sun come out? — gawking like tourists almost, as alert as they'd ever been, as alive as they'd ever been, and the reason both almost jumped from their chairs when the phone behind the bar rang at 6:35.

The bartender gave a quizzical look, put down his fork, and walked behind the bar to answer the phone. He talked for only a few seconds, put down the handset, and walked to where Yakabuski was sitting.

"It's for you," he said.

. . .

Yakabuski sat behind the desk in the office he had used the night before and stared out the window. The thin red line had not budged, although it looked slightly out of focus now, shimmering above the treeline like something electric. He looked at the barometer affixed to the wall outside the office window. Twenty-nine-point-eight and falling.

"This is Detective Frank Yakabuski with the Springfield Regional Police."

"Detective, good morning. This is Colonel Russ Salo with the Department of National Defence. We received an inquiry last night concerning Guillaume Roy."

"That would have come from me, Colonel. I believe Mr. Roy is the victim in a homicide case I am investigating."

"You believe?"

"That's right. I have three bodies in a squatters' cabin near

72

Ragged Lake, a little town north of Springfield. No identification on the bodies or in the cabin. The man was getting a National Defence cheque mailed to him at a fishing lodge here. Payable to Guillaume Roy. Would you happen to know Mr. Roy?"

Clicking noises came through the receiver and there was a long pause before the man answered, "Detective, this was a preliminary call back to ascertain the nature of your inquiry. Now that I know, I can transfer you to our personnel department. Someone there can help you with next of kin information. I'll save you some time and put you in touch with a sergeant major I know over there."

"Appreciate that, Colonel Salo," said Yakabuski, taking a sip of coffee and staring out to where the sun should be. "Before you do that, can I ask you two quick questions? Why is National Defence sending a cheque to someone in Ragged Lake? And why is a Special Forces colonel responding to my inquiry instead of that pencil-pushing sergeant major you want to transfer me to."

This time the pause was so long Yakabuski began to wonder if he had lost the line. Or overplayed his hand. Finally, he heard, "You know me?"

"I've seen your name in the papers, Colonel. And yes, I guess I know you. I did eleven years with the Third Battalion, garrisoned out of Fort William."

"Yakabuski. Right. I've heard of you."

"Then why don't we start over? I need to know everything you can tell me about Guillaume Roy."

"How did he die?"

"Still a bit unclear on the concept here, Colonel. I get to

73

ask the questions. But I can tell you he was murdered, shot to death, along with what we're assuming were his wife and daughter. It's an ugly crime scene."

"Jesus."

"Likely happened two days ago. We have a killer still on the loose. So if you can . . ."

"Bakovici. That poor fuckin' guy . . ."

"Sorry?"

". . . it just kept coming for him."

"Colonel."

"Sorry. It's just a bit of a shock. Yes, I knew Guillaume Roy. I served with him. He was from Springfield originally."

"What do you mean it just kept coming for him? What happened to him?"

"Bak-o-fuckin'-vici, that's what happened to him. Ever hear of the place?"

"Sounds familiar. Can't place it."

"Why would you? There are so many shitholes in the world these days, it's hard to keep track of them. But for a little while, that was the world's number one shithole. Tito's little gift to the world."

When he said Tito, it all came back to Yakabuski. The story, the location — it came back so completely he was looking at forested hills and dirt, the switch-backed roads, the bridges of Sarajevo, the sound of artillery fire, the smells of sweet dough cooked over an open fire, fermented yogurt, peach Schnapps.

"Bosnia," he said.

"That's right."

"An insane asylum."

"Yep. About fifty klicks outside Sarajevo. Guillaume and

74

I were in the company that liberated it. Or found it. Everyone in charge of the hospital had bugged out by then, so you can't really say we liberated anything."

"That's how he ended up in Ragged Lake? I'm not following you, Colonel."

"What the fuck. He's dead, right? You're telling me he's dead?"

"I believe so. Yes."

"What does your man look like?"

"Early forties, blond hair, little over six feet, I'm guessing. Good shape."

"Are you taping this call?"

"No."

"Well, you're ex-military: you should enjoy this. The biggest Special Forces fuck-up you've never heard about."

· · ·

Colonel Salo started by saying the hospital wasn't on any maps. The old Yugoslavia government wasn't keen on letting people know they had crazies. Would have blown the superior-socialist-man argument out the water if they had to admit they had people as fucked up as those capitalist bastards. So Tito kept the hospital a secret. The Canadian Special Forces platoon found it while marching into Sarajevo, surprised to find a building of that size not on any of their maps. They didn't go right in because of that. Not sure if they were looking at some top-secret military base. Put the place under surveillance. And watched while three nurses were murdered.

"They were thrown off the roof of the building with clotheslines tied around their necks," said Colonel Salo, his voice now purposeful and sombre, a man with a sad story he needed to tell. "Our commanding officer thought it was a trap and wouldn't let us move in. Guillaume was furious. As mad as I'd ever seen him. We did nothing. Sat there and watched as those nurses were strung up on the wall like a load of whites."

Yakabuski turned away from the window. Stared at the handset in his hand. Wondered if he had heard right.

"When we finally got the order to move in, it was unimaginable, what we found," continued Salo. "The patients had been running the place for about two weeks. The doctors were all Muslim and had fled from the Serb army, which had the hospital surrounded. We found dead bodies everywhere. In hallways, in beds, some starved, most of them murdered. The stench would knock you out. There were flies and rats everywhere. People had been cannibalized. People had been boiled in the laundry vats. When you walked around Bakovici, you had trouble believing people could treat other people that way."

There was now no stopping the story Col. Salo was hesitant to begin, his words coming out hurried and unabashed, like a confessional.

"We spent a night there and the next morning continued on to Sarajevo. Guillaume was in the company that stayed behind to secure the building and start burying the dead. The night we left, a group of patients who had hidden in a secret passageway snuck out and took the company prisoner. All eight soldiers.

"We didn't get back for three days. When we returned, the only one still alive was Guillaume. It was disgusting, what had been done to our guys. Anyone who saw it probably still has nightmares. I know I do. Two of our soldiers had been boiled in a laundry vat. Four had been tied to posts in the middle of the cemetery and the Serbs had used them for sniper practice. One was never found.

"Guillaume was kept alive, though. For some reason, he fascinated the man in charge of the inmates, a professor from Belgrade who was at Bakovici for raping and killing some of his female undergraduates. He handcuffed Guillaume to a bed and tortured him.

"When I had the clearance, I read the medical reports. I had always wondered what happened to him. The professor would stare at math equations he had written on the wall, then say, 'You see it, don't you? Why don't you tell me what I have missed? It's pain, isn't it? The way it begins?'

"And then the guy would stick a scalpel into Guillaume. Cut him open. Burn him. The doctors who treated him in Sarajevo said that the professor must have been an expert in torture to have done all he did but still manage to keep Guillaume alive.

"It was the worst combat incident in the history of the Special Forces. The brass back at HQ couldn't believe it — seven Special Forces soldiers taken out by a bunch of nutbars in a Bosnian psychiatric hospital. It was a fuck-up beyond imagining. We told the families of the seven soldiers that they had been killed by snipers in Sarajevo. For four of them, it was almost true. The rest of us were told what happened at Bakovici was an Official Fucking Secret. Don't talk about it."

"What happened to Roy?"

"He was sent to St. Anne's Hospital and stayed there nearly two years. One of the doctors there thanked our colonel for bringing him in. Said most of his torture victims were old

77

men whose memory had gone. It was rare to have someone Guillaume's age. Can you imagine ever being thanked for a thing like that?"

Yakabuski would have been in Sarajevo that same spring. Would have been in the hospital where Roy was treated. He dredged his memory, trying to remember if he had heard the story, but nothing came to him. Special Forces would have buried this one deep. Salo was right about that.

"Where did Roy go after St. Anne's?"

"He never came back to the unit, so I'm not really sure. I heard he became a bad drunk. If I had lived through what Guillaume did, I probably would have become a bad drunk, too."

"But he was getting a cheque from National Defence. Not a veteran's cheque. He was still serving."

"That sounds right. If Guillaume had been mustered out, his medical files would have been transferred to Veterans' Affairs. No fucking way that was ever going to happen. Just stay away. I'm sure someone explained that to him."

"Any idea why Roy would be living in a squatter cabin on the Northern Divide?"

"I'm guessing to fall off the planet. Isn't that what you're guessing?"

"Maybe. But there are easier ways to do a thing like that. You can go off-grid twenty miles from Springfield."

"Maybe he went mad?"

"I've been inside his cabin. I've been inside homes where someone has gone off the rails, and your old friend's cabin isn't like those places."

"Maybe you can keep a thing like that hidden."

"Not where you live, you can't. Least I've never seen it. That cabin was a family cabin. Nothing mad or crazy about it.

"I'm out of ideas, then."

"I think there's a third option. For why a man would be living in the middle of nowhere."

"I suppose there is."

"Do you think there could be something to it?"

Colonel Salo took his time before answering. Finally, he said, "If Guillaume was hiding from someone, I have no idea who. Bakovici was nearly twenty years ago, Detective Yakabuski. I wish I could be more help to you."

CHAPTER
FOURTEEN

Yakabuski's first case as a major crimes detective — after working nearly three years undercover with the Popeyes, thinking he had seen every act of depravity and cruelty known to man — was a double murder in Cork's Town, top-floor apartment on North-Western Street. It was a hot day, and he'd had to walk eight flights to reach the apartment.

Lying in the kitchen was the body of a crack dealer who had owed money to a street gang with roots going all the way back to the Shiners. The dealer had tried to run but not been smart enough to run from Springfield. His pants were pulled to his ankles and his severed member had been stuck in his mouth. His throat had been slit as well, and blood had pooled around his head so that it looked as if he had a wild red beard. He had been laid out with his legs straight and his hands folded across his chest, and from a distance — if you didn't know it was blood, didn't know it was his cock — you might have thought he was sleeping peacefully, although on a kitchen floor with his pants pulled down.

The crack dealer's girlfriend was in the bedroom. Eight months pregnant. She had been raped, and stabbed repeatedly. The child had been alive when the first cops arrived, and there had been news stories afterward about whether paramedics in Springfield had the right equipment to have saved such a child, but Yakabuski figured nothing would have saved that boy. Certainly not medical equipment.

His first major crime case, and he had stayed in that apartment for nearly six hours. It was maybe four hundred square feet. He stayed until the smell of blood and static flesh had seeped into his clothing, until the eyes of the young woman on the bed were like the back of his own irises, a thing imprinted. The gash on the young man's throat became as familiar as a path leading from his back door. The baby he only imagined.

When he left that apartment, Yakabuski marched to the Black Ruby Tavern and started drinking. Hadn't left until three in the morning, when a patrol car arrived to take him home.

He had long ago stopped communing with the dead. Worked some cases now from Ident reports. Never saw the bodies. Gained more information from talking to people than he ever did by staring into a dead man's eyes.

Yet Yakabuski was old enough to know there are precious few decisions in life truly left for a man to make, and as he sat in the office that morning, he felt Guillaume Roy walk into the room as surely as if a flesh-and-blood soldier were standing on the other side of the desk.

· · ·

"That was a colonel from National Defence," said Yakabuski, staring at the people sitting in the restaurant. It was nearly 8 a.m. but the lights were still on in the restaurant, the sky outside still a gun-ship grey. The breakfast dishes were stacked in a tray next to the service table, waiting to be brought to the kitchen. People sat at tables with coffee cups in front of them, their legs stretched out; there was already a languor to the day. "The squatter's name was Guillaume Roy. He was a Special Forces soldier who helped liberate Sarajevo."

"The coco?"

"Yes, the coco," said Yakabuski, turning to look at the cook, deciding right then that he didn't like the man. "Roy — that name mean anything to you?"

The cook looked startled to be asked a question.

"No."

"You tried to sell him whisky for two years. You never knew his name?"

"No. He was just . . . you know, the coco."

"You know what you have to do to be a Special Forces soldier in this country?"

The cook stared dumbly at Yakabuski and didn't speak.

"Guillaume Roy. That name mean anything to anyone? Ever been any Roys living around Ragged Lake?"

He stared around the room, but no one moved. No one nodded. No one spoke.

"Well, a hell of a way for a good soldier to die. Finish your coffee. We have things to do today."

. . .

The three cops stood on the porch, staring at the sky, nodding their heads while Yakabuski spoke.

"Donnie, I want you to go over to that expedition school and find out if it's open. If it's closed, come right back and stay with Matt. If there's anyone there, bring 'em back and I'll interview them later.

"Matt, you're staying here at the Mattamy. We're going to put everyone back in the rooms for the morning. I'm going to go get that old Cree woman that lives outside town. We'll head back to the cabin for a second look this afternoon."

"Is there another Ident team coming on the train tomorrow?" asked Downey.

"That's right. A couple of detectives as well. Depending on how it goes today, the detectives could be here a while. You boys are probably going back with the bodies."

"Are we moving them today?"

"No. The train is going to wait for us. We'll move them tomorrow when the detectives have had a look. We don't even have bags right now."

"Are we just going to leave them where they are?"

"No. We'll take photographs, and then we'll cover them up. Or do something. We'll see when we get there."

"Doesn't look like it's going to be much of a day," said Buckham, looking at the sky and turning up the collar of his parka to the wind.

"That sounds about right," said Yakabuski.

• • •

Inside the Mattamy, the cops told everyone they were going back to their rooms. This time they were staying there.

They were to take coffee, water, sandwiches — whatever they thought they would need. They would be there for the morning, at least, maybe most of the day.

As people stood and began to head down the hallway to the lobby, Yakabuski yelled at the tree-marker: "Son, you know where this old woman's cabin is?"

"Yes."

"Get kitted up. You're coming with me."

• • •

The tree-marker took Downey's snowmobile and they travelled along the western shore of the peninsula, beside a frozen bay the size of a decent, high-mountain lake. The main body of Ragged Lake stretched out from the bay. There were few islands on Ragged Lake, a geological oddity for the region, and the view to the north was uninterrupted, a full peripheral scan of frozen water and low-hanging cloud, two equal planes of grey and white that made the two snowmobiles seem small and inconsequential as they hugged the shoreline of the bay, the only things moving.

They passed fishing cottages and an abandoned marina, then cut inland on a trail that ran through a black spruce forest. Soon, they came to the base of a bluff and started climbing, coming within a few minutes to a windswept escarpment with few trees and a 360-degree view of everything. Ragged Lake stretched far to the north like an inland sea. The BMR line ran east to west, following the spine of the Northern Divide. Rivers and creeks bled off the spine, cutting trails through coniferous forests.

Yakabuski looked around the escarpment and found the cabin on the northwest tip, tucked inside a small stand of spruce.

"I don't understand why she lives here," said the tree-marker, once he had parked his snowmobile and was standing in front of the cabin brushing away the snow. "There are abandoned fishing cabins right on Ragged Lake."

Yakabuski looked around and saw what any military officer would have seen. High, defensible land.

"Must be the view," he said.

. . .

The woman who answered the door was someone for whom age was no longer a thing specific. She could have been eighty. She could have been a hundred and eighty. She was dressed in dark-green mill pants and a Cowichan sweater, her grey hair wrapped in a bun that sat atop her head like a pillbox hat. She was a small woman, with a spine that curved so she was smaller still, skin the texture of old pine bark, and eyes a dark black that had begun to cloud at the edges of the irises, as though snow were moving in.

Yakabuski introduced himself and asked if they could come in. The old woman took small backward steps and motioned them inside. Stepping in, they were greeted by the scents of white pine and summer mint, and Yakabuski looked around, finding the small cotton potpourri bags sitting on the windowsills. When they were seated on chairs placed around an airtight stove, Yakabuski asked her name and the old woman said, "Anita Diamond."

"Madame Diamond, I am here because of something that

has happened by the old work camp," said Yakabuski. "It's something bad, I'm afraid. Some people are dead."

"The squatters?"

"Yes, the squatters. Did you know them?"

"I knew her. She came to the cabin from time to time. She brought her little girl."

"Do you know her name?"

Diamond seemed not to hear the question. She rocked back and forth on a Morris chair, her small body hidden beneath her thick winter clothing, close enough to the edge of the chair to be teetering. "What happened to them?"

"It looks like they were murdered, Madame."

"Who would kill a little girl?"

"I'm not sure. That is what I'm trying to find out. Did you ever go to her cabin? Meet her partner?"

"They lived on Cap. That is a long way to go if you don't need to."

"I have been thinking that myself. You lived at the old work camp, I am told, is that right, Madame?"

"Yes. Five Mile Camp, it was called. I ran Anita's Place."

"Anita's Place?"

"Yes, I'm Anita," and with that she laughed. What started as a small titter grew until it was much heartier, the small woman bouncing precariously on her chair, laughing and saying a few more times, "Yes, I'm still Anita."

"Was it a business you ran, Madame?"

"How much do you know about Five Mile Camp, Detective Yakabuski?"

"Not much, I'm afraid. I know it was an off-the-books work camp set up by the Cree at the same time O'Hearn opened a mill in Ragged Lake. That would have been back in the thirties. It was called Five Mile Camp because that's how far it was from the camp to the front gate of the mill. It shut down when the mill shut down. How long did you live there?"

"Almost forty years. When you put it all together. Before and after the mill. You think it strange they would build their cabin by the old camp?"

"I do. There are better places. You could live right on Ragged Lake in a cabin that's already built for you. Or go a mile out and build on better land. I think there is a reason they were living there. You still haven't told me if you knew her name, Madame."

Again the old woman acted as if she hadn't heard the question. Rolled her upper body forward to pick away at a piece of lint on her pants. Then she straightened and said, "I think you are right. There was a reason she was living there. Although, I'm not sure what it was. Would you like to know more about Five Mile, Detective?"

"Yes, please."

And she started talking. A rambling narrative that to Yakabuski later would not seem rambling at all but a lucid account of the building and dismantling of a small village on the Northern Divide, told by an old Cree woman who rocked back and forth like a newborn in a log cabin high on a bluff overlooking Ragged Lake, with the wind skittering and tapping against the window panes, the scent of pine and mint mixing with the dark musk of wood burning in an airtight stove, the sky outside shrinking and turning a flat grey, the first snowflakes starting to fall.

CHAPTER
FIFTEEN

Anita Diamond spoke of Five Mile Camp as though she had awoken in the work camp that very morning. How she would hear the low-gear rumble of logging trucks coming through the forest at all hours of the day and night. How the rivers flooded every spring, so the Cree built their houses on stilts, hundreds of stilted cabins along the Old Duck River with throngs of men heading back and forth to Ragged Lake, the mill running three shifts for many years. How the lichen was so plentiful in the camp it shrouded the gneiss and granite — so much purple lichen you could lie anywhere in Five Mile, wherever you were tired, and be as comfortable as though you were in your bed.

"I came with my husband in '73," she said. "We came down from Kesagami; in skiffs we rowed across James Bay. It took us nearly two weeks to reach Old Duck. Another week to get into Five Mile."

Anita's husband was killed two years after they arrived. An explosion in a bleaching vat that killed two workers right on the floor of the mill left Anita's husband badly burned yet still breathing. He was taken back to the work camp, where he screamed and swore at anyone who approached him for three days before finally dying, his screams ringing out over the camp, and everyone agreeing long before he was dead that it was a tragedy he had not died on the floor like the others.

Because her husband was a hard-working man, Anita was left with a well-built cabin and enough food to get by for two seasons. Maybe longer if she ate only two meals a day. She was twenty-five and liked living at Five Mile Camp. Had no interest in returning to Kes' or in having another man in her bed. She had loved her husband and would miss him for many years.

"I didn't know what to do with my life," she said. "That was the plain truth. I was sitting in my cabin, and I didn't have a clue what I was going to do next."

Given this, it would later seem pre-ordained, the thing that happened next, although at the time it lacked import and seemed a random event. It started with a knock on her door. Anita opened it to find three men standing on her stoop. Two were holding bottles of Bright's sherry. The third had a string of pickerel. The man holding the fish spoke.

"You have to help us, Anita," he said. "Marie is acting like a crazy woman. She has thrown us outside."

"Why would she do that, Eddie?"

"I'm not sure. We're not sure," and he turned to look at the two men behind him, who shook their heads and said in unison: "We're not sure, Anita."

"You're drunk. All of you."

"Yes," they said as one.

"None of you are working today?"

"No," said Eddie Blackstone, a cousin of her late husband. "We have the day off. A day off to drink. But Marie is not letting us. She's being nasty. Maybe we can we drink here, in your cabin, Anita?"

"Why would I let you drink in my cabin, Eddie?"

"Because we can pay you."

And with that, he thrust forward the string of fish he was holding. Anita inspected the pickerel and said they could stay two hours.

That's how it started. Anita's Place. Within a few months, Anita had more fish, herbs, and dried venison than she could store and was accepting only cash money. She was also selling the liquor. She was smart. A single woman with a well-built cabin; she had an asset in a work camp like Five Mile. And she kept on being smart. Got some of the musicians who played the bush camps in the winter to play shanty songs in her cabin in summer and fall. She built a small stage for them outside and had cook fires on holidays and pay days. She let young women spread blankets outside her cabin and hold picnics in the evening, so long as they behaved, so long as they were discreet. Inside the cabin, it was strictly tavern rules — men only.

At its peak, people travelled from as far as Palmer's Junction and Lake Simon to drink at Anita's Place. And it wasn't just Cree and Algonquin. White boys from the mill at Ragged Lake came all the time. Indian and Northern Affairs bureaucrats up on inspection tours were steady summer clientele. Executives from O'Hearn came. The O'Hearns themselves, father and son, more than once. Anita's Place was the best juke joint and whorehouse on the entire Northern Divide.

. . .

It was easy to live in Five Mile back then. The men working at the mill made more money than they could spend. Many purchased trucks and cars at dealerships in High River, although they could drive them only on the stub of land next to the rail line, as O'Hearn wouldn't let the vehicles onto its logging roads. The men bought boats and chainsaws and snowmobiles, expensive hunting rifles and winter clothing made from fabric most of them had never heard of before. Tales of this wealth were well known around Kes', and there were always people arriving at Five Mile. At its height, there were close to a thousand people living at the camp.

"Most of us should have realized it was never going to last," said Anita Diamond, drawing the Cowichan sweater a little tighter around her, staring at the airtight stove as though debating whether to put on another log.

"All the boys thought the shutdown was going to be a temporary thing," she continued, deciding against the log. "You get used to one way of living, you think it's always going to be that way. I don't know if there's ever a good way to prepare yourself for what's coming down the road next."

It was early fall, and the men with cars came back from the mill first and told everyone what had happened. The mill had been around so long, most in the camp thought it was just a seasonal change. There was even a festive mood to the camp that night as men gathered at Anita's Place to celebrate the unexpected holiday.

The next spring, when O'Hearn came to dismantle the company store, the men started to leave. Some went to Buckham's Bay to look for work. Some went all the way to

Springfield, or Minnesota, the Dakotas even. None of them found work. Mill jobs weren't going to Indians anymore. Even white men were looking for work. Most of the men were back at Kes' within a few years. Or they disappeared, rambled so far they never found their way home.

Most of the cars were left behind. As were the boats and snowmobiles. The children's playground toys. The furniture. Anita was the last to leave, after several years of being the only one in the camp. She lived with the abandoned cars and the rusting snowmobiles, the rotting cabins, the cedars pushing through the stilted floors, the windstorms taking out the windows, ripping down clotheslines, the small dock on Old Duck disappearing beneath the snow one winter and not being there come spring. Before the forest reclaimed her as well, she hired John Holly to build her a good, sturdy cabin on a bluff overlooking Ragged Lake. Anita Diamond had no interest in moving to another village. She had reached that age when people stopped looking for better places to live. She did not think that was a bad thing.

• • •

The old woman was silent for several minutes before Yakabuski felt confident enough to finally speak.

"The murdered woman was from Five Mile Camp, wasn't she, Madame?"

"Yes. I knew her as a little girl. Prettiest little wisp you ever saw. I knew her father as well."

"What was her name?"

Again she did not answer. But this time she lifted herself

from her chair and walked to another room. When she returned, she was carrying a book.

"She came to me three days ago. She was alone and she was scared. She said someone had come back for her."

"Come back for her?"

"That's what she said. It didn't make a lot of sense, what she was saying. She was talking crazy and she knew it. 'Better safe than sorry.' She kept saying that. 'Better safe than sorry.'"

"What did she want you to do?"

"She wanted me to look after something. She said she was being silly and she would come back in a few days to get it."

"It's that book?"

"Yes."

She reached over and put it in Yakabuski's lap. He picked it up and fanned the pages. A journal. Black leather and of good quality, although not exceptional. It looked like the writing journals you found in most bookstores. The first entry was dated several years before, May 2, 2010, though most of the journal was a single entry, written under the previous Sunday's date.

Yakabuski went to the front of the journal and stared at the nameplate inside the cover. In perfect penmanship, on the sole line put there for the purpose, was written Lucy Whiteduck.

"Lucy," he said, and raised his head to look at Anita Diamond.

"Prettiest girl I ever saw at Five Mile. Her father was Johnny Whiteduck."

Yakabuski turned back to the journal. Between the first and last entries were few others, and most of those were brief and had no date. The final entry was the exception, a long piece of prose that would have taken hours to write, the sort of writing people did late at night while waiting for the sun to come up, wondering what sort of day was coming for them.

There seemed little sense in reading anything else. Yakabuski turned the journal to the window for better light and began to read.

FIREFLIES IN THE SNOW

I have begun to think I should hide this journal. Put
photos of Cassandra and Guillaume in it and stash it
somewhere. So there is at least a record of what happened.
What Dr. Mackenzie always said was important. A record.

Am I losing my mind? I'm not sure anymore. I see
ghosts. I tell myself that. Lucy, you're seeing ghosts.
You're not thinking clearly. Maybe Tommy Bangles was
a dry-drunk. You never spoke to him. You never touched
him. You're cracking up from the stress of being an adult
in this screwed-up world. Get some rest. The good days
haven't disappeared.

But it seems like the good days are leaving. And if that
is what is happening, would I be doing anything more
than preparing myself, coming up with a backup plan the
way you are taught on the Northern Divide, if I were to
stash this journal?

We will fight. Of course we will fight. It is what Guillaume is doing right now. Preparing to protect our home, our daughter. But if we lose, this journal is the only direct evidence that there was once a beautiful little girl named Cassandra Roy. Is it wrong to want to protect that?

I need to think this through. That was something else Dr. Mackenzie always said. Start at the beginning, Lucy. Think it through scene by scene, see your role in each scene, step back — that is what writing is good for — step back and see where things could have gone differently, if different decisions had been made.

Great advice. But where is the beginning? I have always had a problem with that one. My last entry was more than two years ago. Do I just go on from there?

No. That would be absurd.

Should I start two days ago? Get right to the problem and write about what happened two days ago? How our home is now barricaded and we are living with tripwires in the forest and guns on the ledges of our windows, scanning the land around us with field glasses, searching for what we know is coming?

What would be the point in starting there? That's just a description of the situation we have found ourselves in. How does that help us figure out where to go? No, I need to go back further. The danger we are in has something to do with Ragged Lake. There is a connection. I am sure of it and if I can figure it out, maybe we stand a chance. All I want is a chance.

I'm going to start with the day I got this journal.

• • •

96

I met Dr. Mackenzie two days after I was released from the hospital. Met him at his office in Cork's Town, and that's when he gave me this journal. Our first session.

"I want you to write in this journal as often as you can," he said. "I don't want to say every day and then have you come to the sessions feeling guilty if you fail to do this. But as often as you can. Write about your day. How you are feeling. The decisions you are making. If you stay with it, I suspect you will start to see some interesting patterns. Most people do."

"What sort of patterns?"

"You'll see repetitive behaviour and certain situations that make you act a certain way with almost one hundred percent certainty. If you are like most people, and can stay with the writing, within a few months you will be quite surprised by what you have learned about yourself."

I was not that interested in learning more about myself. I'm still not. If anything, I would like to know a whole lot less. But Dr. Mackenzie was right about the journal. In how writing things down can sometimes help collect your thoughts. Help you come up with a plan.

Dr. Mackenzie was my favourite therapist. He didn't act like he knew all the answers. Was never preachy or condescending. He was a middle-aged man who always wore stiff white shirts with sweater vests, even on hot days. That first session, we talked about why I was in the hospital, the reason I needed to come and see him. At the very end, we went through the court order, making sure I understood all the conditions. My first AA meeting was the next morning.

· · ·

The meetings were every Monday at St. Patrick's Basilica, only six blocks from my apartment, in the basement where they also had Sunday school, so every Monday morning there would be new drawings of Jesus on the wall. The leader was a sheet-metal worker from the French Line called Andre, and he began with the Pledge, then asked if anyone wanted to speak.

A middle-aged woman in a purple pantsuit put up her hand, so she went first. She said she had been arrested in front of her daughter's school the week before. She suspected a teacher had called the police but she couldn't say that for sure.

"Annie saw the whole thing," the woman said. "She was looking out the window of her classroom when the police came. They put me in the back seat of the car and made me take the breathalyzer right there. Can you imagine?" The woman said Annie was quiet and nervous around her now. She was thinking of changing schools.

An old man spoke next, said he was returning to the meetings after an experiment with controlled drinking. We all laughed when he said that. He had his two-year pin when the experiment started.

Then a used-car salesman who lost his job two days earlier. There was a woman sitting in the pews upstairs, crying, and that must have been his wife.

When there was no one left to speak, Andre made some announcements and pins were awarded. A mill hand I recognized from the Silver Dollar got a five-year pin. Andre showed him his twenty-year pin when the ceremony was finished and the mill hand stared at it like it was the Northern Star. He asked Andre if he could

touch it. It was all standard meeting stuff and I only
went on about it because that meeting is where I first
saw Guillaume. He spent that meeting looking out a
window. Didn't say a word to anyone. I remember seeing
him that first day and thinking he must be court appointed.
Like me. I don't remember thinking about him much
more than that.

• • •

The weeks after leaving the hospital were strange times
for me. "In transition" is what my worker at Community
and Social Services called it. In a fog would be more like
it. Nothing was familiar, from my bed to my toothbrush
to how I spent my days. I had no friends the courts would
allow me to see. My apartment was in a neighbourhood
I had never visited before. Every morning when I awoke,
it took me a few minutes to remember where I was.

By our third session, I was looking forward to seeing
Dr. Mackenzie. Just for the chance to leave my apartment
and walk through Springfield. The quickest route took
me through Sandy Hill and the main campus for the
University of Springfield, then over two bridges — one
spanning the Big Green River, the other the Springfield
— and from the Springfield Bridge I could see the exact
spot, far to the east, where a fur-trading post once stood,
the first permanent settlement along the river. After that,
it was fifteen minutes down the cobbled streets of the
French Line to get to Dr. Mackenzie's office.

The third session started with Dr. Mackenzie needing
to fill out some forms the courts had just sent him.

"This should have been done earlier, so I do apologize," he said. "June 10, 1989, is that correct?"

"Yes."

"Born in Kesagami. Full status?"

"Yes."

"Father Johnny Whiteduck, mother Gabrielle Laframboise. No brothers or sisters?"

"No."

"Mother deceased?"

"Yes."

"Father?"

"I'm not sure. I've lost touch with my father."

"No contact whatsoever?"

"That's right."

"Was there a falling out?"

"No. I wanted to come to Springfield and he didn't. That's all."

"When did you last see your father?"

I hesitated when he asked me that, wondering how accurate a person needed to be in order to answer such a question truthfully. Did you need an exact geographic location or would the name of a town or region be enough? I decided to be one hundred percent truthful.

"Last time I saw my dad was at Lake Capimitchigama. That's the headwaters for the Springfield. Not far from Five Mile Camp, where we lived for a while."

"Five Mile Camp?"

"That's right."

"I don't see that here. Your file has you going from Kesagami straight to Springfield."

"The file is wrong."

"Where exactly is Five Mile Camp?"

"It's on the Northern Divide. By Ragged Lake."

"How long did you live there?"

"A little over a year. Two more years in Ragged."

"None of that is in your file. How can something like that be missed? This is not your first time in . . . I would have thought . . ."

And he didn't finish the sentence. Dr. Mackenzie did that a lot, like a thought would enter his head midway through a sentence and he needed to stop and examine the thought to decide if it was the kind of thought you should turn to sound. Being polite like that. Even when it made him look clumsy.

"Well, why don't you tell me about Five Mile Camp?" he said eventually.

I remember thinking there was enough going wrong in my life right then to keep any therapist busy in the here and now, but it was nothing but Five Mile Camp for the rest of that session. Dr. Mackenzie asked all sorts of questions about the work camp, about Ragged Lake, how Johnny and I survived. I was careful with my answers. Only our third session.

Dr. Mackenzie was a bit of an outdoorsman so we talked about that as well, what the fishing was like on Ragged, and at the Goyette Reservoir, which he had heard about. We talked about the way the seasons came over the land up north, how spring arrived and rivers overflowed their banks to run wild through the forests — so much water that people were swept away every spring and never came back. Summer, when the land was nothing but different shades of green. Autumn, when the rivers drained away and the winds came and everything you touched had a covering of grey silt. Winter, with as many shades of white as there were summer greens.

"No hardwood trees?"

"Nothing big. Some ironwood. Some tamarack. Not the trees you know."

"I have always wanted to get to that part of the country. Why did you leave?"

"They closed the mill in Ragged Lake. Everyone left after that."

"Where did they go?"

"High River. Buckham's Bay. Most went back to the reserves."

"No one stayed in Ragged Lake?"

"How could you? Everything shut down. The store. The train station. Maybe you could get a little work guiding, but not enough to make anyone stay."

"You came all the way to Springfield when the mill closed."

"Yes."

"Why so far?"

"I wanted a new start. I wanted a big city."

"And you have been on your own ever since?"

"Yes."

"How old were you, Lucy?"

"Thirteen."

• • •

Arriving in Springfield is one of my most vivid memories. A thing that has clung to me. I was hitchhiking outside High River when a truck driver picked me up and took me the rest of the way. Ten hours, including the lunch he bought me, and the last hour I don't think I said even a dozen words. Just stared out the window at the Springfield River, not believing this river with the white caps on a far horizon was the same river you could walk across just outside Five Mile Camp. Then the first buildings appeared: old warehouses and forward-steerage offices. Lumbermen cottages. An abandoned saw mill. Then we rounded the big bend in the Springfield that turns the flow of water from north-south to west-east and the city was right there before us. As though a curtain had just been raised. I saw silver church spires and high-rise apartment buildings, an east-west highway with eight lanes of traffic, factories by the river with stacks pumping pillars of white smoke, thousands and thousands of houses sitting on every inch of cleared land — more houses than I thought you could possibly put in one clearing by a river.

The truck driver took me around the city for more than an hour, laughing every time I pointed at something that seemed marvellous to me. The Madawaska Hotel, with its copper roof and turrets. The Grainger Opera House. The Springfield city hall, with a courtyard the driver told me was designed after one in Italy, right down to a fountain in the shape of Neptune, although water to the fountain needed to be turned off early November of every year to make sure the pipes wouldn't burst, so it was useless a lot of the time and Neptune seemed to scream all winter for no good reason.

We drove past Strathconna Park and the Claude Tavern, the Lafayette, the outlook for Kettle Falls, the truck driver gearing down as low as he could when we reached the Falls so he could turn around in the parking lot, a manoeuver that took him nearly five minutes to execute, and I looked at the Falls the whole time, the mist from the river mixing with low-hanging clouds so you couldn't see the actual river. Just hear it.

When we were finished, the truck driver asked where I wanted to be let out and I hadn't given it much thought until then, so I asked him where a good place might be. He thought the YWCA in Cork's Town would be good, so that's where he dropped me off after giving me twenty dollars and not asking for anything in return. So he was a decent man, like I said. Looking back now, I would say that was a good day with plenty of good signs, plenty of optimistic signs. My first day in Springfield.

Even though the YWCA was a block and a half from the Silver Dollar. Which maybe wasn't such a good sign. Or good planning in any sort of way on the part of the city.

. . .

I was working at the Silver Dollar within a month. The cops would come by from time to time to check the dancers, but I had a decent driver's licence made and I've always looked older than my age, so the licence was normally enough. A couple times I was taken out and brought to child and family services, but just a couple, and I was dancing by the weekend each time.

I would work at the Silver Dollar, off and on, for the next ten years. That nightclub was my life. It was where you would find me any day. Where you would find my friends. Where you would find my boyfriend. Because of that, it was hard for me to do some of the things the court was telling me to do.

Looking for work was like that. The court order said I couldn't step foot inside the Silver Dollar, or any place that served liquor, but I had only ever worked at a nightclub. At first I tried getting an office job, thinking that might be easy, but there were a lot of girls looking for office jobs in Springfield back then. Boys too. The economy was not in good shape. Another thing I never had to deal with before. When you work as a dancer in a nightclub, it's the same guys spending the same money the same night after night. Nothing changes. There is no recession. There is no depression. Economists should come down and study it. Maybe they already do.

One company seemed interested in hiring me, an insurance company downtown — or, the man doing the interview seemed interested — but when I came back a second time, there was a woman there who must have been his boss and you could tell she was annoyed to be there. She even rolled her eyes a couple of times. Before the meeting was finished, the man from the first interview was being nasty to me, like I had tricked him into coming back.

I started looking for a store job after that. The closest I came was a kids' store in the Springfield shopping mall called Tiggy Winkles, which brought me in for a group interview with the Tiggy Winkles personnel committee. That's what the owner called it. The committee consisted of him, two women who worked at the store, and his grandson. The owner said his grandson was there because children had always played an important role in the running of Tiggy Winkles, the reason for the store's success, really. He told me this in a whisper, to make sure I understood I was hearing important stuff. Children are important to a children's store.

I sat on a mushroom-shaped chair and regretted wearing a skirt. The other women wore sweatpants. Sat with clipboards on their knees. It was the grandson who did most of the talking, an eight-year-old boy named Xavier whose first question was, "Would you describe yourself as a Knex person or a Lego person?"

Everyone seemed disappointed when I couldn't answer. One of the women put away her clipboard. The interview ended a few minutes later with the owner saying the successful applicant would be contacted by the end of the week. If I didn't get a phone call by then, there was really no sense in trying to reach him. Xavier stuck out his hand and said it had been a pleasure.

I went to a meeting that afternoon. Found one on the AA website taking place at a hockey rink in the French Line, in the upstairs banquet hall. I sat at the back of the room listening to stories until the urge to get drunk and burn down Tiggy Winkles had passed.

. . .

I think I knew, even in those first few months, that I was kidding myself about starting a new life by avoiding the Silver Dollar, going to the meetings, getting a new job, and pretending I was a new person. I knew but didn't know. Maybe that's what hopeful is. I'm not sure.

That all ended when I returned to my apartment one

afternoon and found a parcel outside my apartment door. A small, wrapped box about two feet square, no postage or courier stamps, no name or street address.

I opened it on my kitchen table and inside was the contents from my locker at the Silver Dollar. I started bringing the items out one by one. A mesh shawl. A change-making belt. Black Chinese slippers. Magazines and crossword puzzle books. I had not used the locker in years. There was no need to return any of this stuff, and whoever had access to my locker would have known that.

I kept emptying the box — a pair of silver pumps that had cost $1,200 in New York City five years ago. A bundle of showbills for featured dancers at the Silver Dollar. Business cards, either dealers or marks, no way of remembering now. I didn't know what it would be exactly, but I found the message at the bottom. It turned out to be a half-full bottle of Glenlivet with a handwritten note wrapped around it.

> *Darling, you left some things behind. Not sure if you*
> *still need the Scotch. You need to phone me.*
> > *Love,*
> > *Tommy*

I put down the note and looked at the junk on my kitchen table. On my best days, I thought I would be forgotten. They had bigger fish to fry. If they were going to do anything at all, I was hoping for something minor league. Anthony coming over and suggesting I leave town, saying, Call us when you get somewhere. Maybe it wouldn't even be that. They'd watch me for a while, see no cops had approached me, see I was being a stand-up girl, and then they'd move on. I wouldn't be forgotten, exactly. And I wouldn't be safe, exactly. I would be somewhere in between. Which would have been fine with me.

I looked at the note and realized it was going to be none of these things. Tommy Bangles. Of all people.

• • •

Why didn't I leave town the next day? It seems crazy to me now, but I managed to convince myself Tommy's note was actually a good thing. A clear sign I had some breathing space. Nothing would come at me from out of the blue. I had received notice and there was a process that needed to be followed. I had seen it often enough. Nothing would be decided and nothing would be done until Tommy talked to me.

I was in no hurry to talk to Tommy.

I don't know if there was a connection, but after getting the parcel I finally spoke at a meeting. I had put it off for months. Not because I was shy, but because I didn't know what sort of story to tell. The whole truth? Half a truth? Something I made up?

I was leaning toward made up. Because there is something false in most confessions, and I am not sure if personal details even matter. I heard so many stories at the meetings, I got people confused. Was it the purple-pantsuit lady who ended up getting a divorce? Was it the mill hand who had tried controlled drinking? And who was it again who told the story of going on a four-day bender and waking up in the cockpit of a private plane on the runway of an airport in Montgomery, Alabama? The man didn't know how to fly. Had never been to Alabama. Just woke up one morning, opened a plane door and fell to the ground in Montgomery. He was a big fan of Hank Williams. Only clue he ever had.

I can't remember who told that story.

So, I got up at a meeting one Monday morning and described how a person becomes a drunk, leaving my name out of it. Could have been any person there. Wake up after more than three years sober and find you want a fun day so badly you go to a liquor store and purchase a mickey of Crown Royal. Don't agonize over it much. Don't stand at the front door of the liquor store wondering if you should walk inside. Don't stare at the bottle before opening it. None of that nonsense you see in bad movies.

And that mickey of rye was like being given a bus station locker. A secret place to stow away every worry, regret, and bad memory I woke up with that morning. Suddenly I was alive again. Hopeful instead of worried. It was the right decision to make. Am I supposed to be a liar and pretend it wasn't?

But it doesn't stay the right decision. That's the damn problem. Before long the fun drinks need maintenance drinks and then the maintenance drinks have to start at ten in the morning, then nine in the morning, before you roll free of your sheets. After that come the blackouts, the shakes — the days when everything around you is spinning like a deck of cards thrown into the air. Reason is gone. Cause and effect is gone. All that shit.

How does it end?

There seemed no easy way to keep me out of that part.

So I told them. In the saddest, sorriest voice I could make up, I told them how I woke up one morning beside the Springfield River, coughing up blood and silt, two cops staring down at me asking where I had come from, puzzled looks on their faces when they stood to look around, the mist so thick we couldn't see the Kettle Falls, just hear it roaring down the canyon.

• • •

Guillaume came to me after I spoke. The first time I saw him talk to anyone at the meeting.

"That was the most honest story I've heard at a meeting," he said.

"Well, thank you. Are we ever going to hear yours one day?"

"Not much to tell, really. Wouldn't want to bore people."

"You're court ordered?"

"No."

"Angry wife?"

"No."

"Here of your own free will?"

"As much as such a thing is possible."

I think that's when I first noticed him. Most people at AA meetings fall into one of two categories. There are your earnest types, the people who have gone through the Shadow of the Valley of Hard-Core Drinking — mainlining Listerine, three-year blackouts, all that crazy stuff — but they manage to survive, and, because they survive, they have no interest in being loud and brave or even noticed. They're just glad to be here.

The other ones are your stone-cold desperate types. The people just starting the journey. Looking at the road ahead and freaking a little every day at how impossible it seems to them. No drinking. Ever.

Those are your two AA types. Awkward-earnest or hopped-up desperate. But Guillaume was neither. His speech was different too. Not slow or stuttering, the way it was for so many people at the meetings. He seemed sure of himself. Damaged goods certainly; I remember thinking that. But sure of himself for some reason.

We went for a picnic the next week. It was after a meeting and Guillaume asked if I wanted to grab a coffee, and when I said yes we went to a nearby Second Cup where he bought coffee, date squares, juice, and panini, and we turned it into a picnic. We walked to Strathconna Park and sat beneath a crabapple tree in late bloom, the last petals blowing out over the river. The air smelled of apples and lilacs and fresh water and every once in a while of peat and musk from a nearby flowerbed a city work crew was turning over. There were kayakers in the river and they were making their way down a course that ended at a bridge not far from where we sat.

"Why do you go to the meetings if you never speak?" I asked.

"Why do I have to speak? Don't the people talking need an audience?"

"I suppose. Although I think telling your story is part of the therapy, something that helps you stay sober."

In a far channel of the river, some kayakers were making their way down a stretch of white water, the brightly painted boats bobbing in and out of view. When the kayakers reached the flat water underneath a bridge they came ashore. Some stopped there and rested although most were quick to put their kayaks on their shoulders and return to the start of the course. We watched them go back and forth like that, as though a procession.

"How would your story begin if you were to tell it?" I asked.

"Just the beginning?"

"That would be easiest, right? Maybe you're not sure where your story goes, but everyone knows how it begins. Why not start there?"

Guillaume looked at the kayakers before saying, "I'm not sure you're right about that, Lucy. I met an old man once, after soldiers had come to his village and taken away every other man. Raped and killed the women. Burned and blown up whatever they hadn't raped or killed."

"My God, where was this?"

"Bosnia. Although it could have been anywhere. Doesn't matter where. I've seen other villages just like it. The man was allowed to live because he was old. That's funny, right? Because he was the oldest, he got to live. He wasn't worth taking and wasn't worth the effort to kill.

"I asked the old man where the soldiers had gone, but he didn't know. He had been knocked unconscious, and when he awoke his village was gone. That was all he knew with certainty. Probably the only thing he would know with certainty for the rest of his life.

"I wanted to leave the old man alone, but my

commanding officer insisted I ask more questions. Ask him when the attack began, he said. Surely he must know that.

"So I asked him. He said the attack began when they built the village. It had been a provocation, building where they had. I looked it up later, and that village was three thousand years old."

Guillaume and I stayed in the park until the city workers left and the sun slipped below the treeline. The wind picked up right before dusk and changed direction, so it swept across the river and blew the last of the kayakers off course. As we walked out of the park we were holding hands.

• • •

Tommy phoned a week later. I have no idea how he got my number and he wouldn't say. He was drunk. It was a Saturday night, so of course he was drunk.

"Lucy, darliiin," he said when I answered. "It's been a while. We're all missing you down here at the Dollar. You shouldn't turn your back on old friends, darliiin. Why don't you come down for a drink tonight?"

Dr. Mackenzie thought turning my back on old friends was exactly what I needed to be doing right then. Although no one should need a therapist to tell them Tommy Bangles is the sort of person you avoid in this world.

"That's sweet, Tommy," I said. "I got your note, by the way. I've been meaning to phone. It's just a bad time right now. I've been out of the hospital less than three months, you know."

"Three months! Shit, that's a lifetime. Do you know what you and I could do in three months? Have you ever considered a thing like that, Lucy?"

"Tommy—"

"Shit, they'd be writing songs about us forever if we had three months. That is fuckin' forever."

"Tommy. You're not listening. I'm not in a good place right now. I'm in recovery. The Silver Dollar is the last place I should be."

"Well, sure, I respect that. You being in recovery and all. But it's Saturday night. Can't you slip out for just one drink? Do you know it's Saturday?"

"Yes, Tommy, I know it's Saturday," and I laughed when I said it, hoping it would sound like a carefree laugh, me amused at something Tommy had just said. As if anyone who knew Tommy Bangles ever thought he was amusing.

I could hear the sounds of the Silver Dollar in the background: tinkling glass, laughter, the badly mixed sound of Steve Miller's "The Joker."

"So are you coming?"

"It's not a good time right now, Tommy. I've already told you that."

"Ahhh, Lucy, come on. There are people down here who are dying to see you."

I didn't say anything. In the background: cash registers, pool balls, the rat-like laugh of men not accustomed to laughter, the shrill laugh of girls who laugh too much.

"Is he there now?"

"No."

"He's not at the club?"

"I just said no."

"Then why are you phoning me now?"

"I already told you, Lucy. It's Saturday night, and I thought it would be nice to—"

"Bullshit, Tommy. You wouldn't be phoning me unless he told you to phone me. And if he's not there now, that means he ordered you to phone me. What else has he ordered you to do?"

"Don't start freakin', Lucy. We were just drinking last night and he said it would be nice to see you. You haven't been around in a while. There's nothing formal about this phone call."

"It's still a bad time."

"Well, don't take too long recovering, darliiin. That's all I'm saying."

There was an awkward silence after that, ended only when Tommy said, "Have a good night, Lucy."

"You too, Tommy."

• • •

Again, why didn't I leave town the next day? I have been driving myself mad thinking about it, and I suppose the short answer is I thought it would be a dumb thing to do. Running would have been like putting a target on my back. Telling them they did indeed have something to worry about.

I also convinced myself — and it is a wonder how a person can do this, take a bad set of facts and convince themselves it's really not *that* bad — that the phone call from Tommy was another good thing. He as much as told me he didn't have free will. He couldn't do whatever he wanted. I needed to speak to another person before any decision was made about me. Knowing this, I made a promise to stay out of the Silver Dollar. A promise I had already made, so the next few weeks were not that different from what they would have been without Tommy's phone call.

I got a job the next day. At a McDonald's. Something I could not have imagined doing a few months earlier, although I could have said that about so many things. My worker arranged the job interview, helping with my curriculum vitae (that's what she called it), and although my work experience could be written with two words — Silver Dollar — we managed to stretch it out to a full page, complete with my name, address, and phone number in bold type on top of the page, like it was important.

"You have restaurant experience?" asked the McDonald's manager, his eyes peeking over my CV.

"Restaurant and bar. Yes."

"You are . . . where is it here . . . ?"

"Twenty-two."

"Yes. Twenty-two. Is it part-time work you're looking for?"

"No, full time."

"You're not in school?"

"Not at the moment."

"I see. Well . . ."

The interview was held in the manager's office in the back of the kitchen. His name was Roger Rodriguez and he was mid-thirties probably, had a hairy stomach that hung over his belt. You could see it easily because of a missing button. Everything in his office was metal. Desk, chairs, window blinds. A burnished silver metal. Like every stove, fryer, and appliance in his kitchen.

He didn't know what to make of me. I did not present as a typical McDonald's job applicant — that was the word my worker kept using: "How do you present, Lucy?" Talking as though I were a gift being offered, which maybe is more right than I care to admit.

When the manager hadn't said anything for a minute, I fidgeted in the chair and said, "I need a job, Mr. Rodriguez."

"Yes, well, there are things I need in this world as well, Ms. Whiteduck. One thing I certainly do not need is to spend money training an employee who will be gone in a month."

"You don't think I'll stay?"

"I do not understand why you are even here. Look at you."

We didn't say anything for a minute. I waited to see if he would hit on me but he didn't.

"I promise you I will stay for one year, Mr. Rodriguez."

"One year?"

"Yes."

"You promise?"

"Yes."

He laughed, put down my CV, rubbed his eyes, and looked out at the people working in the kitchen. It looked like I would be one of his older employees if he hired me.

"Ah, why not? Can you start Thursday? There's a training session that evening. You would need to be here by five."

The old starting time for the Silver Dollar, if you were dancing in the evening. I thanked him and told him that five would be fine.

. . .

Guillaume stopped coming to the meetings around then. Said he had heard all the stories. He would meet me afterward in back of the church with a Woods rucksack packed for a picnic. One hot July day, a summer storm blew in, coming with no warning, no distant thunder or flash of sheet lightning, no gradual darkening of the sky. One minute it was clear and humid. The next, rain was pelting down and we were running toward my apartment.

When we got there we both knew what was going to happen, but there was none of the games you normally have the first time. No made-up stories. No uncertainty or give-and-take. We took our time about it, like we knew we were starting something that would be with us forever, so there was no need to hurry.

We stopped after every button and tug of denim, our tongues warm in each other's mouths. When we had undressed, we made love on sheets turned cold from the dropping temperature, in front of white walls that danced with the late afternoon shadows cast from my windows — leaves blowing past, rain bleeding down.

His body was like nothing I had seen before. There were dark blue pockmarks on his legs that looked like the ridges of fresh-cut metal holes before they are ground down. On his back were large red welts and more unfiled holes. On his chest were dozens and dozens of criss-crossing cuts.

"My Lord, Guillaume, how did this happen?"

"Bunch of ways. Don't worry about it."

"Was it during that war you were talking about?"

"During. Right after. Depends who you ask."

"Do you want to talk about it?"

"No."

"You can if you want."

"I don't want. I did that once. Talked a man's ear right off telling him all about it. Didn't help me any. And I know it didn't help him."

"How could you know a thing like that?"

"Because he came to me once and apologized for not being able to help me. The day before I left his hospital. He came and apologized. This was a man who had four university degrees on his wall, each one saying he had learned to be a helpful man. I think I broke his heart."

I held Guillaume that night until I thought my bones would snap, a pressure so intense it scared me, as though something inside me might rupture and I would die. A need to hold another person, to couple, like I had never experienced before. Was it love? Was it fear? You would think I would know by now.

• • •

Dr. Mackenzie was worried right from the start. As soon as I told him about Guillaume, our sessions changed. He began to talk about the addictive personality and how it manifests itself in different ways but is never anything different. Drunk on this, drunk on that, doesn't make any difference. Addiction is always addiction, even though it has a pecking order, with shelter drunks at the bottom and coke-sniffing CEOs at the top. But an addict is an addict. Don't ever be fooled.

After several sessions like that, I confronted him.

"This is about Guillaume, isn't it?"

"You don't know that much about him, Lucy."

"I know he has a good heart. I know he is a good man."

"He is an addict. He has stopped going to the meetings."

"I have never seen him drink. He knows what he is doing. He is not a stupid man."

"You know what you are saying right now, Lucy?"

"I do."

"And you think he is worth the risk?"

"I do."

Dr. Mackenzie looked at me for a long time after I said that, assessing me, not even trying to hide what he was doing. No other therapist ever did that. Most liked to keep the conversation moving. Therapists working on billable hours are no fans of silence. When he started again it was all about co-dependence, and after a few moments of that, I asked him, "Can there ever be something that completes you in a good way?"

"I'm not sure there is. You should never be that dependent."

"What about religion? Isn't that a way to complete a person in a good way?

"You should have gone to university, Lucy. Have you ever considered it?"

"Please, Dr. Mackenzie, I'm serious."

"Well, yes, religion would be a way to complete a person in a good way. You're right about that. And it is a natural desire to want to belong, to have companionship and shared beliefs. But for the addict, this natural desire is twisted and out of balance."

"It becomes an obsession."

"Yes. That would be a good way of describing it."

"Every saint was obsessed."

"Lucy, where are you going with this?"

"It is the reason I stay with Guillaume. Why I need him. You must see it."

"I'm not sure I do."

"You just said it. Saints are like addicts. Drug-zonked, crazy addicts, but we don't call them drug-zonked, crazy addicts. We call them saints. That's because they know what they're doing."

"I'm still not following."

"If I know what I'm doing I can't be an addict. Self-awareness changes addiction into something else. Something good."

Dr. Mackenzie nodded but didn't ask the question. Leaned back in his chair, stroked his beard, and said it for me:

"Faith."

• • •

Tommy was out of town most of that summer, and it was after Labour Day before I heard from him again. He came to the McDonald's. Drunk. Cranked. Right to my cash register. Pushing people out of his way to get there, and then he yelled, "Fuck, it's true. Someone told me you were working at a McDonald's but I didn't fuckin' believe him. I said he was a lying fuck, for only in my fantasies have I seen sweet, sweet Lucy in a uniform. Very becoming, darliiin."

It's hard to describe how Tommy Bangles looks exactly, his physical appearance, because most people never move off his face. Couldn't tell you how tall he was or what pants he was wearing because they just keep staring at his face. He has long hair that turned grey in his twenties. A big Roman nose. Two front teeth made of solid gold. And last time I knew him, fifteen teardrop tattoos running down his cheeks. Not a tear for every person he killed. Tommy only inked the men and women he respected.

"Tommy, I'm working. Please don't do this."

"I would have preferred a nurse's uniform."

"Tommy, please don't make a scene."

"A scene? What are you talking about?"

And he started laughing. A sneering, mean-spirited laugh that must have changed course and backed up on him on account of how mean-spirited it was, because suddenly he was hacking and spitting out snot, pushing his long grey hair away from his face.

"Sir, is everything all right?"

Mr. Rodriguez. Standing right beside me. Jesus.

"I'm good," said Tommy, and he grabbed some napkins from a dispenser. Spit a ball of snot into them. Bunched up the paper and threw it on the floor.

"Sir, you can't throw garbage on the floor!"

Tommy looked around before saying, "I don't see any garbage cans."

"I don't see how that—"

"If you don't give me a fuckin' garbage can, it's rather on you, Pedro."

"Sir, there are children here. Are you sure you're feeling all right?"

Oh shit.

"I told you I was feeling all right. Didn't you just hear me say I was feeling all right?"

"Yes I did, but—"

"So why would you ask me again?"

"I just thought—"

"Just thought I was lying to you? Or maybe you thought I was a man who says things he doesn't mean, like some fuckin' Indian begging for change on the street, is that what you thought, Pedro?"

"Tommy, nobody said that," I almost screamed at him.

"Pedro here said it."

"His name is not Pedro, Tommy. He's my boss. Please."

"Do you think I care what his fuckin' name is? Or that he's your fuckin' boss?"

I turned to look at Mr. Rodriguez, and the expression on his face was sad to see. Tommy was already laughing at him. There was fear there, but mostly confusion, my boss no longer sure of his next move, wondering what sort of creature stood before him, how Tommy had been sired and raised and imagining the worst, some Gothic horror brought to life and just come marching through the front door of his McDonald's. Terror was washing through his body. Causing his arms and legs to tremor. A thing so noticeable it looked like he was convulsing.

I placed my hand on his shoulder and said, "I can

handle this, Mr. Rodriguez. I promise you. This man will be leaving right away."

My boss turned to me with a helpless look on his face, but then some sort of decision must have been made because he suddenly gave a firm nod of his head, turned, and strolled past the fryers and microwaves to his office. Walking as though in no hurry. Making a precise right turn at his office, going inside, and closing the door behind him.

"Why are you hanging around with shits like that?" said Tommy. "Wait till I tell him it's true. You're working at a fuckin' McDonald's."

"Why do you care, Tommy? Why does he care?"

"I have no fuckin' idea, Lucy. This is between you and him. I just know he needs to see you."

"Tell him I'll come when the doctor says I can. When he thinks I'm strong enough."

"He'll want that doctor to feel that way real soon, Lucy."

"I hear you, Tommy."

"Real, real soon, darliiin."

"Message delivered. Please, cut me some slack here, Tommy. Do you want something to eat? My treat."

And Tommy Bangles stood there weaving on his feet, a line of people behind him trying to avoid eye contact, a confused, young boy's look coming to his face for a second before he yelled.

"Have you ever seen me eat this shit, Lucy? Ever? A Big-fuckin'-Mac? Honestly darliiin, you are losing your fuckin' mind."

• • •

I tried to put it out of my mind. I was stalling for time. Stretching it out and hoping the answer would come to me. I had begun to think Guillaume was going to be part of any answer, although I didn't see how yet, and of course I feel bad about what happened and where we are now. I should have told him right then. It seems obvious looking back, but it didn't seem obvious then, and by then I had begun to live for Guillaume. The only part of my day that did not seem drab or threatening, too hot or too cold, too rushed or too slow.

If I did not have Guillaume I would have had nothing in my life but a McDonald's uniform and $179 in a chequing account. Not enough clothes to fill out a carry-on suitcase. My home would have been a sublet apartment with three side windows looking out on an identical building twelve feet away. No other windows. No horizon. No way of tracking the sun.

To get out of that apartment, we used to go for long walks through Springfield, cutting through the French Line, walking beside the canals, over the Champlain Bridge, sometimes all the way to the unincorporated townships the other side of the river. During those walks it was easy to pretend I had slipped away from everything that was going wrong in my life. Guillaume is from Springfield and loves the outdoors. He grew up in Britannia Heights, not much better than the Nosoto Projects but surrounded by hardwood forests, quarries, a six-mile-long escarpment looking out over the Springfield River. He is as good in the bush as any guide I knew up north. He joined the army when he was eighteen and that makes a lot of sense to me. I don't understand why he left. He won't talk about it.

That's not true. He has never brought it up, and I have never asked.

We would stop for a picnic when we went on those walks, Guillaume bringing a red woollen blanket for us to sit on that was so old the fabric was no longer coarse but the texture of a shammy rag. We made love many times on that blanket. Moving it after our picnic to a dark spot in the forest Guillaume had found, a spot often covered with pine needles, a hidden furrow that deer probably used for a bed during the winter. Afterward, I would fall asleep in his arms. Middle of the day. A sound, dreamless sleep. Only time I ever did that. I tell you — and I am not making it up — there were days back then when I thought everything was going to be all right.

• • •

I got the phone call I had been dreading about a month after Tommy came to the McDonald's. After I had returned from work one night. While I was still pouring water into a coffee pot. A sense of timing so perfect I stood in the kitchen and tried to remember what cars had been parked on the street when I walked in. Wondering if I had missed something.

"Hello, Luce."

Only one person ever called me that. There was a catch in my throat even I heard when I answered.

"Hello, Sean."

"It's been a while."

"It has."

"You good?"

"I'm good. Good enough, you know."

"Yeah, that's what people tell me. Good enough. Course, it's a bit strange, people telling me this and you not telling me this. That part doesn't seem so good to me."

"Sean, I'm sorry about that. And I'm sorry about how everything ended. I'm sorry about a lot of things. But I report to a PO now. Where I've been and all. How can I come and see you?"

"Who's the PO?"

"Why do you want—"

"Maybe I can cut you some slack there. Is it Dagenais?"

It was Dagenais. No way I was telling him that. Last thing I needed was to have my PO stomped in an alley somewhere, Sean Morrissey walking around thinking he'd just done me a favour.

"That's really kind of you, but, honestly, the guy hasn't been a problem. I'm going to the meetings again. I'm working steady. There's nothing to report."

"Those bastards report whatever they want, Luce. You know that. You're being foolish if you don't let me help you there."

"Sean, I'm good. And I'm sorry for not coming down to see you by now. Tommy dropped by to see me and—"

"Yeah, Tommy says he was pretty clear about the message he gave you. I don't understand why I'm phoning you, Luce. Why haven't you come to see me?"

"Sean, this is starting to stress me out. Why do you need to see me?"

There was silence when I asked the question. Complete silence. As though Sean Morrissey were phoning from some vacuous space no one else was allowed to enter, a world that held nothing but Sean Morrissey's voice. My heart skipped a beat right then, gathering the strength it knew was going to be needed.

"You been talking to any doctors, Luce? As part of your recovery?" he finally said.

"I . . . I go to the meetings. I'm in therapy. Yes, I see a doctor. Don't you think I should?"

"Your little swim over the Falls. Yes, that was quite something, Luce. Never heard of anyone doing that before."

"I wouldn't recommend it. But because of my little swim over the Falls, as you call it, yeah, I'm in therapy. It's not the first time, Sean. You know that."

"I know. But last time, you were sleeping with me, girl. Not so much now, right?"

"What difference does that make? I promise you, on everything that is—"

"Save it, Luce. You're embarrassing yourself. You need to come and see me. We have unfinished business."

And there it was. The words I had hoped never to hear. Never hear if I could just start over, be a good girl, do unto others, recite the pledge.

"Unfinished business?"

"Stop it, Luce."

"You want a final scene? That doesn't sound like you, Sean. Why would you want—"

His voice turned cruel and angry. Like a bad drunk poked awake. "Fuck off and listen, Lucy. People are worried about you. I don't need the fuckin' headaches. You get your ass down here or Tommy will bring it in for me."

Then there was a click, and I was left standing in my

kitchen for several minutes like an idiot wondering what to do next, the phone in my hand, water pouring over the lip of my coffee pot. The silence in my apartment was complete and total. As though Sean Morrissey had just blown everything in my life away.

. . .

I should have run right then. That night. As far from Springfield as possible. At the very least, I should have warned Guillaume. That part seems so unfair to me — he's a good man. He loves me. Loves our daughter. There are things in the past that trouble him, and because of this it seems an extra cruel thing I have done — given him more ghosts. And never told him.

I was not thinking clearly. In my defence, I was not thinking clearly. I even remember laughing at the next thing that happened, telling myself it never rains but it pours. One of Johnny's favourite expressions. I tried to see the humour in the situation, blaming it on my mother, a woman I do not remember and have seen only in a photo, a group photo at that, taken in some tavern, my mother standing next to Johnny and looking nothing like me. A short woman with a big chest. Broad face. Although you can see, in the glow of her intoxicated eyes, a bit of my future.

She met Johnny Whiteduck in a bar in High River and stayed with him four years, leaving just before I turned two. According to her sister, another woman I have never met, she died during a bad storm on the Francis River, drowned when her boat capsized. Her body was never recovered. My aunt phoned to tell Johnny this, at the band office in Kes'. I was there and I heard Johnny ask if there were papers he needed to sign, then thank my aunt for calling, and hang up. That was the last time I ever heard my mother's name. So I'm being silly when I say she is to blame for what happened next.

Although, on another level, you could argue my entire life has been little more than a subconscious tip of the hat to dear old Mom. Certainly, I remember the story Johnny often told, when he was drunk and boastful and there were people in our house gathered for one of his parties, and someone asked about me — where I came from, I suppose. About how my mother should have had a dozen children, but no one could get Gabrielle Laframboise pregnant except him. No one except Johnny. Johnny the man. A one-time miracle child courtesy of Johnny Whiteduck. Lucy: Come out here, I want you to meet some people.

I knew the story. And for more than a decade, I behaved just like my mother. Until the day I became her.

• • •

Dr. Mackenzie didn't know what to say. The only time I saw him look confused.

"Eleven weeks?"

"Yes."

He wrote the number in his portfolio. Put a notation beside it.

"How long have you known?"

"I had the doctor's appointment yesterday. I've known for a few weeks."

"What does Guillaume think?"

"I haven't told him."

"When will you do that?"

"There are a couple of things I need to take care of first. Probably this weekend."

"What do you need to do first?"

"Housekeeping stuff, mostly. I also have to tell an old boyfriend, so he hears it from me instead of someone else."

"That's considerate. You haven't spoken to me about an old boyfriend."

That's right. I haven't. Never told you about Sean Morrissey or Tommy Bangles, and I like to think that helped you. If there was ever a knock on your door late at night, that might have helped you.

I don't know if such a thing ever happened. I like to think it didn't, but who knows? Maybe the consequences of what I have done with my life have been rippling out for years, and I just don't know about it. I'm like some faraway shore.

"It's a bit complicated," I told him. "But after I've done that, I'm telling Guillaume."

• • •

For several minutes, Yakabuski had been trying to place her. Recall a face. A meeting. Sean Morrissey's girlfriend. She would have been known.

He had seen Morrissey only two months earlier, at a bail hearing for Patrick Kelly. Morrissey was in the gallery with some lawyers, and they had spoken in the hallway during a break.

"You testifying, Yak?" Morrissey had asked.

"I'm on the list. Doubt if I'll be needed."

"Patrick will be sprung by then?"

"That's not what I was thinking."

Morrissey laughed. He seemed in good humour, dressed in a woollen suit cut fashionably thin, a full-length overcoat thrown just the right way over his arm, so the coat and suit seemed to flow together. His father used to have a walking stick with diamonds inset into the head. Augustus Morrissey. King of the Shiners. Smart men tried never to get within striking distance of that stick.

"You think Patrick is sleeping in jail tonight, Yak?" asked Morrissey. "I thought you knew this town." And he laughed one more time, walked away to join a small throng of lawyers, all huddled with smartphones in their hands, staring intently at the screens.

Kelly was freed fifteen minutes after court had resumed and was out of the cells thirty minutes after that, which might have been a record for the Springfield courthouse. Yakabuski saw him walking down Dominion Street when he went to get his car from a parking lot, shortly after 3 p.m.

He was the last cop to see him. Kelly missed his first court-ordered visit to the police station two days later and a bench warrant was issued, but there had been no sighting of him since. Sometime that spring, Yakabuski guessed, the racketeering charges against him would be stayed. The lawyers had worked out a plea arrangement for Kelly, in exchange for his testimony against Morrissey, but never had the chance to present it to him.

Sean Morrissey's girlfriend. Killed in a squatters' cabin in Ragged Lake. Yakabuski tried to make a connection between the two facts. But he couldn't. There seemed no possible trail that would connect them.

He turned the book back to the weak light coming from the cabin window and continued reading.

. . .

I didn't bother phoning. Didn't get in touch with Tommy. There are old women who are more spontaneous and unpredictable than Sean Morrissey. It was 10 p.m. on a Friday night, and I knew I would find him exactly where he should be if the world were spinning properly — the back table of the VIP lounge at the Silver Dollar.

The club was crowded when I walked in, but I had no trouble cutting across the floor, most people stepping aside long before I reached them, some even pointing at me before I had passed. Being rude like that. As usual, his table was crowded: dancers with mesh shawls pulled tight across their chests. Men with leather jackets also pulled tight across their chests, three-quarter length, so you couldn't see the handguns tucked into their pants. Two were wearing full colours — Popeye, with the Springfield patch underneath. The table was strewn with quart glasses, rock glasses, shot glasses, ashtrays, coins, folding money, smartphones, showbills, wicker baskets of chicken bones, metal trays of congealed cheese, cigarette packs, disposable lighters, balled-up napkins. At the head of all that mess, before a spot at the table clean and polished, nothing more than a rock glass and a napkin, sat a man in white linen pants and a collared shirt, his hair long, framing his face with the perfection only a two-hundred-dollar haircut can give a man, his teeth whiter than the skin of the youngest girl at the table, his skin more unblemished.

"Hello, Luce."

"Hello, Sean."

We went to his office. Whether out of kindness — to get me away from the stares and snickers of the people at the table — or because this was the best way to conduct our business, I am not sure. Sean had been kind in the past, though, and I was rather counting on it happening at least one more time.

"So, I'm here, Sean. What do we need to talk about?"

"Such a hurry, Luce. I would hope you would want to see me. It's been a while."

"This is not where I should be, Sean. According to the courts, this is definitely not where I should be."

"We didn't get much of a goodbye."

"Really? That's why I'm here?"

"No. I already told you — there are people worried about you, Luce."

"Worried about what?"

"What you may say one day to the cops. Or to a crown attorney. Or to those doctors you're seeing, who have to report certain stuff when they hear it."

"That's not happening, Sean. And it won't happen. You have my word."

"Your word? Have you gone crazy, Lucy? Tommy thinks you have."

"I'm not crazy."

"Then why are you talking like a crazy person? What good is your word, Lucy? Think about what you've seen down here. And then you disappear for, what is it now, six months? If it were anyone but you, we wouldn't be having this conversation."

"Really?"

"Yes, really. I don't think you're taking this seriously enough."

"Are you telling me you can't control your crew? Is that what you're telling me?"

"It's not about control. It's more a problem of instinct."

"What are you talking about, Sean?"

"Some people see you as a problem right now. These are not the kind of people who spend a lot of time thinking about their problems. Problem: go away. That's how they like to handle things. It's their natural instinct. They don't understand why you're still walking around."

"Really? Then tell them they have nothing to worry about. I spend all my waking hours trying to forget them. I never want to remember them. They have no problem with me."

"Yes, I tell them that. But you know what, Luce, I must be losing my gifts of persuasion, because they're not buying it the way they should."

"That doesn't sound right either, Sean."

"I know. I agree. So I did what you always did and thought it through, thought about it logically, step by step, and I suppose there is one other possible explanation for what's happening."

"Which is?"

"Maybe I don't believe it either, Luce."

I suppose if anyone ever reads this journal they may think badly of me for what I did next. For what I had planned to do the minute I walked into the club. But no person can be bigger than who they are. I read that somewhere. I think it may be the truest thing I ever read. If Sean Morrissey could save me, how could I not use him? If my unborn child could protect me, how could I not offer her up?

So after staring at each other for a long time, I told him. His eyes grew wide as I talked, the way I was hoping they would, the way they needed to grow if this was going to work. I had been right. He couldn't do it. He was not that sort of man.

"Is this true gen, what you're telling me, Lucy?" he asked when I had finished.

"You want photos?"

"Some people would. We still might be able to reach an understanding here. It doesn't have to be as bad as you've probably imagined it being. If this is a lie, you're going to get caught out real quick. No hope for you, then."

"It's not a lie."

"Well," and he moved some papers around his desk, smiled, shook his head in an I'll-be-damned sort of way. "Congratulations."

He kept me in his office the rest of the night, telling me, as though I needed to hear it, that it wouldn't be safe to leave the room. Like I had never seen a problem disappear behind the Silver Dollar. Kick-marched to the river. Two in the back of the head. Problem drifted away. The Springfield has been getting rid of problems like me for centuries.

So I did what Sean told me and stayed in his office. I

knew nothing would happen to me there. It was unthink-able. Sean's office.

My problem would be getting out of the club.

A half-hour before last call, he came in and said Tommy was the problem. Everyone else had bought into it. No one wanted to go as far as they needed right then to get rid of me. Some of the old boys, with family con-nections going all the way back to Peter Aylin, thought it bad luck. Plus, I wasn't in witness protection. I wasn't an urgent problem. The reason for bringing bad luck down on their heads, it wasn't clear to them.

Everyone except Tommy.

"Well, it's Tommy," was all Sean would say when I asked him about it. "That boy is nothing but instinct."

"Would he really defy you? Openly defy you?"

"Not tomorrow. But this is all new, Luce. What you're telling us. He could say it was a misunderstanding. He was drunk and didn't get the memo. Something like that."

"And that would work?"

"Tommy would walk through a burning building for me, Luce. Yes, that would work."

We didn't say anything for a long minute. Then he said, "Come on. I'll take you home tonight."

· · ·

We parked in front of my apartment building, Sean looking at it with disdain. He lives in a penthouse downtown. When I first met him, he was heading a stickup crew from Cork's Town, Tommy Bangles his right-hand guy. He looked like he could have played in a rock 'n' roll band. Leather pants, a smile that opened doors quicker than Tommy's feet. Sean Morrissey was the only guy I ever knew who told the Popeyes to fuck off. Told Papa Paquette he was sick of being ripped off and he could take his vig and shove it. Sean and Tommy hanged the first crew that came looking for them from the chain-link fence around the Nosoto Projects. The second they nail-gunned to an abandoned garage across the street from the Popeyes clubhouse. Paquette reached an accommodation with them after that, and overnight Sean became a folk hero to every criminal in Springfield, a local boy who did business with the Montreal bikers, the Buffalo bikers, but didn't bother looking like them, dressing like them, or pretending to be interested in anything that interested them. A man who kept his own counsel. Just like Johnny. And just like Johnny, most of the time I had not a clue what was in his head.

"It took some jam walking into the club tonight," he said, after he had finished surveying my apartment building. "Did you know Tommy was coming to get you tomorrow?"

"No."

"Well, some jam, Luce. You always had that."

"Thanks."

"Don't be thanking me too quickly. We need to come to our understanding now."

I stared at him but didn't say anything.

"This has bought you some time, Luce, but that's all it's bought you. No one will come looking for you right now. You have my word on that. And you should be good for a few months afterward. I wouldn't stretch it much past that."

"You think they would still care? It would be nearly two years by then."

"Yes, I think they would still care. It's crazy, Luce, everything you know. I don't want to think about it myself. So don't be sloppy. You've done this before."

"What about you?"

"I can handle Tommy."

"That's not what I meant."

"Oh," and here Sean looked at me strangely, this man I had lived with for nearly a decade, this man who took me in when there was no more Johnny. In a voice that had gone as flat and dead as a late-night radio signal skipping over the arc of the planet, he said, "I'll be looking, too, Luce. No more favours, I'm afraid."

Neither of us said anything for a minute, and then he added, "Stay gone, Luce. Take your man and stay way gone."

• • •

We went to Strathconna Park the next day. Guillaume spread the red blanket carefully on the grass to avoid the crabapples, which were overripe and pulpy by then, end of the season, fruit that now oozed a dark, acidic juice that stained anything it touched. For a long time, we sat on the blanket and stared at the river. Not saying anything. A couple of kayakers were making their way down the middle channel, although they had to cut through ice to come ashore.

I think Guillaume knew what I was going to say before I said it. We had worn warm sweaters and he held me a little tighter while I spoke. When I was finished, he said, "How do you feel?"

"I feel good. It depends a lot on how you feel."

"I feel good."

The grass was long where we sat, the city work crews not bothering to come to the park anymore. There was the smell of musk in the air, and we could see our breath when we exhaled.

"It's going to be quite the change," Guillaume continued. "I'm trying to picture how it will work. Us taking care of a baby."

"We can make it work."

"We probably can. We can make anything work, I bet."

Guillaume stared at the kayakers and didn't say anything for a while. There must have been a hundred thoughts racing through his head right then, and I clung to him a little tighter, trying to get a read from his body on how he truly felt, how much of a good thing this was.

Finally, he said, "Those kayakers seem so determined. I was that way once. Just like them. You wouldn't have recognized me, Lucy. Some days I wish I were still like that. Then I wonder if that is a smart thing to wish for."

"Probably not. Why do we have to be determined about anything? Life should be simpler."

"I agree."

"I don't want to be determined. I just want to belong somewhere. Be left alone. That would be enough for me."

Guillaume nodded and kept staring at the kayakers.

"I feel the same way. I wish the world was better prepared for this baby, but we'll be all right."

"Don't you mean you wish we were better prepared?"

"No, I mean the world. I love you, Lucy. Like nothing I've ever loved before. Having a baby with you is a good thing. How could it not be? I just wonder some days if the world is set up to let good things happen."

"That's a little dramatic, don't you think?"

"Really? Have you never thought about it before, Lucy? How difficult it is to do the right thing in this world? Why can't we live in a world where if you try to do the right thing, that's what happens? All the time. You get what you deserve. Never want to hurt anyone, run scams, fight wars — boom, that's what you get. Why is that so difficult?"

I sat on the blanket and the blood rushing to my head almost made me black out. The adrenaline and fear of the past few months released with a waterslide whoosh through my body, my next move coming to me in a flash of light and memory. So obvious.

"Do you want to disappear, Guillaume?"

"Love to. Know a place?"

"You know what? I do."

CHAPTER
SIXTEEN

The tree-marker was the first to see it. Before sound had travelled up the bluff. Before the grey jays had been spooked from the trees. Small sparks of light on the eastern shore of the bay that reminded him of his dream of fireflies. Several seconds passed before the sound reached them. *Pop. Pop. Pop.*

Yakabuski put down the journal and walked to the window. The snow had started falling in thick white flakes, the criss-crossing winds on the bluff pushing it around so the flakes formed small funnels that spun for a few seconds before falling apart. The light had formed patterns below them — a bright, bracelet-like ring by the shoreline, one flickering point of light to the east. The sound was now constant. Like a bird tapping away at a dead tree.

"Where would that be?"

"The survival school," said the tree-marker.

. . .

They came fast off the bluff, racing their snowmobiles through the forest, the spruce and balsam losing distinction, losing shape, becoming dark shadows that scampered beside them. They were briefly airborne when they hit the level land by the bay, then they were rushing past the fishing cottages, the Mattamy, Downey standing on the front porch with a rifle cradled in his arms, Yakabuski motioning for him to stay there, not motioning to the tree-marker, and so the boy kept following.

It took them only a few minutes. They parked a hundred yards from the survival school. Buckham was hiding behind a snowdrift fifty yards in front of them.

"Stay there," yelled Yakabuski, and then he looked at the tree-marker. He should have told the boy to stay at the Mattamy. In his rush to reach Downey, he had not stopped and given the boy instructions. He sat beside Yakabuski now, on his haunches, hiding behind a snowmobile, staring at what could be seen of the survival school. No obvious fear on his face. More curiosity.

"I maybe should have told you to stay at the Mattamy."

"I don't mind."

"You hunt?"

"Sure. Not bird so much. But I hunt."

"Ever fired a handgun?"

"No."

There was no sense sending the boy back. Yakabuski had already decided that. There could be someone with a sniper rifle and a decent scope inside that building and they had

143

just been lucky getting into position. The boy looked at him waiting for the next question.

Yakabuski rolled his neck and said, "Stay here behind your sled. I'll be right back."

He fell to the ground and began crawling toward Buckham. The snow was falling so heavily Yakabuski could barely make out the survival school, although as he crawled closer he could see the front doors, wide open, snow blowing through. It had been five minutes since he'd heard gunfire.

"What happened here, Donnie?" he said, reaching Buckham.

"Shit, Yak, did you see any of this?"

"Could see it from the bluff. What happened?"

"I knocked on the door. Guy answers and I tell him there's a police investigation going on, he needs to come up to the Mattamy. He says sure, turns around, and all of a sudden people are shooting at me."

Buckham paused a minute. Took some deep breaths of air. Despite the coldness of the day, heavy beads of sweat were rolling down his face.

"You returned fire?"

"Right away. I tried to get the bastard at the door, but he'd already disappeared. I ducked outside and stuck to the walls till I got to the rear, high-tailed it toward the bay, and circled back."

He may have been a young cop on his first posting after three years of patrol but that part had been smart. Buckham hadn't panicked and run in a straight line toward the Mattamy. Hadn't been cut down easy like that. If someone was going to take him out, they were going to need to work at it. A good, tough kid from the Springfield Valley.

"How many do you figure are inside?"

144

"I'm not sure, Yak. Did you see anyone shooting from the second floor?"

"I was too far away."

"I don't know. More than us. And better guns. What the hell is goin' on?"

Yakabuski turned to look at the young cop, then back at the survival school, the large white-frame building a blur in the falling snow, the hard lines getting lost so the building shimmered and undulated and only the darkness inside gave you any sort of steady reference point. He turned and crawled his way back to the sleds, motioning for Buckham to follow him.

. . .

"If I'm right, in a few minutes people are going to come running out of that building."

Buckham and the tree-marker stared at the ground where Yakabuski was etching a map in the snow with the flat edge of his mitt. The tree-marker was holding the Sig Sauer P229 Yakabuski had given him.

"You stay right here," Yakabuski said, looking at the tree-marker. "Donnie, I want you to reposition to the end of the drift. Keep to the ground and no one should see you. Now, if anyone comes out of that building, I suspect they're going to be shooting at you." He stared at them. Buckham would be a few years older than the tree-marker. Not many.

"If that happens, you cannot think what your response should be. You cannot wonder why anyone would be doing a thing like that. If anyone comes out of that building firing a gun, you need to return fire."

He gave them each a long hard look. Then he said it again, using different words, because he wasn't convinced they'd got it.

"This isn't what you were expecting today, I know that. But we need to deal with what we've been given. You boys will need to return fire. Without hesitating. Can you do that?"

"Yes, Yak, not a problem," said Buckham.

"Yes," said the tree-marker, and Yakabuski smiled at the boy. "Consider yourself deputized, son."

"Can you actually do that?"

"No. That's TV bullshit. But if it helps you, yeah, you've just been deputized."

They each chuckled. A curt laugh: just enough to show each other they were men who could laugh on the tough days.

"I'm heading toward the back of this building," Yakabuski said. You'll lose sight of me, but I'll give you a signal for when you should start watching the building."

"What's the signal?" asked Buckham.

"You'll know it."

Yakabuski took one last look at the building in front of him, imagined how the interior may have looked from the many times he'd been inside lumber-company bunkhouses, how the hallways would have run and the rooms connected. He scanned the second floor, confirming as best he could that there were no shattered windows there, and then he pulled the hood of his parka tight around his head, propped himself on his elbows, and started a slow crab-crawl toward the back of the survival school.

. . .

146

For most of his crawl, Yakabuski stayed behind a six-foot snowdrift that ran beside the walkway of the survival school, needing only a short run at the end to reach a maintenance shed. He lay beside the shed and stared at the back of the building. The main-floor and second-floor windows. Back and forth. Wondering if there were better odds for one.

He took a minute to run it through his mind — more convenient on the main floor, but better venting perhaps on the second. Better storage on the main, you would have to think, but it didn't look like anyone had been firing from the second. Eventually, he decided he wouldn't be able to figure it out. There were too many variables. He would go with the main floor.

He reached into his pockets and took out the six emergency flares he had taken from the cargo bins of the snow-mobiles. Using bungee cords he had also taken from the bins, he tied two groups of flares, three to a group. He scooped some snow and began breathing on it, making it softer, moister, until he was able to wad the snow around the flares.

He took one last look at the back of the bunkhouse and calculated the range at thirty feet. Manageable. He wouldn't need to run toward the bunkhouse to get a good throw. And he would have two attempts. Hopefully.

He took out his camp lighter and lit the first group of flares, waited a few seconds, his back turned to the building. When the flares were burning well, he stood out from behind the shed and pitched them toward the middle of the five lower-floor windows.

He ducked behind the shed. No gunfire. No one had been stationed at the rear windows. Or someone was stationed but not doing his job. Good news either way.

He heard the window break. Glass cascading for a few seconds. A high-pitched jingle-jangle sound he could just make out above the wind.

Yakabuski started counting the seconds — one, two, three, four, five, six — then he stopped. Threw the second bundle away.

Main floor it had been.

• • •

The explosion was loud and cacophonous and so bright it seemed to kick a hole through the low-hanging clouds. But it wasn't the noise and sudden fire that startled the tree-marker and Buckham so much as it was the wind that swiftly turned direction and came at them, knocking them down; a wind turned sharp and ferocious, rushing toward the imploding survival school, punching it down as though it were a crash test dummy house in some old nuclear safety film.

After the winds came flames that shot more than a hundred yards into the sky and stayed there for a long time, until running out of whatever fuel was feeding them, and then collapsing back on themselves, falling as though solid, like a wall tumbling down.

Through all that — the wind, the noise, and the light — the tree-marker and Buckham heard Yakabuski shout, "Pay attention, boys. This is the part I was telling you about."

Two men came running out the front door. One was running erect, with flames licking the back of his parka. The other was stumbling blindly. He had the gun — a military issue M16 — his finger pressed down on the trigger, laying down a line of fire with tracer bullets, ratio of three-to-one it looked to Yakabuski, who stared at the red flashes and wondered who would do a thing like that. Tracer bullets. In case they were ever under siege. In case they ever had to beat a hasty retreat in the middle of the night with someone giving chase.

Buckham rose from his hiding position and fired his handgun at the man with the gun. Aiming below the waist. But he rushed the shot and missed. The man with the M16 turned to the sound of Buckham's gun, a smile coming to his face.

But he never took his finger off the trigger. And as he turned, the man standing next to him flew backwards in the air as though hit by a boom.

The firing stopped. The man with the gun stared at where the second man had been. Buckham took his time on the second shot, his mind racing but a voice inside him telling him to stay calm, that he probably had the jump on a near-blind man in shock at having shot his friend.

Buckham hit him in the right knee and the man pitched forward. Dropped his rifle and grabbed his kneecap. Let out a loud scream that he tried to stifle but couldn't completely.

At the same time, what was left of the survival school collapsed behind him. Flames shot back into the sky. There was a plume of ash and soot. Then a gurgling sound, or a sucking sound, it was hard to say what it sounded most like, although it reverberated and roiled and seemed half-human, and when it faded away three men stood and walked toward the fire — Yakabuski, Buckham, the tree-marker — recognizing the finality of the sound.

When they got to what was left of the survival school, they stood in a semi-circle, guns in their hands and no one

149

speaking. Noticing for the first time that the fire had turned the falling snow to rain. For a twenty-yard radius. They were standing in a cold rain.

CHAPTER SEVENTEEN

Cambio heard the explosion. A loud rumbling sound that came from nowhere and then was gone. He held the phone close to his ear and spoke only once: "François?"

Even before he hung up, he saw the flaw in what only days ago had seemed a brilliant plan, one that had worked exceedingly well for, what was it now, four years? He and his business partners had often congratulated themselves on how clever they had been. For knowing some things in life are eternal. Some of those, transposable.

You could look upon his career in many ways, but it did not seem an unfair thing to Cambio, or an inaccurate thing, to say the primary source of his great wealth and power, the thing fundamental, was what a man was allowed to do in a desperate village. What desperate people were willing to do.

He forgot who had said it first, on one of his trips up north, sitting in a private dining room in a hotel in Toronto,

Papa's little brother there, Papa himself speaking on a cell from the penitentiary where they had him locked away, talking about whether ships or planes would be best to bring in product from a new lab near Juarez, trying to figure out the supply line. Someone had said, "Why don't we make the shit up here, in one of our own fucked-up little villages?"

It seemed a silly suggestion. Everyone laughed. An accountant Little Papa brought with him said maybe desperate villages were a "scalable business model," and everyone laughed some more. A few minutes later, they stopped laughing and started talking.

He couldn't remember who had suggested Ragged Lake. He didn't think it was one of Paquette's boys. They were big city through and through, right down to the black silk socks they wore inside their boots. But someone had known about that village. A near-abandoned village on the Northern Divide, with good rail lines, a floatplane base, not even an operational police service nearby. It had seemed a gift.

But the world's best hiding place, once discovered, can become the worst. He sees that now. Seclusion tracks back on itself. Like a wounded animal often does. Becomes a thing easily hunted. It was always assumed the cops would never come, or if they did it would be because someone had been arrested, someone had been turned, and they would know. To be discovered because of crimes they had not committed? It was such bad luck that Cambio wondered if that was all it was.

He was in Houston that night. A tall glass building downtown where he kept an office with a bedroom. He stared down at the Buffalo Bayou River, dusk coming on quickly, the water turning a dark molasses colour. Was he being played somehow? If so, Cambio could not see who would be gaining an advantage. Or what the game might be.

For the next few hours, he sat in his office, smoking hashish and looking at the river, thinking random, contradictory thoughts: a sanctuary turned to a prison, black and white, yin and yang, transformation and transmutation, and change speeding up and taking over the world, out-of-control change, which could be either chaos or momentum. Cambio could not decide.

Eventually, he placed a call.

"You need to go to Ragged Lake."

"All right."

"Tonight."

"There is a terrible storm here, my friend. Everything is shut down."

"Are you asking me to repeat myself?"

"No." A short pause and then the man who had answered said, "It is the complete op?"

"Yes. As we discussed."

"I do not wish to bring this up right now my friend, but—"

"The money will be wired to your account as soon as we are finished here."

"Very good."

"Anything else?"

"No. We kitted up yesterday. We're good to go."

"Phone me before you leave Ragged Lake. If François is still alive, I would like to say goodbye."

Just before the phone went dead, Cambio thought he did indeed hear a storm in the background. A howling, white-static noise that stayed on the phone for several seconds, building and growing louder, even after the dial tone had returned.

. . .

Yakabuski stomped out the fire still flicking on the back of the man cut down by the M16, turned him over using the heel of his boot, and confirmed without needing to bend down that he was dead. The man had no head. Just a charred and bloody ball of flesh trapped inside the hood of his parka, where a head should have been.

The man who had been shooting the M16 was sitting on the porch, screaming and clutching his knee. Yakabuski kicked the gun farther away and knelt to have a look. He stared at the man's clothes. At the ground around him. Then he said, "It's just the knee, isn't it?"

When the man began to nod, Yakabuski punched him, under the chin so his head snapped back, lolled briefly to one side. His body fell backward into the snow.

"What the hell?" yelled Buckham.

"I don't want to hear him right now, Donnie. He has no other wounds. He'll live. Nice shot, by the way."

Yakabuski began to frisk the man. He found a Glock 34 in a front pocket of his parka. He searched the body of the dead man but found no weapons. He picked up the M16 and checked the clip.

"Cuff him to the back of your sled, Donnie, and let's head back to the Mattamy."

Buckham looked at the unconscious man, then to his snowmobile, then back at Yakabuski.

154

"You want me to drag him behind my snowmobile?"

"We're not carrying him," said Yakabuski, and he started walking toward his snowmobile. Halfway there, remembering something he had forgotten to say, he turned to yell, "You probably don't want to be going too fast, Donnie."

CHAPTER EIGHTEEN

The bar in the Mattamy was dark when they entered — a just-before-last-call darkness, although it was only late afternoon. Downey had not bothered to turn on the overhead lights. Or light any of the candles on the tavern tables. He went to start bringing people in from their rooms while Buckham stoked the fire.

Yakabuski sat the biker in the middle of the room, handcuffing his feet to the legs of a chair. He left his hands cuffed. The man had not screamed while being dragged behind the snowmobile. Had not yelled or complained. Indeed, he had yet to say a word.

While people were being brought back to the bar, Yakabuski took off his parka, shook out the snow, draped it over the back of a chair, and walked to the fire. There, he rubbed his hands back and forth to bring some warmth back to them. Although his back was turned, he knew everyone in

156

the bar was staring at him right then. Waiting like patrons in a theatre for the show to begin.

Yakabuski rotated his neck from side to side to work out a kink, gave his hands one last rub, turned, and said, "Anyone know this man?"

"He's from the survival school," said Holly.

"How do you know that?"

"I'd see him in the bush sometimes. He fishes Lake Simon."

"That's right. His name is François," said the bartender. "He comes in here sometimes with some other guys from the school, when they're picking up people on the train." The bartender looked over at the handcuffed man, sneered, and said, "What the fuck happened out there?"

"Well, there was one big mother gunfight," said Yakabuski, "then there was one big mother explosion. Would you say that about covers it, Donnie, what happened out there?"

"That about covers it, Yak."

"And, oh yeah — dead people. We got more dead people."

There was no reaction. None that Yakabuski could see anyway. No sharp intake of breath. No surprise. The room right then was filled with a languor so thick and warm it was almost sensual. Yakabuski had never been in an opium den, but he had read about them and thought they might have much in common with a cabin in the bush when a winter storm was moving in, a fire going in the airtight, and people hunkering down for a few days. He thought there would be similarities.

"I don't know how many dead people we got," he continued. "I suspect we'll find a few more when we sift through what's left of that old bunkhouse. Looks like you're going to need some new drinking buddies, François."

The man had long, greasy hair that must have been

tucked into a toque most of the winter, because it was tangled and misshapen, pushed into geometrical shapes. He had a scraggly black beard that hid a lower cleft of pimples. His eyes hadn't moved off Yakabuski's face since the detective had started talking.

"What do you say, François? Want to tell us why you and your buddy would be shooting at the local law enforcement just for knocking on your front door?"

He would have been in his late twenties. Perhaps early thirties. Well-muscled under the parka. He stared at Yakabuski for a few more seconds, then shrugged his shoulders, as theatrical as could be, turned his eyes to a point on the floor six inches ahead of his feet, lowered his head, and said nothing.

"Yep. That's what I thought you'd do. Well, you're just a sorry sack of shit, ain't ya, François? Making me do all the work. We should have shot you and kept the other mutt." Yakabuski walked over to the handcuffed man, stopped a few inches from his face, turned around to look at the people in the bar, and said, "Has anyone figured it out?"

His eyes travelled around the room. The bartender seemed to be chuckling under his breath. Holly and Gaetan were raising and lowering rock glasses. Buckham was whispering something to Downey. The waitress was staring out the back window. The cook was trying again to dry a rock glass with a wet towel. Nothing in the room seemed quite right. Quite on point. They're tired, thought Yakabuski. Two days now since the bodies had been found in the squatters' cabin outside their town. Two days of bad sleep and worry and now a major storm moving in and they were stuck in a dark bar with three cops and a man in handcuffs, dead bodies lying to the east and west of them. Fatigue. Stress.

Confusion. Yakabuski was probably looking at a lot of things when he looked around this room.

"Are you going to tell them, Frankie or am I?"

He finally got a reaction from the man. A flash of anger that crossed his eyes for only a few seconds before retreating. It reminded Yakabuski of the eyes you saw sometimes on old muskies when they were brought to the surface chasing a lure only to see danger at the last moment then dive back to the bottom. The look a muskie like that would give you before it disappeared.

He didn't like to be called Frankie. Yakabuski almost laughed.

"My Lord, Frankie, are you really going to make me do all the work? Is this what you're telling me, Frankie?"

Yakabuski stared at him hard, trying to get another reaction. But the moment had passed. There was nothing in the man's face now but indifference. Millennia's worth of old-fish indifference. Yakabuski gave his own languid and theatrical shrug of the shoulders, reached into the pocket of his parka and pulled out a Buckmasters hunting knife. He flipped open the blade and put it to the side of the man's throat.

A slight reaction this time. But not much. After leaving the knife there for several seconds, Yakabuski made a quick slicing motion down the man's left arm. Took two more slices, and then he started pulling goose feathers from the sleeve of the parka. Ripped open the sleeve like it was a rib cage on an operating table. When he bent over he let out a soft whistle and said, "Christ, you got two of them."

Buckham and Downey had moved closer and could clearly see what Yakabuski was talking about. Two red thunderbolts. Tattooed on the man's left forearm.

"Yep, you're looking at a read badass, boys. Ain't that right, Frankie?"

The man in handcuffs said nothing.

"Ragged Lake. You must have loved this one." Yakabuski started laughing.

"Detective, do you mind telling us what the hell is going on?"

John Holly. The old fishing guide having enough of the games. Of the pissing contest between the cop and the biker. Yakabuski couldn't blame him. He was getting tired of it, too.

"I'm sorry, Mr. Holly. What we have here, in Frankie, is an officer-class enforcer of the Popeyes Motorcycle Club. And what you had there, in that survival school out back, was probably one of the biggest methamphetamine labs on the northeastern seaboard."

Finally, there was a reaction. The waitress gasped. Buckham and Downey let out near identical loud exhales. Gaetan dropped his rock glass, the ice cubes sliding across the bar. No one made an effort to grab them.

"I'm guessing it was that big from the size of the explosion. And because good ol' boys like Frankie were willing to shoot at some cops just for knocking on their front door. But most particularly, I'm guessing because of Frankie himself, a not one- but two-thunderbolt Popeye assassin, sitting right here in the bar."

Yakabuski kept on laughing. He knew he shouldn't be doing it, that it was sending every wrong message he could — to the cops under him, from whom he didn't want any frivolity for the next few days; to the others in the room, who were confused and scared and wouldn't know what to think of the officer-in-command laughing like a lunatic; to the man in handcuffs most of all, who might feel emboldened by a captor who lacked balance, who was prone to bouts of extreme emotion. But he couldn't help it. Maybe he was as tired as everyone else.

"One last question for you, Frankie," said Yakabuski, managing to stifle his levity. "It would have been your job to protect the lab. You were the security. How does your boss normally react when someone fucks up as badly as you've just fucked up?" The old muskie eyes came back. Yakabuski looked at them and said quietly, "Yep. That's what I thought."

CHAPTER
NINETEEN

During the Second World War, Ragged Lake was a prisoner-of-war camp. The place you sent German sailors plucked from sinking U-boats in the St. Lawrence River. Spies caught red-handed. Nazi sympathizers who got close enough to bad ideology to need to pay a price for it. They were all sent to Ragged Lake to work in the bush camps.

The prisoners were housed in two bunkhouses built next to the mill. A wooden fence was built around them and barbed wire placed atop. Soldiers from the Rangers reserve unit in High River provided sentry duty in the evening. But in the daytime, the prisoners had the same run of the town as anyone else. They worked in the bush next to men who had been working the camps all their lives. Ate meals in the same cookhouses. Any minute of any workday, the Germans could have made a run for it. The POWs were called Krazy

Krauts by people on the Northern Divide, but not a one of them was crazy enough to try to leave. There were nearly three hundred miles of bush between Ragged Lake and the nearest town of any size. How could you escape?

So Yakabuski was being overcautious in his selection of a cell for the Popeye enforcer. He inspected a dry-goods storage room and a janitorial closet. The storage room had a small ground-level window that didn't look large enough for a man to crawl through, and the janitorial closet was good and sound but had a hollow-frame door, so Yakabuski chose neither. Instead, the prisoner was put in the walk-in freezer. It had a metal latch you could lock and hard plastic walls. No windows. If you turned off the power, no one would freeze to death and there was a pipe that vented outside.

With the power cut to the freezer, the light was off even with the door open, and the prisoner stood in the shadows like some back-door-of-the-church penitent, silent and needy, hands tucked behind his back until Yakabuski closed the door with a swoosh and he disappeared. Yakabuski walked back to the bar, and with everyone staring at him, said, "I have to use the phone."

• • •

"Fuck, Yak, what have you stumbled on up there?"

O'Toole had barely stopped swearing since Yakabuski had reached him. The line this night sounded frail and tenuous, the chief's voice hollow and distant despite the anger of his words.

"It's the Popeyes," Yakabuski said one more time. "They've

been operating here four years, I figure. They used the train to ship everything in and out. It was pretty slick. Someone at BMR has to be in on it."

"Four years. That's quite a coincidence."

"I know."

"The drug boys thought it was coming up from Boston."

"Dead wrong. Tell 'em I said that."

"Fuck. And you've taken out how many of them?"

"One that we know of. We didn't actually take him out. It was his buddy who shot him. I would think there are bodies inside the lab. And I've got one guy locked up in a meat freezer."

"How are the kids doing?"

When Yakabuski had left to make his phone call, Downey was sitting in a chair pulled close to the walk-in freezer. He was staring at the metal door with a sneering satisfaction, the sort of smile you see on the face of some hunters posed beside a kill, a look of mean-spirited superiority. Yakabuski had felt compelled to tell him not to try and talk to the prisoner. Buckham was sitting at the bar, where he had sightlines on everyone else. Only occasionally did he look at Downey sitting in the kitchen. And then, as though he didn't like the person he had suddenly seen, he looked away.

"They're all right."

"So, the squatter family, they stumbled on what was happening and the bikers killed them?"

"Looks that way."

"It would take a bastard like a biker to kill a little girl."

"All sorts of bastards in this world."

"Fuck, Yak, you know that better than anyone. What a

fucking mess you've got on your hands. You have reinforcements coming tomorrow. I'll call BMR and tell 'em we need our own fuckin' car. Are you good till then?"

"I'm good."

CHAPTER TWENTY

The cook made sandwiches in the kitchen while the waitress set up three tables. When people were finished eating, Buckham and Downey began escorting them back to their rooms. The Tremblays went first, the old woman holding onto Buckham's proffered arm, the old man walking with a limp Yakabuski had not noticed before. Then the guide, with a half-bottle of Scotch cradled under his arm that Yakabuski allowed him to take to the room, making sure Holly understood he could not leave the room until morning.

"No exceptions this time, Mr. Holly," he said. "We expect you to stay in your room."

"I'll be fine, thank you."

Then the Sports. Even though Yakabuski knew now that they were not Sports, it was hard for him not to think of them that way. They so looked the part. The youngest one looked glum and put out as he was led to their room; the

166

older one read a newspaper, looking up only occasionally to see where he was going, like a business commuter walking beside a morning train. Then the bartender, the cook, and the tree-marker, who seemed to have stopped drinking and brought to his room only apple juice, water crackers, and a badly bound copy of *Riders of the Purple Sage* he had found in a box set aside for such books in the lobby. The waitress was the last one to be escorted to her room. The last because she had insisted on cleaning tables, stacking the dishwasher, working even though Yakabuski told her it was unnecessary. But the girl received such obvious solace from her work that he let her finish.

"Thank you for your help today, Marie."

"You're welcome, Mr. Yakabuski."

"I hope you sleep better."

"Thank you. So do I."

After everyone was gone, the three cops stood in the gloom of the empty bar, and Yakabuski said, "You boys have a preference on the shifts?"

"No."

"No."

"All right. I'll go last."

. . .

Yakabuski took his time walking to his room, stopping to read the brass plaques under the mounted fish. There was a large pickerel halfway down the hallway, caught thirty-two years ago, according to the plaque. The fish glowed like a Japanese lantern in the darkness.

From behind the closed doors, Yakabuski heard rustling

sounds and running water, short bars of whispered conversation. He picked out the voice of Madame Tremblay. The young Sport. He was not sure if they felt relief yet that the murder had been solved, that the killer of that squatter family was now sitting handcuffed and locked inside the freezer. He doubted it. They would still be taking it all in, what had been happening in Ragged Lake the past few years, the people they had been living among — hard thing to process when you find out you've been living cheek-to-jowl with true evil. Or working for true evil. Which was something lots of people had to process. It took time.

Smaller fish were mounted in the hallway. Not the muskie and pike you had in the bar and the lobby. Framed black-and white photos were placed between the fish, archival photos of Ragged Lake for the most part. There was one showing a giant log boom that took up half of Northside Bay, a half-dozen cabins, and a permanent cook fire in the middle of the raft. A POW cabin with a half-dozen men posing with some Rangers, arms thrown over shoulders, a man in the middle holding an old-style football.

Yakabuski suspected that if he took a photo of Ragged Lake today, it would look archival. Right from the outset, he'd be looking at something lost. Out of focus. Half-forgotten. The town had that sort of feel to it, the same feel other mill and lumber towns had these days. When he was in them, Yakabuski felt like he was walking around in the past tense, everything around him retreating and moving backward.

He continued down the hallway, patting a pocket of his parka almost unconsciously to make sure Lucy Whiteduck's journal was still there. Before entering his room, he stopped to look at one last archival photo. It showed the front gates of the Ragged Lake mill, men gathered around the fence, a large banner hanging from a smokestack in the background that he couldn't quite read. Standing in the middle of the knot of men was Charles O'Hearn. Yakabuski recognized him from newspaper photos. He had died about ten years ago. To his immediate left was a tall Cree man wearing a sports jacket and tie. A handsome man with his arm thrown around O'Hearn. Standing to the other side of the lumber baron was another man, tall and thin, his skin pale and sallow, a young man who might even have been a teenager, dressed in a suit that fit him perfectly. Yakabuski stared at the face and thought he had seen it somewhere. He leaned in to have a close look, nodded his head, and entered his room.

CHAPTER
TWENTY-ONE

That night there was no gently twirling snow on the lake. There was utter chaos. A maelstrom of snow and wind that churned over the frozen lake and then charged fast and hard to strike the north wall of the Mattamy like artillery rounds. The timbers in the old building trembled and moaned. The lights flickered and seemed at risk of being extinguished.

Donnie Buckham sat in a chair he had placed near the reception desk, the spot giving him three angles of surveillance. The view out the front windows was a confusing mess of shadows and shifting shapes, nothing he could make out clearly; but out back, because of lights kept on at the biplane dock, there was distinction. Buckham could see the snow billowing and crashing on the lake like waves on an ocean. See a midnight horizon that was remarkably clear and distant because of the blanket of snow. He had never shot a man. His second shot had landed right where he'd aimed, taking out the man's knee, and he knew there would be operations to make him walk right again. If such a thing were possible. He had likely crippled him. A man like that. A Popeye assassin. He sat in his chair with an hour and forty-five minutes to go before Downey relieved him. It seemed an interminable length of time. He was restless, and he sat there trying to grab onto one of the many emotions coursing through him — make one of them stick — so he could relax and concentrate on his work.

Matt Downey had no doubts. He lay in his bed wishing he had been the one Yakabuski had sent to the survival school, the one who had helped destroy a meth lab and shot a Popeye assassin. He knew there would be commendations waiting for Buckham when they returned to Springfield. He had moved his career ahead five years. Maybe more. He would be working robbery, first-class detective maybe, when Downey was still powdering rooms at Holiday Inns in Cork's Town. It wasn't fair. Nor was the rebuke Yakabuski had given him on the trailhead the other day. It had seemed a fair question. Can we just make sure there's a crime before heading all the way to the Northern Divide?

Downey sat there thinking life was unfair, until the thought occurred to him there might be some refracted glory in all this. Which cheered him. It was a hell of a story, what had happened here in Ragged Lake. Downey lay in bed and started practising it, seeing how much of a role he could safely give himself.

John Holly poured himself another drink. Last one tonight, he told himself. He had thought briefly about getting hammered, then decided against it. Comfortably numb would have to be enough for tonight. He needed to keep some wits about him. He sipped the Scotch, closed his eyes and listened to the wind raking its way up and down the exterior walls of the lodge, like the scratching, thumping, and braying of some predator animal. There may be no better feeling in the world. To be sheltered from a bad storm.

He wished he had taken a book from the lobby bin. He read most nights, as he had told the cop, history for the most part, any sort of history book, although if it was a book about the North Country, he liked it more. The week before, he had read for the first time the story of Henry Hudson and how the great English explorer had been betrayed by his crew after they had endured a tough winter on the shores of James Bay. The captain had wanted to explore the New World for another summer, but the crew wanted to return home. And so there was a mutiny. Hudson, his son, and seven others were set adrift in a shallop that tried for four days to keep pace with the sailing ship *Discovery*, rowing until they could row no more, and then they had faded away on a retreating horizon of ice and water, never to be seen again.

For days afterward, Holly wondered how it would have felt to be put into a boat and set adrift, to stare into the eyes of the men who had betrayed you, who had measured and weighed your fate, and decided your time had come. He wondered if Hudson had been surprised. Betrayal seemed to be a constant in history. Some sort of oxygen, almost. So Holly didn't think there should have been any great surprise. He wasn't sure if the men who had pushed away the boat would have even felt guilt.

William Forest stood in front of a full-size mirror looking at his naked body. He made muscles ripple up and down his arms, his legs, then stroked his groin so his member stood upright, and then he stood side to side, looking at that as well. It was time to leave Ragged Lake. That's what he was thinking as he stroked himself, his back turned to the window, the lights low so no one could see him from outside, a habit he had not thought to break, even on a night like this. He wondered about the prisoner in the freezer. A part of him wanted to take the initiative; another part knew that would not be wise. He was here if they needed him. They knew that.

The cook was not moving. He lay on his back snoring. The bottle of Canadian Club he had snuck from the bar lying on the bed beside him, the last few shots roiling in the bottom whenever he moved. The cigarette he had in his mouth when he passed out had smoldered and burned away a hole the size of a baseball in the comforter. The down inside the comforter had burned like incense sticks for a long time and there were even small flames for a while, but the cook was protected for some reason. Kept alive. God making the sort of decision he makes routinely, keeping a worthless man alive while somewhere a good one died in pain. The cook, oblivious to such cosmic machinations, to the eternal riddles of philosophy and religion, woke up to finish his bottle of rye, then went back to sleep.

• • •

The tree-marker knocked on the wall of his room, waited a few seconds, and knocked again. The waitress sounded scared and confused when she answered.

"Who's there?"

"It's me. The tree-marker."

"What do you want?"

"To talk. How are you doing?"

"How am I doing? How do you think I'm doing? There are people killing people around here."

"That's why I knocked. To see how you were doing."

This silenced her. She wondered if it might be true. That he was being kind.

"We could hear the explosion and see the fire from our rooms," she said. "I've never seen anything like it."

"I know. I saw a refinery fire once down in Springfield but this was worse."

"Worse?"

"I'm telling you. The flames out at that bunkie seemed higher to me."

"Did you see anyone get burned?"

"Saw someone came running out of the building who was all on fire. But he got shot right away."

"By the cops?"

"No, by the guy he was with. It was an accident."

"My Lord. I can't believe what is happening here. A meth lab? I've been working at the Mattamy two years. I had no idea. How can you keep a thing like that a secret?"

The boy leaned closer to the wall, almost pushed his ear against the drywall so he could hear the girl clearly.

"It might not be all that hard," he said. "People don't ask a lot of questions around here. Did you know there was an Englishman, who came over here once, came right to the Divide, and he pretended to be a great Apache chief from the Dakotas, and he got away with it. People bought the story."

"You're making that up," said the girl.

"I am not. They got an exhibit of the guy at a museum in Springfield. He was famous. He wrote books and everything."

"Didn't he speak with an English accent?"

"You would think. But people didn't ask him a lot of questions. Hell, they didn't even want to know how he learned to write books."

"I don't believe it. People aren't that dumb."

"You can look it up. And I don't think people *are* that dumb. Sometimes people just don't want to ask a lot of questions."

"You found the bodies of the squatters, too, didn't you?"

"That's right."

"What was that like?"

"I'd never seen dead people before. Now I've seen three of them. Each one shot up. That would be a horrible way to die. Metal ripping you up. Metal coming your way, no accident about it, not getting lopped with a chainsaw or something like that. Cut up with metal because that is the way someone wanted it to go for you."

"What is happening around here?"

"Bikers. They pretty much run High River nowadays. That cop, Yakabuski, he flat out nailed the one we got in the freezer. Sucker punched him cold."

"The cop?"

"Yeah, the cop. Everyone's acting weird right now."

The waitress said nothing for a minute, not knowing what to say next, wanting to say something halfway normal. Eventually, she asked, "How long have you been working for O'Hearn?"

"Same as you here at the Mattamy. Prit' near two years."

"You like it?"

"I like it a lot. I love the bush."

"Isn't it dangerous? Being out there without people?"

There was a wall separating them and no familiarity, so the girl had no way of knowing the tree-marker was smiling right then. Feeling good for the first time in days. Already knowing the waitress came from Buckham's Bay and already reminding him of girls back home, and now for reasons he could not articulate, although he would think about it for the rest of the night, he felt closer to her than he had felt to anyone in a long time. Just by her asking that one question. Wanting to know if a place without people was dangerous. After everything that had happened the past two days.

"It's not that bad," he said gently. "In some ways, it's better."

• • •

The Tremblays took their medicines one after the other, carefully counting the pills, unwrapping the paper around the glass in the bathroom, sharing the water. They had been allowed to bring toiletries, pyjamas, and robes from their home, and they hoped to have a more pleasant evening.

"I cannot remember the last time I was this tired, can you, Gaetan?" asked Roselyn, and Gaetan yawned, not saying anything afterward, as it struck him as a good answer.

"Maybe it is time we left Ragged Lake," she continued. "This place has seemed cursed for a long time. Now this. I do not think this place will ever be good again."

"A place is not good or bad, Roselyn. It just is."

"How can you say something so silly?"

"How can you? Something bad has happened. A few bad things. But it was done by people. It has nothing to do with this place."

"Place is everything, Gaetan. It is who you are. If I were

not born in Kes', would I be the woman that stands in front of you today? Would I be a different person if I had never lived at Five Mile? How could it be any other way?"

"I'm not sure, Roselyn." He sat down on the bed. "I read an article once about twins who were separated at birth. They met each other years later and they looked exactly the same. Even wore the same clothes. Where they lived seemed to make no difference."

Roselyn stared at her husband and pity came to her eyes. Then kindness and love, and she went to lie beside him. Of all people, Gaetan should see the obvious, but for some reason he refused. As if place could be denied. As if newspaper stories ever amounted to anything.

Tobias O'Keefe stared out at the storm, the wind pushing around the snow in great billowing sweeps, like God shaking out a blanket, he thought. David Garrett sat on a bed, untying his boots, gazing not out the window but at the back of the front door. Garrett did not understand why it had been necessary to share a bedroom. It seemed an inconvenience. If he had been sharing a room with anyone other than this man, he would have complained. Surely you've made a mistake. Does O'Hearn need money so badly it can't spring for two out-of-season hotel rooms in Ragged Lake?

But he had said nothing. Tried to see this trip as an opportunity. A chance to further his career. He had been jolly on the train. A good companion during their meals at the Mattamy. A diligent worker when they were out on the field, making note, he was sure, of things others would have missed. Machinery that would be eligible for a recent tax change allowing for faster writeoffs on such obsolete equipment. A treasure trove of old seeding records. Contact information for a manufacturer that O'Hearn thought had gone out of business but had instead only merged, and that alone might speed up a retrofit by six months.

Yet his companion never seemed to warm to him. Looked at his work with the impatient indifference a teacher might show if he were about to go on holidays but still had a dull child's essay to mark. For long stretches of time, Garrett was even left on his own — the other man more interested in exploring the countryside on his snowmobile — to work in the shuttered darkness of the mill over a conical space heater, using a flashlight to find old documents.

Sharing a room made no sense. Why not give him a room to continue his work when he got back to the Mattamy? Why go through this charade? The basest possibility for such a decision left him unsettled, an effect magnified whenever his companion stepped naked from the shower or on the rare times he smiled and seemed to lick his upper plate at the same time.

"Quite a storm," he said once his boots were off, but as usual O'Keefe said nothing. Kept staring out the window. Not even acknowledging his companion's question.

• • •

Yakabuski stared at the treeline of spruce and pine bending in the wind. They didn't look like trees to him. More like summer hay. Or cottonwood strands thrown to air. He had rarely seen wind this strong. The creaking and groaning of ice on the lake was mixed with sounds from the forest. The thunderclap banging of trees as they fell. The whistling of branches being ripped from trunks and flying through the air.

There had been no way to make it back to the squatters' cabin. He went through his day once again, but did not see how it could have been done. He took off his parka, placed it on a chair next to the bed, and tried not to think of the bodies in that cabin. Still lying where they had fallen. How their faces would have looked, for there would be slight differences, even in this cold. He wished now he had turned down the eyes of the young girl. As if that family had not been abandoned enough. Now they were locked in their death poses until the world found the time to collect them.

There seemed to be abandoned people all over the Northern Divide these days. People not connecting to anything anymore. Not working anywhere. Not knowing what they would be doing two months from now. Rootless, desperate people living in a world that had abandoned them, something that had been going on so long now there were people drifting around who couldn't recall any other way of living. Couldn't remember a time when people grew up and always did a bit better than their parents. When people had a job until they decided they didn't want a job. When they knew what they would be doing next Monday morning.

The sure things in this world had vanished. Along with decorum and decency and just plain neighbourliness, it seemed to Yakabuski. Everyone was on the take these days. And how could that be? After ten thousand years of progress, after the fabled march of civilization, most people were still left wondering how to survive. As if we were still cavemen looking with fear upon a dwindling fire. It was almost embarrassing.

Yakabuski took the journal from the inside pocket of his parka and sat on the edge of the bed. He suspected the police chief had seen it by now: bikers killing that squatter family

179

was a convenient story that explained away all the problems but there was no witness. No one you could ask ten thousand questions so you could feel better about the story. Left owning a tale of happenstance and bad luck — wrong place at the wrong time — and they were supposed to be all right with that.

If O'Toole hadn't thought of that already, he would think of the gun soon enough. A heavy-bore shotgun. A duck gun. Used by people — if you believed the story — who used military-grade assault rifles with tracer bullets.

Maybe they were wearing overalls when they killed that family. Chewing strands of hay. Left the turnip truck running outside.

No, there was something wrong about that story.

Yakabuski opened the journal, flipped to the page he had turned down, leaned the book a little closer to the bedside lamp, and began to read.

FIREFLIES IN THE SNOW II

Guillaume loved the plan right from the start. If you were looking for a way to slip off the edge of the planet, it was a pretty good plan. He never once asked a question that made me think he was unsure of what we were doing. That he had doubts. He was tired and it was time to move on. We both felt that way.

I never heard from Sean or Tommy again. Guillaume moved in with me and that helped me feel safer. I thought about telling him the whole story but never did. I was confident again.

I worked at the McDonald's until I was eight months pregnant, and on my last night Mr. Rodriguez took me to an Irish pub in a strip mall across the street where there was a cake waiting for me and three tables of people who worked at the McDonald's. There were baby presents wrapped in expensive paper and a card they had all signed.

It was rather sweet. I wasn't expecting it. Although I knew we would be leaving Springfield and would not have Guillaume's truck much longer, I made up a story about him struggling to fit a car seat into the truck and they all laughed. It seemed the least I could do for them.

I had my last session with Dr. Mackenzie the next day. We spoke like people about to part for summer holidays or some long journey. I miss him some days and hope he is well.

"I have you blocked out for two months, Lucy," he said when I arrived. "I have the missed appointments starting the week of the eighth. Is the fifteenth still the due date?"

"Yes."

"It looks like you could come any day. How are you feeling?"

"I feel fine. Better than I did a few months back."

"You saw the doctor this morning?"

"She says I'm fine as well. Healthy baby girl. She won't be a small child."

"Well, you look good, Lucy. You must know that. I don't think there is a way, really, that you could ever look anything but . . . good."

He stammered the last word, as though he had come to the end of the sentence and regretted where he had found himself. Wishing he could start over. After blushing for a second, he asked me about Guillaume.

"He's good," I said. "I know you have your doubts about him, Dr. Mackenzie, but he's a good man. I love him and he's good for me. We're at the same place in our lives. This only works because of Guillaume. I know that's the sort of thing you don't want to hear, but I feel lucky to have him."

"Well, I only want what is best for you, Lucy. Guillaume may well be a good man. From what you have told me, I am inclined to believe he is. But be careful. Be aware. You know what you are dealing with. You know what your diagnosis is. No therapist has ever told you anything different." He stared at me and I didn't like him right then. For sounding like a doctor.

"Do you think I'm going to be a good mother?" I asked.

To his credit, he didn't hesitate. Didn't take off his glasses and think for a minute, make out like this was a question that needed to be pondered, considered, reflected upon with all the time you need to reflect upon the big stuff, the stuff you're not certain about.

"Yes. I think you will be a good mother, Lucy."

"Why do you say that?"

"Because you will love this girl. You will protect her. You will always have her best interests as the thing that motivates your actions. She will never feel unloved or . . . abandoned."

Again, he stammered out the last word. As though saying something he wished he had had a bit more time to think about. We hugged at the end of that session, and I promised to bring my daughter with me when I came back for the first appointment after the break. Guillaume would come as well. I told him we had already bought a car seat.

• • •

Guillaume went to collect the midwife the following Monday, one of those early spring days that lacked warmth but felt like spring all the same. A day so clear it was disorienting after a season of dull winter skies. There were no shadows or clouds that day, and the wind built steadily so that by early evening, when my water broke, it was a high keen outside our window and the stop signs on the street below were rattling.

We had found the midwife at the Odawa Friendship Centre, an old Cree woman from Kes' who lit sticks of cedar incense when she arrived and made me lie on our bed, where she wrapped hot towels over my body as I listened to the storm move in. Shortly before midnight, the rain started. Splats of water that landed on my window with so much force it could have been children throwing rocks. There was thunder in the distance, and the midwife started to chant an old song I remembered hearing as a young girl, not sure where it would have been, not from Johnny, couldn't have been Johnny, a Cree lullaby about the founding of the universe, three brothers setting out on a journey, two to die, one to prosper. The wind was now rattling the stop signs with so much force the sound had become a constant metal clanging, a thing out of control, rising in pitch and intensity until it mixed with the wind and the rain to become some new sound, some mad, high-pitched scream announcing the cleansing of Springfield.

The midwife was still singing a sad song about three brothers setting out on a journey when our daughter was born at four in the morning. She was born at the high point in the storm, when trees were being ripped up along the shoreline of the Springfield and tossed like cabers into the river, when cars were crashing on the Trans-Canada

Highway and power was going out in every home and business in the Upper Springfield Valley.

We had already chosen her name. From a children's book of myths and fables we had purchased at a second-hand store, both of us loving the name and the story that went along with it. There was nothing about her birth to make us reconsider. Cassandra.

. . .

We left Springfield ten days later. Drove Guillaume's truck to High River and sold it to a dealer on the edge of town who drove us the rest of the way to the train station. For the first two hours, the train travelled the southern tip of the great boreal forest, rising and falling on the uneven grade, going around granite hills and over trestle bridges that spanned rivers we could only dimly see in gorges far below. The forest was spruce mixed with some outlier maple and oak at first, but after that came the grand sweep of the Upper Springfield Valley and the white pine, the white pine that towered and shimmered over other trees, the trees that brought lumber companies this far north in the 1800s, when they were looking for squared timber to build English naval ships. There were some old-growth stands still ringing the train-line. Looked like mountains when we passed. The height unknown.

We travelled on and before long passed the last access road to the Goyette Reservoir. The land began to change after that. Flatten. Could see the horizon in the distance, past pebbled riverbeds and clear-cut land. Soon we were travelling down the Northern Divide, the sound of running water so loud you would have thought you were in a ship. The conductor stopped the train at mile 372, where there was a thick stand of spruce, a gravel embankment, and a culvert with a creek running through it. The conductor told us when he was lowering the stairs that it had been "ten years, lordy, it must be more" since he had last stopped his train at mile 372 of the Northern Divide Line.

"There used to be an Indian camp in there. Is that where you folks are heading?"

"No," lied Guillaume. "We're heading to Old Duck to do some fishing. Make our way over to the Goyette after that and get a ride home with some friends."

"That's quite a trip."

"We've been planning it a couple years."

"You don't have a canoe?"

"Friends have left us one on Old Duck."

"Good friends. It's not easy getting into that stretch of river."

"They work for O'Hearn. They drove right in."

"Well, that'll do it. Take care of yourselves. Looks like you'll have the weather on your side."

"Thank you."

"And you have a real sweetie there. What's her name again?"

"Cassandra."

"Yes, a real sweetie," said the conductor, although our daughter was swaddled and he had seen nothing more than her eyes. With that, he pulled up the stairs, closed the gate on the train, pulled a cord, and the metal wheels started to turn. In a few seconds, the train rounded a bend, the engineer sounding his whistle once before he rolled out of view, and we were left standing by the side of the railway tracks, the sound of rushing water filling our ears.

. . .

It was strange, walking the old trail again. No longer a clear path through the forest but something hidden that needed to be divined from time to time. Once, we lost it completely, and Guillaume needed to take a compass bearing to find our way back, but we never worried. We were travelling river country. In river country you are never truly lost. You follow water and you arrive somewhere.

We reached Five Mile Camp just before dusk. Most of the cabins were gone, long fallen to the ground, although there were a few walls still standing. Some even had roofs, badly sagging but still supported by rough-hewn logs you could see through holes in the walls. An evening mist was coming in from the Old Duck River and it swirled around our feet as we walked past the cabins, the rusted cars, the broken pieces of dinnerware, a clothesline which had, almost as a miracle, a badly faded pair of jeans still clipped to the end of it. The jeans flapped in the wind, making the sound a large injured bird might make.

"How many people lived here?" Guillaume asked.

"A few hundred. Maybe close to a thousand for some years. It was a big place. People were always coming and going."

"It was never an official town?"

"No. The Cree never wanted to live in O'Hearn bunkhouses. The company built bunkhouses, when the mill first opened, but they sat empty. So they tore down the wood and built a company store instead, here in the camp."

"How long did you live here?"

"A year. Another two in Ragged Lake."

We stepped around wooden planks that had rotted to mulch. Bicycles with only strands of rubber left hanging from the wheels. Piles of clothing so badly faded you could only guess what the original colours might have been. That first night, we stayed by the shore of the river, not even bothering to pitch our tent, hooking up our sleeping bags and sleeping with Cassandra nestled between us. As we fell asleep, we heard the hoot of a barred owl and both of us took that as a good sign.

At first light, we finished the hike to Capimitchigama. The trail to the headwaters was even less obvious than the one into Five Mile. It was possible no one had come this way in years. Even less of a reason to go to Capimitchigama than there was to go to Five Mile.

Guillaume never asked why we were walking the extra distance. Why we were not staying in the camp. So I never had to tell any of the stories I had rehearsed. We walked side by side down a trail I had not walked in twelve years, a day I remembered well, in spring, too, but later in the season, with buds already turned to small leaves that cast filigreed shadows on the trail. Two people walking in silence then as well.

In a few minutes we crested a knoll and saw Capimitchigama, a small dollop of cold blue water with ice still ringing the shore. Still not speaking, we walked toward the far shore of the lake to a dense stand of spruce, the trees crowding in on us the closer we came to the water, eventually forcing us to twist and switchback, the air turning colder, the world seeming slightly detached, slightly untethered as we moved through that forest, the way I remembered it. When we were twenty feet from the shoreline, still surrounded by trees, we stopped.

Guillaume put down his rucksack, and I paced in small circles with Cassandra bouncing off my chest. When he had rested a few minutes, Guillaume started the hike back to Five Mile Camp. I lay Cassandra on a blanket and started removing rocks from the spot we had chosen for our cabin.

• • •

We lived in a tent the first six months. Guillaume purchased it at an army surplus store in Springfield, the oldest one in the store, I think, but he had insisted on buying it, saying the thick, stiff canvas would serve us well and he wasn't concerned about the weight. This was not a fishing trip, he said. This was not a vacation. We were going somewhere and staying. How heavy could anything be, really?

I was laughing at that, when we paid extra money to buy the oldest tent in the store: how heavy could anything be, really? Guillaume can get by on six hours' sleep. Less than that. And he likes to stay busy when he's up, can't stay still, so hard work tends to be a thing he welcomes. He's practical, too, could see the utility in that old tent, so of course he'd see no problem in hauling it all the way to the Northern Divide. It ain't heavy. It's my home.

He was right, of course. We were never wet in that tent. Or cold. Not even in November, when the lake had frozen and there was already snow on the ground. In the morning, the canvas sponged up the dew, and at night, it gave off the scents it had gathered through the day — white pine and wood smoke, lilac and wild mint. I cannot recall a room I have lived in that I loved more.

Guillaume fashioned a sled from sheets of plywood he found next to the old company store, and he used that to start hauling out the lumber we used to build our cabin. Two-by-fours. Two-by-sixes. Support beams. He would pry the wood from the collapsed cottages, looking for any that had been covered up or fallen a certain way, that hadn't been exposed to twelve years of rain and snow.

The tools were all there. As I promised him they would be, explaining that people would have left everything behind, taken not much more than the clothes on their backs, certainly nothing heavy. Guillaume thought about that for only a few seconds before saying, yes, he could see people doing that. He found a crosscut saw hanging from the branch of a white pine, as though someone had placed it there that morning and would be coming back after lunch. Screwdrivers of every size and description. Nails. Pry bars. Mallets. An ash-handled hammer was found in the trunk of a car, the head balanced against the shaft so perfectly it swung on its own weight. It was the only thing Guillaume found at Five Mile that truly surprised him. That someone would leave behind a tool like that.

While Guillaume built our cabin, I prepared the cooking area and the hearth, picking rocks from the shoreline of the lake, organizing them by size, small boulders to fine pebbles, then burrowing a circular trench, laying the stones down largest to smallest, pacing atop the pebbles and tamping them down. Like Guillaume, I do not mind work and I take my time when doing a job, knowing I will be looking for another task as soon as this one is completed, preferring to do a proper job anyway.

"Do you know that is a macadamized rock line?" Guillaume asked me one afternoon. "What you're building there, that's what it's called."

"I didn't know it had a name."

"Laying down rocks largest to smallest, tamping it all down so it becomes a level surface. Those were the first roads. Before gravel and asphalt."

"How do you know that?"

"They still have roads like that over in Bosnia."

He stopped what he was doing and helped me with the cook pit. We paced side by side. In perfect unison.

The company store had been built with roof trusses, and Guillaume separated them and brought them back, but they were difficult to align and we briefly considered building a horizontal roof. But we knew that was being lazy. The weight of the snow would be too much. So we hung the trusses as best we could, not perfect, but solid, and after that Guillaume lay down plywood and Typar, then shingles he made from old pop and beer cans.

He found the cans in an old dump, thousands of them, half-buried in peat moss and pine needles, lying in the remains of green garbage bags. Guillaume brought back several sleds of cans that first week and worked on them for months. His last chore of the day. He liked the work

— labour that came with a number, that could be assessed and judged by simply counting the number of flattened tin cans stacked beside the hearth when we rose for bed. I enjoyed seeing him do it, the hammer ting sounding through the forest, the moon taking shape overhead, and the pickerel rising to the surface of the lake, their long sleek bodies cutting across dark water.

By the time the snows came, it seemed as though this had always been our life. I had no memory of another time or place. I tell you that honestly. It really did feel like I had been reborn.

. . .

The first person to visit us was an old fishing guide. John Holly. I remembered him from the Mattamy, one of the guides that showed up each spring and pitched a tent beside the lodge.

"Morning," he said, and Guillaume stopped working on the roof, came down his ladder, and shook the guide's hand.

"You're putting up a cabin," said Holly. "You with O'Hearn?"

"No."

"They have timber rights to this land. Did you know that?"

"It's government land. Timber rights can't stop a man from building a cabin. You got to be logging the land to do that."

Holly looked over at me and nodded.

"Been a while since I seen any Cree out here by Five Mile. How you doing, Miss."

"I'm doing well. My husband is right about the timber rights."

"Of course he is. O'Hearn has timber rights to half the known world. Means fuck all. He may not like you taking stuff out of his work camp, though."

"It was never his," I said. "That was an old Indian camp. And it's abandoned. When was the last time anyone lived there?"

"Been a while. You're right about that, too."

Cassandra woke up right then, and I don't think Holly had noticed her until then. She was wrapped in a blanket and lying beside me. He smiled when he heard her scream and then walked over and squatted on his haunches to watch while I lifted her up and began to rock her.

"How old?"

"Three months."

"She's beautiful."

"Thank you."

Then he stood up and turned back to Guillaume. "Well, good luck to you. I heard people were living out here, and I just wanted to drop by and see. You're cashing a cheque at the Mattamy?"

"That's right."

"We'll probably see you in town. My name is John Holly. I guide out of the Mattamy."

They shook hands one more time. When Holly left, we went back to work. We knew people would come eventually to see what we were doing, and we both thought it a good first visit. Holly had neither threatened us, nor tried to be our friend.

O'Hearn sent someone later that month, a bull rigger from the bush camp at Simon Lake. The man had never been to Five Mile but, when he toured the old camp and saw what we had built he laughed and kept slapping Guillaume on the back, calling him a "ruddy genius."

He spent the night in a tent he pitched by the lake and left early the next morning, saying as he packed up his ATV that we were no doubt crazy, but the stuff we had taken was junk and we were living on government land — even if O'Hearn had the timber rights — so if we fucked up in any serious way it would be someone else's problem, not his.

"So, have yourselves a right ruddy life," he yelled, and with that he took off. This visit also pleased us. It seemed that we were well on our way to falling off the edge of the planet.

. . .

For the next twenty-seven months we never had another visitor. Never heard a noise outside our home that was anything but animal or weather. Never saw a face in the morning or late in the evening we did not love. A seclusion and a repetition like I had never experienced before, as though the good moments of the day had expanded and pushed everything else aside. Love. Work. Family. The fine high rise of that. Those were our days.

We grew herbs and root vegetables in a plot of land I cleared by the lake and there was always pickerel or smoked venison in crockpots that Guillaume buried in the ground. He'd brought a Remington 870 with us and several boxes of shells. He is a skilled marksman. He has yet to waste — I do not believe I am exaggerating — a single bullet. He hunts in the fall for the most part, preferring to fish in spring and summer. He checks the maps we have brought and sometimes goes in search of new lakes. When he is hunting, he will sometimes be gone a night or two. He reminds me of the old hunters from Kes'. Not the young ones, who fly around on snowmobiles and drive around the village with heads mounted to the hoods of trucks owned by a finance company down south.

Cassandra began walking before she turned one and by the time she was two was already helping us around the cabin. She works with me in the vegetable and herb garden, helps her father stoke the cook fires. She looks like me. Not her grandmother. A part of me wishes she looked like Guillaume, so a circle could be broken.

It has been a time of healing. We both needed it and I am glad it came for us. Even Guillaume's body has healed. When we arrived I talked him into trying an herbal press, and although he didn't think it would make any difference, he agreed. I made the press with golden root and white cedar and made him wear it for two weeks. When we unwrapped the press, the scars on his chest looked like lines of ink from a writing journal left outside in the rain. Today, you can barely seem them at all.

The only interruption to our routine comes when Guillaume goes to Ragged Lake to cash his cheque and get provisions. Sometimes we accompany him. The old village has changed almost as much as the work camp.

Not halfway toward becoming forest again, but leaning that way. The roof on the community centre built by O'Hearn in the late '50s, a large building that used to have a hockey rink, tavern, and two twenty-desk school-rooms, has caved in. No doubt from the weight of snow. During the winter there always used to be men shovelling snow off that roof at the end of their midnight shifts. A task given to mill hands as a reward and rotated every week, a chance to finish their shift outside the mill instead of inside with the chemical smells and noise. Snow now blows through every window. The tavern has been looted of all its wood. The desks are gone.

The railway station is just as abandoned. The small building where you used to buy tickets is boarded up. A train goes through the village three times a week but stops only when needed — to deliver mail and supplies to the Mattamy or to a survival school that has opened up in one of the old bunkhouses. The conductor on the train has the waybills. And passenger tickets, if anyone ever wants to leave, although everyone did that years ago.

The two-storey homes that used to surround the railway station are also boarded up. The wraparound verandas — the thing that used to distinguish the homes of the rich from the homes of the poor — have gone, use-less appendages winter storms must have obliterated years ago. The cottages by the lake, where I lived with Johnny for two years, are in better shape. The Mattamy rents them out as fishing cabins, but it has been a long time since anyone painted one, or changed a curtain. All of the curtains are yellow and tattered, like rags hung on a rod.

In the centre of town, right by the shore, is the

mill. I'm not sure if a thing not living, not breathing and moving around, should be able to scare you. You wonder how such a thing would be possible. Yet there is something about that mill that frightens me. Perhaps it is merely the size of the thing, a red-brick building the length of two football fields, a building that would seem large even in Springfield. Or maybe it's the smoke stacks that are blackened and chipped and don't have a purpose anymore, that remind me of hardwood trees stripped of their leaves, as though we are always living in late November. There is something about that mill that leaves me thinking of hospital rooms and bad smells and uncertain futures. So it must be possible. For a thing not living to scare you.

The Mattamy is the only place still living, still breathing. Guillaume cashes his cheque at the bar and we will pick up items we have ordered from the Stedman's catalogue or buy provisions from the kitchen. We do not need all the money the government sends, and we try to overspend so no one will think we have money stashed in the cabin. The cook is a greedy man but he is stupid as well, because he could be far greedier. A few weeks ago it occurred to me that it had been years since I had thought about money. I sat there confused, like a child might be, trying to remember why it had once seemed so important.

In the summer there are more than a dozen people working at the Mattamy, not counting the guides, but in winter there are only three. A bartender, a cook, and a waitress who also works as a maid. I do not like going to the lodge in winter. I went once, a year ago, and ended up sitting in the bar while Guillaume was in the kitchen bartering with the cook. The lights were turned off to save energy and there was no sun that day so the room was filled with shadows and gloom, the bartender staring at me even after I said we didn't need any drinks. Just staring until I felt so uncomfortable I shifted Cassandra on my lap so she was blocking his line of vision. Even then he kept staring at us.

"Do you like living out there?" he asked eventually.

"I like it well enough," I answered.

"Seems silly building a cabin way out there. We got abandoned cottages right here in town."

"We like the lake."

"You don't like people?"

"I like people fine. I just like the lake, too."

"I suppose. Do you never get lonely?"

Just then the waitress came in — a young girl, perhaps still a teenager. She came over and made a silly face for Cassandra, who cooed and held out her hands to be picked up. Guillaume came in from the kitchen a minute later and I stood to leave. I gave the waitress a quick hug and she hugged me back with enough force to make me think it had not been a coincidence, her walking in the room when she had.

• • •

Ragged Lake holds the key to the trouble we are in. I know it. It was a mistake to have gone back there, and I need to figure out the connection.

When it comes to actual homes where people still live and still have Ragged Lake as their mailing address, I count three. John Holly has one, a fishing cottage by the lake. An elderly couple has another cottage. The man is a former mill hand, the woman someone I remember from Five Mile, an old woman even back then.

The third house is Anita's. I am not sure I would have said — had I been asked before I returned to Ragged Lake — that Anita would still be living here, although I think I might have. There is logic to it. An unfolding I can easily imagine. When I stumbled upon her cabin, high on a bluff overlooking Ragged Lake, I was not surprised, nor was I by the old woman who walked out of it.

"Hello Anita," I said.

"Hello Lucy," she answered.

We went inside and stayed more than two hours. Cassandra played on the mandala rug I remember from Anita's Place, the one that sat beneath the circular table with the punch bowls. She is smaller and older than I recall, but she has the same friendly laugh, the same look of mischief in her eyes that I remember so well as a young girl when she would lean over to whisper something scandalous in my ear, keeping a child amused in a room full of adults. I think I was the only girl, or woman, ever allowed inside Anita's Place. Johnny's little girl.

"Things are better for you?" she asked, and I told her they were. It seemed genuine, the smile that came across her face when I said that. I go to visit her from time to time and have told Guillaume about her, this old Cree woman living high on a bluff overlooking Ragged Lake, although I have not told him the whole story. I have come to the conclusion I am not a whole-story-telling sort of person.

And that's it. Everyone who lives in Ragged Lake.

Everyone who works in Ragged Lake. And everything we have been doing the past twenty-seven months.

Now I just need to figure out why people are coming back. All at the same time. As though summoned.

• • •

The first one came a month ago. It was Lucinda. Johnny's old girlfriend. For a couple years anyway, before she drowned in the Old Duck.

So, it was a ghost I must have seen when I was out picking chokeberries, Cassandra having an afternoon nap in the cabin, Guillaume fishing, and there she was, standing beside the trail, dressed in the stained, dark-red evening gown Lucinda favoured for Saturday nights.

"Well, lookie here, if it isn't sweet little Lucy. Come here, child, and let's have a look at you. Your father is around here somewhere."

I jumped and spilled the berries, turned my eyes to the ground when it happened, to see them rolling away, and when I looked back up, she was gone. For the rest of that day, I saw flashes of red moving through the forest. A red not the hue of a cardinal or a maple leaf still clinging to a tree but the dirty red of Lucinda's weekend dress, a colour I would recognize anywhere, no other colour quite like it in the world, not even the blood-red satin you find sometimes inside a coffin — and if anything were to come close to Lucinda's party dress, it would be that.

The next day, she came back. While I was by the shore of Cap, Cassandra again having a nap. This time Lucinda did not run away after startling me. She stayed and talked.

"How long has it been, child?"

"Twelve years."

She was smoking the clay pipe she always had, dressed this day in her work clothes, denim overalls with large metal buckles, good leather hiking boots, a straw hat.

"There's no one living at Five Mile anymore?" she asked.

"No."

"They're all gone."

"Yes."

"You don't even live at Five Mile. Why you living at Cap and not at Five Mile, or back in Ragged like you did with Johnny?"

"I like the lake."

"You got the river at Five Mile."

"I prefer the lake."

"You got a man and a child now, too. Your husband ain't from here?"

"No."

"Why would a man who's not from here ever want to live here? No one ever came back here. Why you come, Lucy?"

"I got tired of living in the city."

"Your man?"

"He got tired, too."

"How old is the girl?"

"She's staying away from you, Lucinda. She's never talking to you. You're dead."

I stared at the apparition in front of me, wondering for a moment if I were having a dry drunk, the way people talked about having such things in the meetings, having

201

all the crazy, disconnected mania of a week-long drunk, but you're stone-cold sober. Your body just remembering how it used to be, something tricking your mind into remembering. That would explain what has been happening. If I were a drunk again.

"Why you actin' so uppity, Lucy? I was just askin' 'bout your little girl. Your dad is around here somewhere. Maybe he'd like to meet her, too."

"You're not ever coming close to my little girl. Same for my dad."

"Oh, child, he loves you. You know that. Anyway, I'm not here for that," and she laughed.

"Why are you here, then?"

"I think you know."

She laughed one more time, hiked up her overalls, and walked away. I watched her go deeper and deeper into the forest until I lost sight of her, could only hear her voice singing an old shanty song:

Where you going, my child?
To the pines, to the pines
Where the sun don't ever shine

Where you going, my child?
To the hills, to the hills
'Fore my baby comes to kill . . .

. . .

It made sense, Lucinda being the first to come back. She was with us at the beginning, coming in a locked-oar skiff

202

from Kes', travelling the western arm of a great Atlantic Ocean bay and then down the Francis River to the northern tip of Ragged, another week of rowing after that to reach the mill.

After Johnny got hired, we stayed with one of his cousins in Five Mile. Lucinda was drunk all the time, Johnny and his cousin when they weren't working, so half the time. The cousin's wife despised us for the chaos we brought to her house. Most mornings she would run out of food before she reached my bowl. Her two daughters were ugly and stupid and never spoke to me. Her four boys, when they noticed me at all, would try to pin me down and put their hands down my pants.

Johnny caught them doing it one day and was so enraged he beat them silly, stomping the oldest boy's head until I thought it was going to pop. The cousin was angry when he came home and learned what Johnny had done, but after he was sure the boy wasn't going to die, he agreed his son had done wrong. No one bothered me again, and no one spoke of it.

No one except Lucinda, who for days afterward said it had been my fault the young boy almost got killed.

"It's the girl that done it," she would scream at my father. "You can't have a girl like that walking around boys and drinkin' men."

"What do you mean 'a girl like that'?"

"Are you blind Johnny? No, you ain't blind. That's why you nearly killed that boy."

"Since when do you care about boys?" and Johnny would grab her, Lucinda laughing and hitting his chest with feigned punches. "You quit worrying about boys and quit worrying 'bout my daughter. I'm enough for you to worry about."

Johnny was protective like that. Or, he was for a long time. Longer than most men in his position might have been, and it's hard to fault him for some of the things that happened later, because I never saw another single dad at Five Mile. I think Johnny was the only one who could have pulled it off. Always a little quicker than the next guy coming up the road. Always a little ahead of whatever game was being played. I don't think I was ever a burden to him. I don't think much in life ever was.

By the time Lucinda went and drowned herself, we were living in Ragged Lake. We were the only Cree to live full time in the village and we moved after Johnny got promoted to foreman, the only Cree to have that happen as well.

We moved into a cottage on the shores of Ragged Lake, which was just goofy, having a place like that. Our neighbours were the VPs at the mill, the railway agent, the family that owned the Mattamy back then. Even the O'Hearns, when one of them came up to Ragged Lake, would stay at the cottages.

Shortly after Lucinda left us, we started having what Johnny called "cocktail parties," which was just drinking at home, like I had always seen it, except the liquor was store-bought and there was ice in a silver bucket with tongs people were supposed to use and normally did, until the third or fourth drink. The railway agent was a bad drunk and always came to Johnny's parties. One of the VPs was single and usually came, although the other VP had a wife and two daughters and came only occasionally. Once he brought his two daughters, but the girls looked like they wanted to run away and wash their hands as soon as they arrived. They stayed hidden in the corner for most of the night like bad furniture. The O'Hearns came from time to time, the old man and his son, always polite, always staying until the last drink. I served the drinks, dressed in a skirt and white shirt, my hair pulled back in a ponytail the way Johnny taught me.

I'll always remember those cocktail parties. The way Johnny would drink and slap the backs of the drunken railway agent, the timber company VP, the government Indian and Northern Affairs bureaucrat passing through, all those men sitting in our living room laughing at anything Johnny said, my dad dressed in a jacket and tie some Sport had given him, the tie with a flying duck pattern on it. I am just Indian enough to think that may be the strangest sight I will ever see.

· · ·

Then one day the mill closed. And just like that the world changed.

There had been warning signs it might happen, but nothing anyone took seriously. Shifts had been cut back, sure, but the same thing had happened in the recession of '92, and in the early '80s, even further back than that some people said, although no one could remember when that might have been. It seemed unlikely anything like that had happened in the '60s and '70s, when everyone read newspapers and newsprint mills may as well have been banknote companies. When did all that start to change? That feeling of invincibility everyone used to have around here?

Suddenly three shifts were cut to two, the second became an on-call shift, and then there was only one shift left, and before anyone had much time to think about it, O'Hearn closed the mill.

Everyone was summoned to a meeting at nine in the morning. It was a Tuesday in early September and as soon as the men walked onto the mill floor, everyone knew something extraordinary was happening. I heard about it later from Johnny. The presses were not running. The vats were not burbling. There was not a piece of machinery in the entire mill that was making a sound. A silence no man had heard before. So foreign and disorienting they were immediately struck mute, and the human resources man who had flown up from Springfield for the announcement didn't need to use the PA system that had been set up for him.

"Newsprint isn't coming back," he said after talking for a few minutes about commodity prices and the state of the newspaper industry. He shrugged his shoulders and added, "I'm afraid this is the end of the road, boys."

Each man was given two weeks' pay for every year worked. The men queued for their money, forming three lines that arrived eventually at a foldout card table with a woman sitting behind it who had also flown up from Springfield that morning. The men gave their names and the woman searched through stacks of envelopes, eventually giving each man an envelope with his name on it.

"The company bank," the human resources man continued saying, marching in circles on the dais, looking a bit like a television evangelist on a slow day, "will stay open until the end of the week. Same for the company store and the bunkhouses. Anyone wanting to use the train has free passage until the end of month."

. . .

The night they shut the mill, I lay in bed listening to Johnny arguing in the kitchen with another man. My father was talking quickly. Already hustling. Johnny wasn't fooled. He knew that mill was never going to reopen. The other man shouted at him.

"It's a little fucking late in the game, Johnny."

"It's whatever time I say it is, Tommy. Maybe you're forgettin' some stuff."

"I forget nothing."

"Then you know we have a problem. I'm not fuckin' off back to Kes'. Is that what you think I'm doing?"

"I don't know what you're doing, Johnny. I don't know why I should give a fuck what you're doing. There is no more fuckin' mill. Maybe we can get to that, Johnny. Why am I still fuckin' here?"

"You know damn well why you're still here."

"You're a bastard."

"We need to reach an understanding. That's all I'm saying."

Before long, I put my hands over my ears and tried not to hear. Johnny was just trying to survive. I knew that. And I loved him for it. A feeling of love came over me right then that I think could have washed me away like a spring flood if I had let it, me loving Johnny for not being deceived, for thinking ahead, for everything he had done since my mother left, for raising me. I have wondered sometimes why he did that. Was I some exotic thing he liked having around? Like his Tony Lama boots and his $1,000 watches? I'm not sure. It's probably best not to think about some things too much.

I kept my hands over my ears until I fell asleep and by then I had my plan. Knew what I had to do if I was going to survive, if I was going to put my father's problems behind me and have a life of my own. For a while the plan seemed cold and frightening and kept me from sleeping, but then I asked what my father would do if the roles were reversed, and I never came up with any answer different than mine. Sleep came just as the man in the kitchen was leaving, telling Johnny he would see him tomorrow.

Four days later, a truck driver was letting me off in front of the YWCA in Cork's Town. That's how quickly it all happened. The last person I saw before leaving was Anita. I had my rucksack on and was heading to the train station. She was in the low meadow running between Five Mile and Capimitchigama, picking herbs for the potpourris she hung around Anita's Place.

"You're leaving, Lucy?"

"I am."

You're a smart girl. That mill is never going to reopen."

"I know."

"The boys are fooling themselves."

"Johnny says the same thing. Will you be leaving, Anita?"

"No. I have money saved, and I've been here a long time. I don't know where else I'd go."

That day it was sunny but the sky was stuffed with high cumulus clouds, so many clouds the sun was constantly being blocked, and shadows moved across us like slow rain.

"Where are you going to go, Lucy?"

"Springfield."

"I didn't think Johnny cared for Springfield."

"He's not going."

"Well, my heavens, so you two are finally splitting up. Where is Johnny going?"

I didn't answer right away. I hadn't expected to run into Anita or ever hear the question. A world of strangers awaited me that afternoon.

"I think O'Hearn is getting him a job at the bush camp on Lake Simon."

"Lordy, things are moving quickly. Where were you just coming from?"

"I wanted to have a look at the headwaters before I left. I'm going to be travelling down the Springfield. All the way to the Kettle Falls. Did you know we used to pray to the gods at those falls?"

"Not just us. The Algonquin, the Iroquois, the Long Hairs. We all did."

"Nothing unusual about what I'm going to do, then, heading down that river."

"Nothing unusual at all."

Anita offered me some herbs, a few of which I took for the journey, and in a cheery voice she wished me luck.

. . .

A week ago someone else came back. Not a ghost like Lucinda. Not a friend like Anita.

It is this person who has kept me up all night writing. Even though as I sit here, nothing seems clearer to me and I am beginning to think I am playing games with myself. That this is a problem that has no solution. That maybe there is karmic weight to bad decisions and it catches up with you after a while, leaves you waterlogged and useless, unable to get out of the way of danger, two thousand pounds of every bad move you ever made weighing you down.

It was bitterly cold most of January, but it changed last week. Warm air pushed its way up the Valley and was finally able to push over the Highlands and reach us. So I bundled Cassandra in layers of clothing, put her in the toboggan Guillaume made from old barrel slats, and we went to Ragged Lake to pick up his cheque.

When we got to the Mattamy, I stayed outside so I could avoid the bartender. I have wondered about this, but I don't think it would have made any difference. There was no way he was going to miss me. With all the things that needed to line up right for him to be there in the first place and then for him to not see me? No way that was going to happen. At least outside I wasn't right away trapped.

I was standing by the biplane dock with my back to

the lodge, Cassandra holding my hand, and we were looking at the lake. I was trying to will my eyes past the horizon, like I've been doing since I was a girl, and I heard the kitchen door of the Mattamy open and shut. Heard two men arguing. The cook and someone else.

The second voice sounded familiar but I couldn't place it. I was standing about fifty yards away, with the wind blowing in my face, so there was no surprise in that.

But I must have sensed something, because my back stiffened, all my limbs went straight as a board, and I stood for a long time feeling threatened for no reason that seemed obvious. Cassandra looked at me with a puzzled look on her face, a look that seemed to sense danger, and I wondered how a three-year-old could do that.

Finally I turned around to see the man the cook was arguing with. And there was Tommy Bangles, staring right at me.

I couldn't have hidden if I'd wanted. There were no buildings anywhere near me. No people. Nothing in Tommy's line of vision. I stood there as though placed in the foreground of a painting.

And Tommy didn't do a thing. Just kept staring out over the lake as though that was the only thing he was doing, as though that lake was fascinating right then, in the middle of his argument with the cook, utterly fascinated by that frozen lake. Then he tilted his head, a small gesture you could easily miss, and went back to swearing at the cook. A minute later, they were back inside the Mattamy.

I ran to the front of the lodge, where Guillaume was walking down the front steps muttering about the cook not being able to see him that day. I took him by

211

the hand and started walking away. Then I began to run, saying Cassandra liked it that way, the faster the better, let's all run. I'll race you back to the cabin. I strapped her to the toboggan and took off. Running down the trail. Guillaume following. Me looking back every few seconds to make sure it was only Guillaume following us.

That was two days ago.

· · ·

What is Tommy Bangles doing in Ragged Lake? What in the world? If Tommy had come looking for me, then things would have gone differently when he saw me. He had been surprised. I could tell that, even though he tried hard not to show it. Which is what Tommy would do. He told me once surprise was the look a man had on his face right before he died. So Tommy tried to never look surprised.

But if he didn't come looking for me, what in the world would bring someone like Tommy Bangles to Ragged Lake? Tommy hates the outdoors. He and Sean were Irish kids from Cork's Town, and I don't think either of them had gone much beyond the eight blocks of workers cottages, diners, and bars that made up Cork's Town until they were teenagers. I remember Tommy rolling up windows on cars during drives in the country, because he didn't like the smell. Complaining whenever he and Sean had to meet Papa or some other high-ranking biker, because the bikers tended to like secluded farm-houses down country roads.

He isn't here visiting. He isn't here planning a fishing trip. He knows the cook. Tommy knows the cook.

This thought paralyses me. Leaves me gasping for air. The cook has never struck me as a man who is where he belongs. He is a poor cook, his kitchen always a mess — dishes not put away and utensils scattered. Perhaps the cook is in Ragged Lake trying to disappear, just like we are. He was a bad drunk and something catastrophic happened to him. He owed money and had run, but now Tommy had found him.

The more I think about this, the more sense it makes to me. Tommy was always the one who collected debts. Tommy was the one who tracked people down. He was talking to the cook as if the man were someone he'd just tracked down.

If I play it out, with this being the right assumption — Tommy came to find the cook, not me — how much time does this give me? Tommy likely left on yesterday's train. Which means the earliest he could have been back in the Silver Dollar was last night.

If I were starting cold, with no one having thought of me in more than two years, it would take time to build. The need to do something. Men would hear my name and remember. Some would smile. Tell a story. That Lucy. Then it would come back to them — a thought long dormant, not coming to them right away — that they had been worried about me once. That's right. The last time I was living in Springfield, they had been worried about me.

This is my best-case scenario. That it will take time to rouse them. If I am lucky, I might have as much as a month before someone comes back.

My worst case is they never forgot. They went looking for me after the birth of Cassandra, but I was gone. The men Tommy is drinking with might already be thinking I am an unresolved problem.

That gives me a week.

. . .

Last night I dreamed someone had entered our cabin, rummaged around, come to our bedroom, and stared at us while we slept. It was a dream that seemed so real, when I awoke I had the sensation someone was still in the cabin. I was scared to turn around and kept my arms straddled around Guillaume's chest, my face buried in his hair. I took deep breaths and waited several moments until I threw off my blankets.

And maybe it is delusion, or maybe I have no proper recollection of where I live, but it seemed to me a curtain was drawn where it had been left open the night before. A teacup was on the stand beside the sink, something we would not normally do. And there was what appeared to be a footprint in a knothole of dust in a plank of flooring beneath the kitchen window, a plank I can never clean properly. I looked at that knothole a long time but never thought I was looking at anything other than a footprint.

We went for a long walk that afternoon, Guillaume pulling Cassandra in her toboggan, me saying I wanted to get outside, we had been staying in the cabin too much.

We were outside for hours, but I saw no sign of something out of place. The spruce and white pine refracted the same weak light they had refracted the day before. The rivers made no different sound when I bent to listen, still the soft moan of a thing trapped, some old thing complaining. The snow slanted the same way in the wind and the horizon was still a grey-blue ridge of low hills. I still heard grey jays and ravens, and, on this day, with little wind, gulls from the Bay.

No sign of an intruder. Until the walk home, when we crested a small hill and in the distance saw a snowmobile heading from our cabin. Guillaume shielded his eyes, looked over the plain the snowmobile was travelling across, then dropped his rucksack and took out a pair of binoculars. He stared at the snowmobile for several minutes, adjusted the ring a few times, and said, "Whoever it is, they're wearing a hood. I can't even tell if it's a man or a woman."

"What about the sled?"

"It's a Polaris. It's white. Can't tell anything more than that. It could be one of the sleds from the Mattamy."

"Why would anyone be at our cabin?"

Guillaume shrugged. We watched the snowmobile hook up with the S and P and turn toward town. As we continued to the cabin, we looked for tracks, and it was Guillaume who found them, twin-skied tracks that did not approach our cabin, but circled and stopped fifty yards away. For several minutes it must have been, judging by how far the snow was pushed down. For no good reason, when you stood in the exact same spot and looked around, than to stare at our cabin.

Fifty yards away. For several minutes. Whoever it was, they had been using binoculars.

Less than a week.

• • •

"People are coming."

I said it quietly, sitting on the rug by the airtight, my head nestled on Guillaume's chest. We hadn't spoken for several minutes and I knew he could sense it, or perhaps even know it with certainty. Our quiet days are finished. The days of peace and rest are finished. We were given twenty-seven months, and maybe one day that will seem like a good deal to us. More than either of us had been given before.

"What sort of people?"

"People you would never want to know."

"Why are they coming?"

"They're coming for me. Because of stupid stuff from a long time ago."

"Is Cassandra in danger?"

"Yes. I would think so. Yes."

"What makes you sure they are coming?"

"I saw one of them. Two days ago. At the Mattamy."

"The man arguing with the cook?"

"Yes."

Guillaume didn't say anything. It was a cold night and we were wearing Cowichan sweaters, thick flannel pants, two pairs of socks. We stared into the fire in the dull-witted way people have about them when they stare into a fire too long, not thinking clearly. I had the first wave of remorse and self-pity, wondering why, no matter how much I try to do the right things, I always end up back in the same spot. Maybe Guillaume was right about this being the wrong world in which to expect good things.

"I don't think you've ever asked me a single question

about my past," I said, turning from the fire to look at him. "Do you know that? Not a single question. Why is that?"

Guillaume shrugged. I already knew the answer. Don't ask a question and you won't have to answer a question. Johnny taught me that — Johnny, who was always of the opinion that people asked far too many questions in this world. If you ever stopped and thought it through, you would soon realize there are only a handful of questions that truly need answering. Maybe fewer. I don't believe Johnny even wanted to know how he was going to die.

"It's never mattered to me," said Guillaume. "And that's no bullshit, Lucy. It's never mattered. You're free to tell me what you want, when you want. I don't need a history lesson to tell me what sort of person is standing in front of me."

"I don't need one either, Guillaume. I've always known you are a good man."

"And I've always known you are good, too, Lucy. History can just muddy the waters, don't you think?"

I came the closest to crying than I had in years. As though sensing it coming, and wanting to keep my mind focused, Guillaume asked a question.

"What do I need to know about these people?"

"They're bad people," I said. "They don't operate with rules or anything holding them back. I was told once they would come looking for me. I should have told you. I was hoping it would go away. That it wouldn't be true."

"It still might not be true. We don't know why he was here. How bad are they?"

I thought for a moment before saying, "Tommy, the

guy I saw at the Mattamy — I saw him kill a man once behind the Silver Dollar. He stomped the guy unconscious, then left him in the mud, went back into the club, and came out with a Drano bottle. He opened the guy's mouth and poured the Drano down. Then he sat on him with his hand over the guy's mouth to keep him from throwing up when he started to convulse.

"I was hiding in the shadows and Tommy didn't know I was there, but I saw everything. The look on Tommy's face when the guy died, bucking around on the ground . . . Tommy got off on it, like he was a cowboy at some rodeo. I've never forgotten it. It comes to me in dreams sometimes. That exact moment."

Guillaume didn't say anything right away. Stood and stretched. Went to the kitchen to refresh his tea.

"There's some work we should do to the cabin," he said, when he returned.

"When should we start?"

"Probably right away."

• • •

There is nothing to do now but wait. Guillaume has set up trip lines on the three approaches to the cabin, strung twine and tin cans, and there is no way a person or animal can approach and not set off a warning. The lake is trickier, but Guillaume has rolled boulders to the shoreline, placing them in such a way that the easiest approach would be to skirt the boulders and cut through the forest. If a man is smart and scurries over the boulders, then we have a problem. The back of the cabin has a large window.

There is a good view of the lake. Guillaume has left his gun on a ledge above the window. We are telling ourselves we have done all we can.

This journal has come to matter a great deal to me. Dr. Mackenzie told me it would one day, and I never believed him. Now I am sitting here, waiting to see if Tommy is coming back to Ragged Lake or if they'll send a crew, and it occurs to me that if this is a complete op, our bodies may never be found. The place where we die may never be found. Our lives the past two years may never be known. I get angry when I think about this. One more unfairness. In a world that is about to steamroller over us with its constant, flattening, fucking unfairness.

Cassandra. When I think of my daughter, my anger grows. She will be forgotten as well. No, it is worse for my daughter. She will never be remembered. She will disappear more completely than her parents, who may have a distant aunt somewhere who will remember them one day, if anyone cares to ask. For Cassandra, there will be no one.

Maybe that's why I have been writing all night. To make sure there is at least this record. And if I did all that work, then stashing this journal is the right thing to do. The right, crazy thing to do. I need to find a safe place.

I guess this will be my last entry for a while. Maybe my last entry for—

I hadn't thought of that. If we lose this fight . . . I need to say something.

I am grateful for my time with Guillaume. I want to say that. I still have faith but wish things had played out differently for us. Sometimes free will is real and sometimes it isn't. My last thoughts on that subject.

Cassandra would have been a beautiful woman.
I regret Guillaume and I are the only ones to know this.
If someone ever reads this journal, perhaps it will be
possible to remember her in some way. There was a spot
in Strathconna Park, in Springfield, where you can watch
kayakers run a course. That place meant something to
her parents.

We came close to making it. I honestly believe we did.

CHAPTER
TWENTY-TWO

There was no sun the next morning. The snowstorm continued unabated and the darkness of night did not disappear or retreat come morning but merely turned a lighter shade. The wind stayed strong and hard from the northeast, and the snow still fell from low-hanging clouds, thick, wet flakes that were too heavy to be swept out over the lake. When people awoke that morning, they found the village blanketed in snow, the rail line disappeared, east-facing windows shuttered, and the drift outside the back door of the Mattamy so high the door would not open.

It was a day that could have come from a book of fairy tales, with everyday reference points vanished and boundaries obliterated; a fantasy day of cloistered rooms and heightened emotion, slow-moving action and out-of-focus seclusion; a day when it would not have seemed all that strange to learn a princess was sleeping nearby, or that a sad king was looking down from a watchtower somewhere as a winter storm moved across his land.

Yakabuski had read the journal most of the night, stopping only when the darkness outside his window had begun to turn a mottled grey. He put down the book, stood, and stretched, counting the popping sounds coming from his back. Then he grabbed his service revolver from the nightstand, put on his shoes, and went to Downey, who was sitting at the end of the hallway.

"How you doing, Matt?"

"Doing good, Yak. It's not time for you to relieve me."

"I know. I want to grab a coffee before we get the day started. You up for some fun?"

"What sort of fun?"

"We're going to throw that cook and that bartender into the storage closet."

• • •

It was two in the morning when the crew assembled at the Buckham's Bay trailhead. They had drilled the day before, so there was little talking. Tommy Bangles took what he needed from a roofer's trailer that an old man had driven to the trailhead, doing only a cursory check of the guns and clips, the GPS machine, and the satphone. Most of the kit still had the rubber bands and numbered paper he had placed there the day before. The three men standing with him did only a cursory check of their kit as well.

The old man was a mechanic from a garage in Cork's Town and was extra careful when he drove the sleds off the trailer. There could be no mistakes with these men. When he was nearly finished checking the fuel levels and the lights, Bangles walked away from the group, pulled a cellphone from his pocket, and punched a pre-set number.

"Are you at the trailhead?"

"Yes."

"I spoke to our friend yesterday. He suspects something. He doesn't know what."

"I'm not surprised, Sean. There *is* something odd going on up there. "

"You've spoken to him. What is he thinking?"

"How can you tell with that guy?"

Sean Morrissey looked out the window of his office. The snow was falling as heavily as it had been twelve hours earlier. This would turn out to be one of the biggest storms of the season.

"Have you stopped to think how odd this is, Tommy?"

"'Bout every minute."

"Of all the places for Lucy to try and hide."

"She must have had the same idea we did."

"Looks that way. She never had much luck. If the cook hadn't run up such a fuckin' debt, you never would have had to go up there and see him. What are the odds?"

"It's a freakish thing. I hear what you're saying, Sean."

"Do you think it was François?"

"He says no. Says he was just keeping an eye on her, like we asked."

"If he had a good look at her, that might have been all it took."

"I was thinking that, too."

"Did she look the same?"

"Yeah. Pretty much."

Tommy Bangles didn't say anything for a minute. He had known Sean Morrissey since memory began — never a time in his life when Sean had not been there protecting his back. He stayed silent, knowing a dark shadow was passing across his friend's heart right then.

"What were the orders Cambio gave you, Tommy?"

"Full op. That's right, isn't it?"

"That's right."

"Any special instructions for Lucy?"

"No. You can leave her where she is."

• • •

When Tommy put the phone in his pocket, a man approached him. He came cautiously, stood a distance away before saying, "It has to be tonight, Tommy?"

"The cops are there now, Bobby. It looks like they've shut down the lab." Bangles kept his back to the man, staring down the trail they would soon be travelling, the headlights of the four snowmobiles the mechanic had lined up by the trailhead illuminating the way.

"Shut it down? What does that mean?"

"We're not sure, Bobby. One of the reasons we have to go up there."

"But the cops are there for sure?"

Bangles stretched his body to its full height and cocked his head. Took some deep breaths of air. If he had been a forest animal, you would have thought he was trying to detect a scent right then. Slowly, he turned, and as he did the headlights from the snowmobiles caught him full in the face.

The other man gasped in spite of himself. He knew Bangles well. Had looked into his eyes many times. But the teardrop tattoos running down both cheeks would never seem familiar.

"Yes, the cops will be there, Bobby. It is the full op tonight. Are you up for it?"

"I'm always up for it, Tommy. We should take scalps."

Bangles laughed and slapped the other man on the back. "Time to go, my brother."

CHAPTER
TWENTY-THREE

Along the east wing of the Mattamy, people stayed in bed late that morning, in no hurry to start their day. Roselyn and Gaetan Tremblay embraced, the old man's legs tucked into the back of his wife's legs, his right arm thrown over her chest, his head buried deep in her long black hair.

"It is evil," said Roselyn one more time. "Can you not feel it, Gaetan?"

"It feels no worse than any bad day, Roselyn."

"Any bad day? There are people dead, Gaetan. One of them was a little girl."

"A very bad day, then."

"It is evil. There is someone in Ragged Lake who is nothing but evil."

Gaetan pushed his nose a little deeper into his wife's hair, enjoying the smell of the oils with which she bathed, the sweet talcum with which she powdered, the fine ridge of the powder dusting her shoulder. He took a deep breath and prepared himself for the day. He would be surprised if there were only one.

Tobias O'Keefe had risen early and had already done one hundred push-ups, fifty sit-ups, and a dozen near-perfect chin-ups from the doorframe of the bathroom. Which wasn't that much for him, but he had worried about the wood splintering. He had showered and dressed while Garrett slept — either real or feigned, O'Keefe didn't know or care. Garrett was right to assume he had no interest in talking to him. The mere sight of the man had begun to repulse O'Keefe. The whiteness of his skin. The fatness of his body. So much fat there were rolls on the backs of his legs.

O'Keefe did not understand how a man could let himself fall apart like that. Become as weak as that. Not through the actions of an enemy, but by his own hand. His own sloth and banality. His father had done a hundred pushups every morning until the day before he died, so the story went — might even be true. Certainly, he was doing them well into his eighties. There are two secrets to success that only successful people know, his father had once told him. The first: success comes only to certain people, to those who are special, who can make the tough decisions you need to make to reach a goal. The second, and this was just as important: never feel guilty about being special, about being better than other people; never waste time feeling sorry for people or wondering why most people are losers. That's just the way God planned it.

O'Keefe turned from the storm and stared at Garrett asleep in his bed. He had thought, when they had first arrived, that he might find some pleasure there, but he had never warmed to the idea. That happened sometimes. He did not know why. He stared at Garrett and wondered how many days his father could have shared a hotel room with this man before starting to think of ways to get rid of him.

John Holly was also staring at the storm, marvelling at the strength of it, at a wind that came in fast and mad across miles of clear ice and then crashed into the forests and buildings of Ragged Lake with such force the trees seemed to shake and the buildings trembled. The snow was thrown around in patterns he had never seen. Funnel formations that spiralled either up or down, he wasn't sure.

He laughed once he realized he was looking out a window trying to figure out what was up and what was down. Freakin' Divide. No other place like it in the world. Holly laughed again. He was anxious for the day to begin.

The waitress lingered in her shower, enjoying the steady stream of hot water. The showers in the staff cabin were never warm. When she was finished, she dabbed herself dry with a plush terrycloth towel and examined her body in the full-length mirror. She was nineteen and had nipples that pointed upward from the shower, a curve near her buttocks that had collected a small pool of water, long legs that let the water course down her skin when it finally dropped, a lazy track that curved and twisted and touched as much skin as possible.

She was thinking about the tree-marker. They had talked for nearly two hours the night before, a strange conversation, speaking to someone through a wall, yet she could have spoken all night. He was from Buckham's Bay and she had struggled to find an image of him in her memory, thinking back to group events, hockey games, street parties . . . but nothing came. She was surprised. The tree-marker was handsome.

When she had this thought, she felt a pang of guilt. It did not seem right having a pleasant thought right then. She told herself to think of the day ahead, a trick that normally settled her mind. But not this morning. When she finally sat on the edge of the bed, dressed in her waitress uniform, waiting for a police officer to knock on the door and collect her, she decided it was all right to think about the tree-marker. If that kept her from thinking about other things.

The cook lay in his bed, grunting and coughing and trying to dislodge a thick, coppery ball of phlegm from the back of his throat. He was on his stomach. His head hung over the edge of the bed. He spat into a soup bowl.

The cook spit until he started coughing and then the cough turned into a dry heave. He kept his head over the bed and beads of sweat formed on his forehead. His stomach started to convulse. His limbs twitched. Finally, he rolled onto his back, gave one last great cough, and looked at his watch. Quarter to six in the morning. He sat up and threw his legs over the side of the bed. Started to dress. He was hoping he could sneak another bottle out of the bar while he was making breakfast.

William Forest was in the first room of the east wing, a standard room but with a few extra square feet, and so it had a bay window. He had spent most of the night in a chair pushed in front of that window. The light by the wharf allowed him to see the storm, and he sat transfixed. That storm would kill an unprotected man in . . . what would he give it? Two hours? Less than that?

The bartender had respect for power like that. Such indiscriminate power, too. That blew him away. It didn't matter who you were, what you had done with your life, who your friends might be, how much money you had in a bank account or how much you had stashed from the bastards at Revenue — you went into a storm like that and you were dead. Any geographic location. Any person. Dead. That was mission certainty you just never saw. One hundred percent guaranteed balls-out devastation. The bartender laughed and marvelled at what he was seeing. Occasionally, he would bend over and use a bar straw to snort from a plastic bag he had perched carefully on his lap. Then he would light a cigarette. The bartender was pretty sure he and God could be friends.

• • •

The tree-marker awoke feeling better than he had in days. No longer hungover. No longer frightened. He lay in bed remembering his conversation with the waitress. Searched his mind for an image of her standing somewhere in his hometown. You would think such a thing could be done. She was beautiful.

He quickly felt bad for what he was thinking. How could you have a happy thought on a day such as this? The boy got dressed and ran the problem through his mind. Decided eventually it was all right to think about the waitress. Didn't rationalize his decision the way she had, by telling himself it would help him get through the day. Figured there was probably not much he could do to stop thinking about her anyway, so why fight it?

CHAPTER
TWENTY-FOUR

Yakabuski waited until everyone had left their rooms and gathered in the restaurant, until the cook had finished breakfast and the waitress had started to clear the tables. Then he walked to the bar, pulled his service revolver, and pointed it six inches from the face of the bartender.

William Forest said nothing. Yakabuski gave the gun a small wave and the bartender started to back up toward the kitchen. Heads in the restaurant turned, one by one, as they passed their tables. The cook was the last one to see it. Standing with his back turned, pouring rye into his coffee cup, turning like a fool with the bottle clearly visible in the pocket of his jacket when the bartender backed into him. The cook stared at the gun in Yakabuski's hand. At the gun in Downey's hand, who had also come into the kitchen.

"I haven't been able to figure you boys out," said Yakabuski, who seemed neither perplexed nor worried by this failure. "I suspect I'm not going to have much time to work on it today, so we're just going to park you boys somewhere."

"Are you fuckin' whacked?" said the cook. "I haven't done anything." The man's right hand was now trying to hide the bottle of whisky.

"I'm afraid you're going to have to leave the bottle behind too."

"Now I know you're fuckin' whacked. No fuckin' way that's going to happen."

Yakabuski fired his gun. Three quick shots, because the gun was a semi-automatic and why waste a thing like that? The bullets hit a toaster on the counter and it flew through the air before clattering across the floor and then landing with a metal thunk against the back door. "Bit of a hurry, boys," he said, pointing the way with his gun. The two men started moving.

On his way back from the storage closet, Yakabuski banged on the freezer door and heard a lusty "fuck you." He didn't bother checking any further.

He went back to his coffee. Sat at the table and stared out the bay window. Then out the back window. At the biplane dock. It was hard to see much of anything because of the falling snow.

"The train won't be coming today, will it?" he said. He looked at Holly, not sure why he had bothered to ask the question.

"No. It won't be able to get past the first gorge outside High River. It'll come the day after the storm ends."

Yakabuski needed to phone O'Toole. But as he got up from the table, the lights went off in the restaurant. Behind the bar. Out by the biplane dock. At the same time, there

232

was the sound of machinery shutting down in the lodge. The hot-water tank stopped burbling. The furnace fan went silent. A machine somewhere made a loud knocking sound, like the busted rods of a car engine, a clanking that extended and extended until it faded away, leaving everyone listening for one final clank that never came.

"You missed your phone call," said Holly. "How's your satphone working?"

"Not at all."

"Didn't think so. This is a bad storm."

"You always lose power during a storm?"

"Not usually."

"The power comes in on a trunk line running down the S and P. Is that right, Mr. Holly?"

"That's right."

Yakabuski looked at his watch. Refreshed his coffee. Zippered his parka and walked outside. Stood on the front porch and stared through the storm to where he knew the S and P line ran.

Maybe it was nothing. How could you be surprised at losing power in a storm like this? Or maybe it was exactly what the adrenaline coursing through his body told him it was.

. . .

He saw it shortly after 10 a.m. At first it was nothing more than a slight disturbance in the snow. An anomaly so small and distant he couldn't say with certainty it was even there. And if it was, maybe it was nothing more than a difference in wind speed. A difference in the density of falling snow. But

233

slowly the anomaly grew, coalesced, took shape and definition, and before long Yakabuski was looking at a white orb.

He tracked his line of vision back from the orb, heading west, and soon he saw another pinprick anomaly. Then another. And another. The rest of the men inside the Mattamy had by now gathered on the porch to stand beside him, and each man found himself looking at the same thing. A line of headlights heading toward the lodge.

"I thought the cops were coming on the train," said O'Keefe.

"They are."

"Then who the fuck are these guys?"

Yakabuski didn't answer. Kept staring at the line of headlights. He watched in silence when the headlights stopped a half mile away from the lodge. Peering through his binoculars at the far-off cluster of shimmering lights, he started counting the seconds. He had not reached ten when two sets of headlights veered away from the main group. One heading north. The other south. He stared and tried not to let fear show on his face.

A planned deployment. Executed in less than ten seconds. In a blinding snowstorm.

"What is going on, Detective?" asked Garrett, the younger Sport. "You seem to know something you are not telling us. You knew these people would be coming?"

"I suspected. I wasn't sure."

"Who are they?"

"They're bikers. Or they work for bikers."

"Why have they come out in a snowstorm like this?"

"They've come to get rid of that lab."

"Get rid of it?"

"That's right, Mr. Garrett."

"But you've already destroyed it. There's nothing left to get rid of."

Yakabuski put down his binoculars and turned to look at the men surrounding him. There was no sign of fear yet, so he knew they had no clue what was happening.

"That's not completely true, Mr. Garrett."

A flash of surprise passed over Garrett's face. It was the other Sport who said, "The guy sitting in the meat freezer. He's still left."

"That's right, Mr. O'Keefe."

"They need to get rid of him."

"That's right."

Yakabuski didn't say anything else for a minute. Kept staring at the set of headlights heading north, a far-off light shimmering in the falling snow, disappearing whenever the snowmobile dipped, reappearing when it crested a drift. Would the man driving the machine be smart enough to go all the way to the shoreline? Yakabuski needed to think. The men with him needed to think as well, needed to realize how a door had just opened and they'd been shoved outside into a world probably none of them knew even existed. Where the spinning building blocks, the subatomic things, were different, came together to create a deadly, remorseless alternate world.

By now each man had fear on his face. Downey and Buckham, who had not asked a question, not wanting to appear out of the loop, looked as fearful as the others. It was the tree-marker who finally spoke.

"They need to get rid of him? What do you mean?"

"They've come to kill him, son. And anyone else who worked at that lab."

"You can't be serious."

"I'm afraid so. Someone has decided to shut down this operation. The guys coming would have blown up the lab if we hadn't done it already. They want nothing left. No equipment. No witnesses. It's a complete scrub today. That's the only reason you'd come out in a storm like this."

"How could they keep something like that a secret from everyone else in the village?"

"They have no intention of keeping secrets."

Fear grew on their faces. But it was the wrong fear — the kind someone has when he sees a dangerous animal in the distance, or the photo of a mass murderer in the newspaper. A detached fear. Wondering what might have happened to you if that grizzly had crossed the river one day and come toward you. If that killer had been walking in your direction one night. No ownership.

It was again O'Keefe who figured it out. Yakabuski knew it as soon as every muscle in the Sport's face tightened as though he had just been given a cortisone shot.

"They don't want any witnesses at all," he said.

"That's right."

"It's not just the lab they've come to get rid of. It's the entire village."

Yakabuski didn't bother answering. Garrett shouted, "Come on, you have to be—" then stopped when he saw the expression on Yakabuski's face.

CHAPTER
TWENTY-FIVE

When Yakabuski was a boy, his father would sometimes lose him in the bush, find a way to dart ahead to the trailhead where Yak would find him hours later waiting on the tailgate of his truck. Having a beer. Smoking a cigarette. Shaking his head at the boy.

Yakabuski knew it was coming. Knew every time the game was about to be played. Yet his father had always managed to slip away. Outran him when Yakabuski was a child. Outsmarted him when he was older. Some of the trails in the early days, when the game first started, were crazy dangerous. Alcove Canyon in the spring. Source Lake, where the switchbacks were marked only by coloured rocks that would often roll away. It wouldn't be fair to say children in the Upper Springfield Valley were raised as if by Spartans, marched regularly to the edge of cliffs to have their fate pondered. But it wouldn't be completely unfair, either.

Later, his cousins started playing the same game. Yakabuski came from a small family by Yakabuski standards — just him and his sister — and maybe that was why he was always assigned the role of fox on the run, his cousins figuring he wasn't tormented enough at home. The cousins were quick to add new wrinkles to the game as well, lying in ambush for Yakabuski when he tried to find them, pelting him with pine cones and sticks when he appeared on the trail. On a day when he seemed deserving of extra travails, he got rocks or chunks of mica.

As he had with his father, Yakabuski tried to avoid this fate by sticking close to his cousins. By not giving them a chance to slip away. But it was even easier for the cousins to pull off this trick, needing nothing more than to tie Yakabuski to a tree and leave him there to be released by the next person coming down the trail. Yakabuski could never detect when the ambush was about to happen. Could never track his cousins afterward, all of them being some of the best bushmen in the Valley.

He considered himself a fast study, so he groaned when he thought back to those years, at how long it took him to figure out the riddle. Close to three years. Two full summers, certainly, of getting pelted with pine cones and mica, too dumb to figure it out. How to beat his father. How to beat his cousins.

Don't give them a chance to attack. Get off the trail before they do.

Now Yakabuski stared at the headlights, noticing the one going north had started to curve, wasn't going to go all the way to the shoreline. The two in the main group were still stationary, waiting for the two other men to take position.

238

He put down his binoculars and was surprised to discover there was only one thought in his head right then — what would have to pass for his plan. Exploding like a mantra. No room for anything else.

Get off the trail. Get off the trail.

. . .

They had no more than a few minutes. Yakabuski began shouting, pushing the men inside the Mattamy.

"We're going to be splitting up. Mr. Tremblay, I want you to take your wife and Marie and go hide somewhere. Mr. Holly, you're going to be staying here in the lodge with Constable Downey. I want you to follow his instructions, sir."

Yakabuski ran as he shouted, making his way to the gun locker in the main office. They'd inspected it the first night, so he already knew there were two lever-action hunting rifles in there and two Colt target pistols. No shotguns. He opened the locker, scooped the guns, and ran back to the bar.

"Donnie, you're going to take the Sports and head toward that headlight going to the lake. We don't have time to get kitted up for snowshoes, so stay low, spread your weight, and don't start cussing when you keep falling through. You need to get in behind the guy. Here's a rifle, and a pistol for the sports." Garrett looked like he wanted to throw up. O'Keefe stroked his chin, not taking his eyes off Yakabuski.

"You're coming with me, son. Here's a rifle," and Yakabuski tossed a .223 Remington to the tree-marker. "Mr. Holly, here's a gun for you," and he threw one of the Colt target pistols. "Matt, I need you to keep those bastards out of the lodge until we get into position. Chances are they'll come right to the door and try to bullshit you. They won't do anything, though, until they've come up with some sort of sit-rep. So keep them talking."

"Will do, Yak."

"Frequency is set to 23. Let's go. Let's go." And with that, Yakabuski started pushing men out the back door of the Mattamy, all of them clambering over the snowdrift that had formed overnight, running clumsily into the storm.

It was a gamble right from the outset. Enough of a gamble that other men would have opted to fortify the Mattamy and hunker down for a siege. If Yakabuski had seen that strategy work even once, he may have considered it as well.

If they were spotted leaving the Mattamy, the crew would come in right away, knowing they had the advantage, and their workday would be cut short. Men travelling on foot in a snowstorm, against armed men on snowmobiles? Yakabuski knew they wouldn't stand a chance. It's why you couldn't hunt animals like that up in the Territories.

If they weren't spotted right away, if they survived the initial gamble, Yakabuski liked their odds of getting into position. The bikers would have their attention on the Mattamy. Downey would be able to stall them because the two men coming wouldn't be sure what was inside the lodge. How many people. What sort of guns. It was reasonable to assume they would have some sort of intel, but the situation had been fluid for two days at least, so it wouldn't be good intel. Not the kind you went to the wall for. So they would sniff around a little.

Yakabuski kept crawling toward the southbound light, the tree-marker beside him. When they were within two hundred yards of the light, the driver ran the snowmobile to the top of a drift, spun around a few times, then angled the machine with the headlights shining toward the Mattamy and killed the engine. Yakabuski looked east and saw the two snowmobiles that had been stationary start to move toward the lodge.

They were in position two minutes later, with the snow-mobile parked on the drift twenty yards in front of them. The biker crouched behind the machine, a pair of binoculars in his hands trained on the Mattamy. He was oblivious to everything behind him. As Yakabuski had been hoping.

"So what do we do now?" asked the tree-marker. "Shout 'put your hands up'?"

Yakabuski remembered what had happened to his father when he had shouted the same thing in the toy aisle of a Stedman's store in High River.

"No," he answered.

They turned their gaze toward the Mattamy and saw Downey walk onto the porch, a rifle cradled in the crook of his left arm. As Yakabuski had told him to do, his right was in the pocket of his parka, holding down the button of the walkie-talkie so he and Buckham could hear what was being said.

"Bad day to go sledding," they heard Downey say.

• • •

The two men who had arrived at the lodge had parked their snowmobiles and were swatting snow from their suits. Stretching and raising their arms. One had taken off his helmet and his long grey hair twirled in the wind. The man used a gloved hand to push the hair away from his face.

"Ain't that the truth, son," he said.

"Where you coming from?"

"The S and P."

"You must have set off in the middle of the night. Why would you do a thing like that?"

Tommy Bangles gave his head another shake, arched his back, and stretched his arms over his head as far as they could go. He acted as if he had not noticed the rifle pointed at his chest.

"It's a long story, son. Something has happened at the Northern Divide Expeditions school. Would you know anything about that?"

Downey said nothing. Kept staring at the man in front of him, whom he had seen only in police mug shots and once in the hallway of the Springfield courthouse, surrounded by full-patch bikers, more than a hundred yards away and walking quickly out of the building. He felt a hypo-like surge of adrenaline course through his blood. Gripped the rifle a little tighter. No one knew the Popeye assassin Downey had helped capture. Every cop in Springfield knew this guy.

"It burned down yesterday," said Downey, keeping his lips tight together, working hard to contain his excitement.

"Anyone survive?"

"Don't know if that's your concern."

"So someone did survive. He's in the lodge? I'm going to need to see him."

"Don't think that's going to happen."

"Ahhh, I wouldn't be saying stuff like that, son. You never know what life has in store for you. Where's the detective?"

"Not sure what you're talking about."

"You're Ident, son. I can smell it off you. And you'd be the dumbest fuck of an Ident cop I've ever met to go to the wall

242

for whatever mutt you're holding inside. You don't want this fight. So, where's the detective?"

Tommy Bangles was acting as though he were chairing a meeting, and this irked Downey. The biker was asking all the questions. Ignoring the rifle pointed to his chest. A cavalier disrespect, it seemed to Downey, not taking him seriously. One of the reasons he wore the uniform was so he wouldn't have to put up with that anymore.

"Sir," said Downey, "I'm taking what you have just said to me as a threat and I am going to arrest you now."

Bangles didn't bother answering. Turned his back on Downey and stared into the storm, not bothering to shield his eyes, taking the snow and ice pellets full in the face. Then he started to laugh. In a few seconds he was laughing like a deranged man.

"Fuck. He's already out there, isn't he? What shit-ass Springfield dick would have the jam to go into a storm like this?"

"There are people in the lodge with guns trained on you," said Downey. "I want you to drop to your knees right now."

Again, Bangles ignored him, turning his head toward the other biker instead and shouting, "You know who's here with us today, Bobby? In fuckin' Ragged Lake?"

The second biker, who had taken off his helmet but was still patting snow from his suit, didn't say anything. There were now two of them ignoring him, thought Downey, who said without thinking, forgetting for a moment that his purpose in life was to stall these men: "If you're not on your knees in the next five seconds, I'm going to shoot you and bring you to your knees that way."

"Ahhh, it is a sad fate God has in store for you, son," said

Bangles, turning finally to look him in the eyes. "Some people prefer it. To die and not know why. Myself, I think it would be the worst."

Downey had no more than a second to think about what was said. A second that encompassed much, although he never had the chance to reflect upon it. Snow funnels twirling in a mid-morning storm. A branch being snapped from a tree somewhere and banging its way to the ground. Two bikers smiling at him. And a sound that in ordinary circumstances would have been lost in the howl and roar of the storm but right then had the volume and pitch of a clarion horn summoning Downey home. The sound of a footstep behind him.

CHAPTER
TWENTY-SIX

You spend a lot of time waiting. Yakabuski was thinking that as he watched Downey talking to the two bikers. When you're fishing, it's almost all waiting. The seasons, when you're tired with one and ready for the next — more waiting. Any road trip is just waiting for the end, hopefully with some adventures thrown in along the way.

Maybe it's no different anywhere, but anticipation seemed a thing born of the North Country, came with it as surely as seasons, storms, and rivers. Yakabuski wondered from time to time if this might be what kept so many people on edge. All this waiting. For the next thing to surprise you. The next thing to battle. Waiting every day for things as simple as weather reports, because you lived someplace where the weather could kill you, and not by being extreme or any-thing, just by being February.

So part of what he was doing right then did not strike him

as strange. Sitting in a snowstorm with his service revolver in his lap, his gaze moving back and forth between a biker in a snow furrow twenty yards in front of him and two more bikers speaking to a young cop on the front porch of a fishing lodge. Waiting. Wishing he could be there to tell Downey to tone it down. Waiting to see what would happen now.

As so often happens, he didn't see it coming. Was surprised when he saw John Holly walk onto the porch with his target pistol in his hand. Yakabuski thought for a second he was coming to stand beside Downey. Thought for a second that was courageous. Watched in disbelief as Holly raised the gun; pointed it at the back of Downey's head, and pulled the trigger.

What they had been waiting for.

. . .

Everything happened quickly after that. Downey teetered for a second with a chevron of blood and goose feathers flying from his parka hood, then fell to his knees and toppled forward. Beside Yakabuski, the tree-marker yelled in surprise.

The biker in front of them turned. Not out of curiosity or surprise, but to attack. He was already firing his assault rifle. The bullets thudded in the snow in front of Yakabuski and he gave the tree-marker a push, then rolled in the opposite direction. "Split up," he yelled, "split up." When he had stopped rolling, he raised his service revolver but the biker was gone. Already repositioned. A good crew and that was one more sign of it.

To the north, where Buckham and the Sports would be hiding, Yakabuski heard the clatter of automatic gunfire. He strained to hear the single shot of a hunting rifle or a target pistol but couldn't. This could be over in five minutes. With bad luck, maybe two. How had he missed Holly? Yakabuski had taken the bartender and the cook off the playing field because they were obvious, but he hadn't thought it through all the way. That meth lab would have bought off anyone it could. Corrupted anyone it could. Why had he stopped with just the cook and the bartender? He should have thrown every man in Ragged Lake into that storage closet. Thrown every woman into a locked room.

The gunfire in the distance stopped. Yakabuski raised his head to look at the porch of the Mattamy. It was clear now except for Downey's body. He had no idea where the two bikers had gone. They could have gone into the lodge. Or they could have headed into the storm. He suspected the lodge, although he knew that might be wishful thinking. The other option meant the bikers were in the storm looking for them.

Just then, the biker he had been watching reappeared. Rose straight up from a snowdrift not more than ten yards away. His gun already sighted on Yakabuski and already firing. Yakabuski rolled to his right but wasn't quick enough. Could feel the bullets ripping into his leg. He screamed in pain and dropped his revolver. When that happened the biker stood fully erect and pushed back his parka hood. A smile spread slowly across his face.

"Not your day, my friend."

"Do you know I'm a police officer?" yelled Yakabuski.

"I know who you are. You just made me a rich man. Papa says hello."

The biker wasted no more time talking. Or gloating. He

raised his rifle. This was a top-notch crew and Yakabuski knew he had just been beaten. He wasn't going to act like that cell-block prisoner twisting on the ground.

He lay still and thought of what memory he wanted to take with him, flashing back and forth from Dorion Lake in early September to a Christmas morning when he was a child, sitting around a tinselled spruce with his mother, father, and sister, flashing back and forth between those two images, thinking for a brief second that if he opted for Dorion Lake, he was going to die alone.

Just then he heard a rifle shot. Single shot. Far away. No, closer than that.

The biker, still with a smile on his face, only his eyes registering surprise, rocked on his feet and pitched forward. Standing behind him was the tree-marker, the Remington rifle in his hands. The expression in the boy's eyes was not much different from the surprise in the eyes of the man he had just killed.

CHAPTER
TWENTY-SEVEN

Yakabuski was already bandaging his wound when the tree-marker approached. He cut the bandage from the parka of the slain biker, twisting the Gore-Tex fabric into twine that he used to knot the bandage. He had been lucky. It was not a bad wound.

"You all right?" he asked the tree-marker.

"Is he dead?"

"Yes, he's dead."

"Fuck."

"He was about to kill me. Don't feel too bad about it."

"He really was about to kill you, wasn't he? I saw him raise his gun and everything."

"Yes, he really was. So thank you."

"What is going on here? Has everyone gone crazy?"

Yakabuski didn't bother answering. Just kept twisting and

knotting his bandage. He looked at the dead biker and wondered if he would need more fabric.

. . .

Yakabuski tried the walkie-talkie. When he didn't get an answer, he and the tree-marker began to crawl. They took a wide flank around the fishing lodge. The windows of the lobby showed no lights inside. No motion. They kept going, crawling past the access road to the biplane dock, the fenced area for the garbage dumpsters, along the shoreline of the lake, on their bellies, burrowing through the snow like gophers. Finally, they came to the top of a windrow and found Donnie Buckham.

A bullet had caught the young cop square in the forehead. A neat, half-inch diameter hole with no seeping blood, no brain matter, not even a rough edge, a wound so neat it almost looked like a birthmark and that Buckham was merely sleeping.

Yakabuski stared at the young cop's face for a moment, the tree-marker behind him, not trying in any way to look around the giant cop and see the body.

"He's dead?"

"Yeah, he's dead," said Yakabuski. "Would have been dead before he hit the snow."

He sat on his haunches and rotated his feet so he could make a complete turn without standing up. He took in every angle. Every sight line. When he was finished, he rocked back and forth on his haunches a few times and did it again.

"How far do you figure the Mattamy is from here?" he asked the tree-marker.

The boy looked before answering, then said, "A hundred yards maybe. Probably a bit less than that."

"I'm going to say eighty."

"I wouldn't argue with you."

Yakabuski calculated the angle at thirty-five degrees. It was a bad storm, so there was no sense leaving a marker, and not knowing what else to do, he turned down Buckham's eyes, wrapped his scarf around his face, and turned his body into a fetal position, back to the wind. With luck, the drifting snow would leave a small pocket of air before Buckham's face. So he wouldn't be buried twice. A dignity that could not possibly matter to the dead, and Yakabuski wondered why he was bothering, even as he was positioning the body and sweeping away mounds of snow.

The tree-marker, crawling over a drift twenty yards farther on, nearly bumped into Garrett. The Sport was no more than twelve inches away — his face, anyway, what was left of it. The boy screamed in surprise and terror and did not stop until Yakabuski wrapped a massive mitt around his mouth.

"Calm down, son," he whispered. "We don't want to let people know where we are."

He hugged the boy, waited until his tremors had passed, until the shallow breathing had turned full again, until the whimpering had stopped, and then he waited another minute so it wouldn't be the last thing they heard.

"Sorry," the boy said, when he was released.

"Nothing to be sorry about, son. This is fucked up. You're right to scream about it."

Yakabuski looked at Garrett. Crawling up on a sight like that would have scared anyone. The back of the Sport's head was little more than a butcher's slab, a thing lacking such distinction it could only be called meat. He had landed chin-first in the snow, so the bottom half of his face was buried and only his nose and two surprised eyes could be seen, like some grotesque Harlequin mask.

Ten yards beyond Garrett was the biker, lying on his belly, his legs splayed upward, a small ring of blood pooling around his head.

Two dead men. Both shot from behind. That was quite the trick.

Yakabuski pushed the tree-marker to the ground, then lay beside him for several minutes not moving. Eventually, he took his binoculars from a pocket of his parka and started to scan the ground in front of him. The windrows and furrows. The parked snowmobile atop a drift. The dead biker. He was making a second pass of everything when he found him. No longer hiding behind the snowmobile. Standing up. Raising his arms. Waving them in.

"He's not dead," said the tree-marker in surprise.

• • •

O'Keefe did not appear frightened or panicked when they reached him. He pushed back the hood of his parka and calmly answered questions, sitting on his haunches as Yakabuski had done a few moments earlier.

"Constable Buckham stood up when Constable Downey was shot and ran toward the lodge," he said, looking directly at Yakabuski and ignoring the tree-marker. "It was not a smart thing to have done. The biker who was talking to Constable Downey turned and shot him. With a handgun he pulled from his pocket. It was rather an impressive shot."

Yakabuski looked back to where Buckham was lying. Almost eighty yards away, he calculated. Erring on the short side. Using a handgun and hitting Buckham square in the forehead. That was more than an impressive shot. That was genius.

"You saw it all happen?" asked Yakabuski.

"We both did. The officer was with us, then he was running toward the Mattamy, then he was shot. Garrett and I saw it all."

"What did the biker you were watching do when all this was happening?"

"Nothing. He kept his position. He was better trained than your young officer, I am afraid."

"You know something about police training, Mr. O'Keefe?"

"I know when emotions get the better of a man. I mean no offence."

"So what did you do?"

"Well . . ." and here O'Keefe hesitated a second, a thing that did not seem natural to him, that seemed to confuse him. Eventually, the trace of a smile came to his lips, fled just as quickly as it appeared, and he said, "I think I made a mistake. That's what happened next. I asked Mr. Garrett to check on the fallen officer."

"Check on him?"

"That's right. It didn't seem right to leave Constable Buckham lying there. Maybe he was still alive. Even if he wasn't, it didn't seem right to just leave him there."

"So you sent Garrett out to inspect the body?"

"Yes."

"Why didn't you go?"

"I wish now I had."

"The biker you were watching, he saw Garrett moving toward the body."

"Yes. I told Garrett to be careful. But we figured the biker would have his attention on the Mattamy."

"You and Garrett figured that?"

"Yes."

"But the biker saw him and crawled up behind him. To get a good clean head shot."

"Yes."

Yakabuski looked to the biker, then Garrett, saw the sightlines measure up. Saw the furrow of packed snow where O'Keefe would have been positioned. Saw how perfectly everything would have lined up for him.

"He didn't know there were two of you," Yakabuski said quietly.

"I think you're right about that."

O'Keefe looked sad right then, although he seemed to have trouble holding the emotion. It waxed and waned. Battled with other emotions that twitched the corners of his mouth and danced across his eyes. A sad-happy man he seemed right then, a thing so incongruous Yakabuski kept staring at his face, waiting for it to fall to one side of the spectrum.

CHAPTER
TWENTY-EIGHT

Yakabuski glassed the Mattamy. Still no lights. No sign of anyone moving inside. The tree-marker had another pair of binoculars and was watching possible approaches behind them — the shoreline of the lake, the lake itself. Yakabuski told him twice not to forget the lake. It would be smart to come in that way.

For the longest time no one spoke. O'Keefe had asked what he could do, and Yakabuski had told him to sit there and do nothing. A nerve in O'Keefe's left cheek had started to twitch, and it wasn't hard to figure out that the Sport was used to giving the orders. Saw a role for himself in any situation greater than that of passive observer.

When it looked like he was going to complain, Yakabuski said, "Absolutely nothing. I don't want you even moving without checking with me first. Are we clear on that, Mr. O'Keefe?"

Both cheeks started twitching, but O'Keefe nodded his head and stared out at the Mattamy, wishing he had a pair of binoculars, but not saying anything.

They waited more than an hour before Yakabuski finally saw a man with long hair pass before a window of the lodge. It was not the sort of day when you would be happy about anything, so relief is the better word to describe how Yakabuski felt right then. Relief to know the bikers were inside the lodge. Not outside hunting them down. Relief that was pretty close to happiness.

The feeling lasted only seconds. As Yakabuski watched the Mattamy, the front door opened and Tommy Bangles walked outside. Yakabuski could see his face easily with the binoculars. Could almost count each teardrop tattoo. He had suspected, but now he knew.

Tommy Bangles unzipped his parka, pushed back his hair, and yelled out, "Yak! It's been a while. Why don't you come in for a beer?" He started laughing. Stared down at the body of Matt Downey and gave it a little push. "Take a shot at me right now and everyone in this lodge is dead," he yelled, still looking at Downey. "Everyone with you is dead. They will be hunted down and quartered over a cook fire. Are we clear on that, Yak?"

Bangles raised his head and stared into the storm. Seemed to rise on the balls of his feet and cock his head. Then he turned to look at the front door of the Mattamy, gave a wave of his hand, and continued. "This is the drill, Yak." When he said that, John Holly walked through the door, pushing Gaetan Tremblay in front of him. The old man's hands were tied behind his back. His John Deere cap was missing and his head was bald except for wisps of grey hair around the edges that blew in the wind.

Bangles walked up to the old man and placed his hands upon his shoulders. Bent to talk to him, a gesture that seemed almost gentle. After talking a few seconds, Bangles braced the man and pushed him down, forcing him to his knees. Than he drew a handgun from the pocket of his parka, and walked behind him. Stroked the old man's head, another oddly gentle gesture.

"It's a one-hour drill, Yak," he shouted. "I think I'm being generous." With that, Bangles' hand twitched almost imperceptibly and Tremblay pitched forward. The old man fell with drill-parade precision, his two legs flipping up at a forty-five-degree angle so precise it looked geometric. Then the old man's legs lost inertia, collapsed to the snow, and the symmetry was lost.

Bangles gave a little salute with his gun hand and strode back inside the lodge. Holly followed him.

. . .

The tree-marker was in shock. Yakabuski wasn't sure about O'Keefe. It was hard to tell with him.

"You can't lose it, gentlemen," he hissed. "Cannot lose it. That's what they're hoping for. You cannot give them an easy win."

He put his arm on the tree-marker's back to make sure the boy did not rise and do something foolish.

"Can't lose it, gentlemen," he said one more time. "We can't make it easy for these bastards. I'm not going to let you make it easy."

No one spoke for a moment, and then O'Keefe asked, "What did he mean, it's a one-hour drill?"

"He means we have one hour before he brings someone else onto that porch."

"One hour?"

"Fifty-five minutes now."

Yakabuski laid out his plan. The tree-marker didn't understand how the cop's instructions could be so detailed, how he could not ask any questions, or hesitate even once, everything said in a low whisper that did not change pitch so much as half a tone, that did not inflect or add drama, that could have been reciting the best way to reach a nearby grocery. When Yakabuski finished talking, he began to crawl away, leaving the tree-marker and the Sport hiding behind the snowdrift.

· · ·

Yakabuski had seen a one-hour drill once before. In a farmhouse in the Laurentians. It was the sort of drill used by bikers and criminals for the most part, not so much by warlords and mercenaries. In war zones, you played for some distant endgame, with politics thrown into the mix, so there were advantages to holding onto a captive, sometimes for years, before you executed them.

Bikers either were interested in retribution and intimidation or needed to know something right away. So everything was a little hopped up. In that farmhouse in the Laurentians, seven men were locked in a bedroom. They were the full-patch members of the Sherbrooke Popeyes chapter, and after numerous transgressions and outright breaches of the Popeyes' code of conduct (all seven were intravenous drug users), Papa Paquette had issued a cull order against the chapter.

They could have been lined up and shot together, but Papa wanted to know where they had been buying their heroin, so the one-hour drill was held, one man brought out of the room every hour.

The executions happened in the living room of the farmhouse, a dump of a room with overstuffed furniture and overflowing ashtrays, a lacquered pine floor that had long ago lost its sheen. Each man was forced to kneel before Papa on the dung-coloured floor. Late afternoon sunlight through the spruce and red pine that surrounded the farmhouse cast long thin shadows across the floor. Each man pled for his life, had walked into the room believing he could strike a deal with Paquette, that his life mattered, that God would make an exception — believing this even though the dead bodies of the men who had gone before were lying by the kitchen door, stacked like cord wood, waiting to be weighted down and thrown into the lake.

Not one of the captured men had known the supplier; the only one who had was the head of the Sherbrooke chapter, who had been tipped off about the cull order and had flown to Mexico the day before.

Yakabuski had sat in that living room for all seven executions. It was the crime that would send Paquette away for life when Yakabuski, sitting behind a green screen with his voice altered, testified via video about what he had seen. Not that any of the precautions had made a difference. Paquette had known his true name and identity within six hours of being arrested.

During cross-examination, Yakabuski was asked repeatedly, by Papa's lawyer and then by each lawyer for each of the six men charged with him, how he could have sat there and done nothing during the Sherbrooke Cull. As though they would have done something different, would have stood up in the middle of that farmhouse living room and said, "I'm a cop, I can't let this continue."

It was a stupid argument and Yakabuski had said as much on the stand, careful to let only a little of his anger show — not the seething anger he felt when he heard the question, for it was one of the few good questions any of the lawyers had to ask.

How *could* he have sat there and done nothing? Even though it was seven bikers who were killed, each one deserving to have that as his final chapter, and even though he had been trained in the Third Battalion for just such situations — human shields and civilian executions being the norm for a while in Bosnia and Afghanistan — the question wouldn't disappear the way logic said it should.

Yakabuski ran a little faster through the snowstorm. Logic would be no help to him that morning if he were late. He knew the next person to be executed was not a biker but an elderly Cree woman, widowed for less than an hour.

• • •

Yakabuski had been surprised to find her at the end of his run. Sitting in her Morris chair, rocking back and forth, a pair of old binoculars in her lap. She had been watching what was happening at the Mattamy and knew he was coming.

Bangles should have gone and collected her. Or killed her where she lived. Yakabuski ran the entire distance, not knowing if he was wasting his time, and when he reached the cabin, he was panting and couldn't speak for a minute.

Finally, he said, "We need your help, Madame."

"You will need my gun?"

"Yes."

"Should I get dressed?"

"Please."

She didn't say anything more. Pulled her gnome-like body up and out of the Morris chair, padded in her woollen socks to the closet, and took out the shotgun Yakabuski had seen there the day before.

Anita Diamond slid her child-sized feet into a pair of mukluks and took down her parka. As she was doing all this, she listened to Yakabuski explain what they needed to do, already knowing for the most part what he was going to say. Not the details. Not names and places. But what had happened, what needed to be done now — in every way that mattered, she knew.

The tough days had returned. It was a simple enough story to understand. Returned along with the tough decisions that always accompanied the tough days. As she put on her coat, Diamond remembered a cousin who had been making the fall migration down the Francis River one year, leaving the summer fishing beds, going to the inland village of Kashawana. His three sons went with him in the sixteen-foot locked-oar skiff. Halfway home, a rogue wave capsized the boat.

Her cousin had been the last boat out that season. There was no one coming behind them. And there was a six-day hike ahead of them to reach Kashawana. In the fast-moving river, her cousin rescued one son, then a second, but when he swam for the third boy, his dry-goods sack popped up from the river, directly in front of him. Without that bag — which had their fresh water, kindling, flint and food — they would likely die before reaching Kashawana. He reached for it. Knowing it needed to be done. Trusting there would be time to rescue his last son.

But there hadn't been. Her cousin had watched the boy drift away, listening to him call his father's name until the boy's voice could no longer be heard. Her cousin's heart became so heavy, he had trouble walking to Kashawana. Needed to be supported by his other sons every step of the six-day hike.

The day they reached the village, her cousin killed himself with his favourite hunting rifle. Diamond believed her cousin had known what he was going to do as soon as he grabbed the dry-goods bag. On a good day, she believes the young boy knew as well.

She zipped up her parka, put a toque on her head, pulled the hood of her parka over the toque, and hoisted the shotgun over her shoulders. She looked at Yakabuski and nodded.

"Thank you, Madame," he said.

"There is no need," she answered.

• • •

O'Keefe and the tree-marker were crouched behind the snowdrift staring at their watches when Roselyn Tremblay was brought outside. Unlike her husband, the old woman had her arms free. She walked unescorted with short, purposeful steps to where her husband lay. She knelt and turned over his body, held his hands and bent to kiss his face. She paused here, then leaned back and raised her head to the storm.

Behind the old woman were Bangles and Holly. Bangles

had a smile on his face. Holly now wore a black balaclava against the storm.

"You just cost me money, Yak," Bangles yelled. "I bet John here that you would have the balls to come in before we killed this old woman."

Tremblay did not flinch when Bangles said it. Bangles' smile grew larger. He looked over at Holly, pointed the gun at the old woman's head as if to say, "Will you look at that?" and continued talking.

"Yeah, I thought you had the balls. But you're a cowardly bohunk dick, aren't you, darliiin? You'd let us kill your own mother if it meant you could save your ass. What do the men standing beside you think about that, Yak? Do *they* want this old woman to die?"

Bangles placed his gun on the back of Tremblay's head. Like her husband, her head was uncovered, so her hair blew freely, coiled around the handgun like strands of seaweed in a strong current. No one on the porch moved. It seemed for a second as though they were posing for a photo.

• • •

"Are we really going to let this happen?" The tree-marker looked at the man crouched next to him.

O'Keefe kept his eyes trained on the porch. "You heard what the cop said."

"I also heard him say he'd be back."

"You heard him say he'd try to be back. He warned us he might not get back in time."

"I don't know if I can do this."

"You're going to have to do this, kid."

"Would you shoot me if I couldn't?"

"I might."

"Why would you do a thing like that?"

"To keep you from surrendering. To keep you from giving away our position. Because I don't know you that well. Take your pick."

"Shouldn't surrendering be my call?"

"Almost never."

"How can you do it? Watch and do nothing?"

"Might not be that hard. It's doing nothing. Just like you said."

The tree-marker thought it took courage for him to keep watching. Then thought it was something perverse and maybe it had nothing to do with courage. He was just starting to work his way through a mental list of all the ways courage and perversity were different when Bangles' hand twitched.

Nothing more than that. Roselyn Tremblay fell over the body of her dead husband. A short woman, she was left perched on his chest, like a teeter-totter, rocking back and forth in the wind, her small feet kicking up drifts of snow you could almost see in the storm.

The tree-marker turned his head and threw up.

Bangles stood over Roselyn Tremblay's body and after staring for a few seconds laughed, lifted his head, and shouted, "You're a fuckin' coward, Yak."

His parka was unzipped and he was wearing long underwear underneath, red, no sweater, his upper chest exposed. He was hopped-up on adrenaline or something more synthetic, the tree-marker thought, hoping it was synthetic, that it was unnatural, because a man standing in a storm like this, killing and laughing and not seeming to notice the elements, was just not right.

"I don't know why I'm surprised. Papa said you were a sneak-up-on-you-in-the-middle-of-the-night coward. Said he would have respected you if you'd brought him down like a man, drawn a weapon and stood in front of him. But it's always a trick with you, isn't it?"

Even from a distance, the tree-marker noticed Bangles' body change right then. Saw it tense and become rigid. Saw the man's mouth open and close a few times, and then Bangles spun around, moving in a 360-degree arc, scanning the countryside, as if such a thing could be possible in this storm.

"You mother-fuckin' bohunk bastard. You're not even there, are you? Always fuckin' games with you, Yak."

Bangles was kicking the body of Matt Downey as he screamed, full-throttle kicks that lifted the young cop's body several inches off the ground each time, kicked and kicked until Downey was off the porch. Then he grabbed Holly by the arm and the two men ran inside.

The sound of gunfire crossed the distance from the lodge to the tree-marker and O'Keefe. They watched as Bangles and Holly reappeared on the porch, dragging the body of the prisoner from the freezer. After that, the body of the cook. After that, the body of the bartender. Holly dragged each man's body across the porch and threw it off to land on the one before, Bangles kicking the bodies as they were dragged and making the job more difficult than it needed to be, kicking and stomping and swearing. The tree-marker and O'Keefe could see that Holly was frightened, keeping his distance, positioning himself on the porch so he could jump clear of it with one running step if needed.

"Fuckin' bohunk bastard. You get half a fuckin' hour for the waitress, Yak. Half a fuckin' hour. Then we start the cook fires and hunt you down." He turned and stormed back into the lodge, kicking at the bodies of Roselyn and Gaetan Tremblay before entering — though not with enough force to fling them off the porch. As though something inside him had been sated. Or the old couple belonged there. It was difficult to tell.

CHAPTER
TWENTY-NINE

From behind a drift closer to the lodge than the tree-marker and O'Keefe, Yakabuski had also vomited after witnessing the execution of Roselyn Tremblay.

He had been late getting back. Despite his exertions. Despite some measure of success. He had not been able to get back in time and an innocent person had died. The way he had been trained as a soldier, he had done nothing to stop it. *Which says something about the decisions you make as a young man,* thought Yakabuski. *To have ever been trained for such a thing.*

But a soldier never added himself to a body count. Not willingly, anyway. You never make it easy on an enemy like that. A warrant officer who had served in the Vietnam War told Yakabuski this one day, when Yakabuski had asked questions about the training, saying he wasn't sure if he could do it — stand down and do nothing when another person was executed.

The warrant officer had thrown his arm around the young light infantry soldier and told him in a cheery voice that sometimes soldiers can't be in the saving-people business.

"Sometimes soldiers can only be in the paying-bastards-back business," he said.

Yakabuski kept the warrant officer's voice rolling through his mind as he crawled back to O'Keefe and the tree-marker. It helped a little. Not enough to take away the sadness that had overcome him. Just enough to let him focus on the mission ahead — pay the bastards back.

· · ·

Lying beside the tree-marker and the Sport, Yakabuski looked at his watch. Ten minutes before the waitress was due to be brought out.

"What just happened?" asked the tree-marker, his voice frail and shaky.

"They've started the sweep," said Yakabuski. "Looks like the cook and the bartender were part of the gang. Or were helping them."

"Why kill them now?"

"Bangles doesn't — the guy with the gun is Tommy Bangles — he doesn't need them anymore. They'd just be in his way." A second later, he added, "He also looked a little pissed."

The next ten minutes could have been an hour. Could have been a hundred hours. The tree-marker thought he was floating for a while, time and other sensations vanished, an untethered feeling as he kept staring at the front porch of the Mattamy, which now resembled some back-alley boxing ring, blood and unidentifiable pulpy flesh scattered around; flint-eyed, indolent men running the show.

When the waitress was brought outside, Holly had her arms pinned to her sides and the young girl was screaming, a pitched lament you could hear easily above the storm. Holly was still wearing the black balaclava. Bangles came out behind them, not even wearing his parka anymore, his red long underwear bright in the falling snow.

Yakabuski had explained the plan, but only the parts they needed to know, so both O'Keefe and the tree-marker looked at him right then, the tree-marker with a quizzical expression on his face, O'Keefe's face unreadable. Yakabuski didn't say anything. He couldn't ask either of them to do what needed to be done next.

If he had things figured out right, he wouldn't need to.

"This is the last one, Yak!" Bangles yelled out across the snow. "The last one you can save. After this, we hunt you down like fuckin' pigs. She's young, this one. We know you don't care about the old ones. What about this one?"

Marie was struggling against Holly, trying to kick him in the groin. It seemed unlikely she would kneel before her executioner the way the Tremblays had. Yakabuski wondered if they had already worked out a plan to compensate for that.

"This one has much to offer, Yak. If we weren't in such a hurry, we'd bounce her off a few walls, I think."

Through his binoculars, Yakabuski saw Bangles leaning in to run his tongue down the waitress's cheek, an action that caused her to scream as though scalded. She screamed and screamed and Bangles laughed, and while this was happening the tree-marker rose.

The tree-maker rose and stretched his hands above his head. Stood for several seconds with the snow swirling around him. Then he started walking toward the Mattamy.

O'Keefe reached for the rifle the tree-marker had left behind and then gasped in surprise when Yakabuski put his service revolver against his temple. He turned to see Yakabuski putting a mitt to mouth, motioning for him to be quiet. The two men stared at each other for a long minute, then Yakabuski lowered his gun. They turned to look at the tree-marker, who was taking slow, laborious steps through the high snow, his arms raised in surrender, not bothering to look behind him, his eyes fixed only on the waitress, not even noticing Bangles laughing and motioning with his free hand for the boy to keep walking.

After a few seconds, Yakabuski said, "Were you going to shoot that boy?"

"I was thinking of it."

"It's that important to you? Your own survival?"

"Don't be precious with me. You watched that old couple get executed, same as we did."

"That couple couldn't be saved. That boy can be saved."

"What makes you so sure?"

Yakabuski didn't say anything right away. Kept staring at the tree-marker trudging through the snow like some sad supplicant. Then he said, "There's a photo hanging in the hallway outside my room in the Mattamy. A bunch of men by the front gates of the mill. Some sort of banner on a smokestack. You're in it."

O'Keefe kept his eyes on Yakabuski but didn't say anything.

"What was the celebration?"

"The one millionth roll of newsprint to come off the presses here," said O'Keefe. "That was nearly twenty years ago."

"It must have been quite the party. Old man O'Hearn came up for it. He's right in the centre of the photo. I didn't notice the resemblance until I saw the photo. You worked here at the mill?"

"Four summers. While going to university. A full year after I graduated. My dad insisted on it. Who have you told?"

"No one."

"Why not?"

"I was still trying to figure it out. And you weren't going anywhere."

Yakabuski stood. Threw his service revolver into the snow. Raised his hands and turned to where the tree-marker was trudging toward the Mattamy, almost there now. He cocked his head and said to the man still hiding behind the snow-drift, "Come on, Mr. O'Hearn. We need to go in."

CHAPTER
THIRTY

Yakabuski had been captured twice before. The first time had been in Afghanistan, his last year with the Third Battalion, clearing caves on a mountain called the Whale — third day of doing that, and they hadn't found a single Taliban fighter. Just munitions and supplies left behind. Each cave and each tunnel between the caves — an elaborate system that would have rivalled anything built by the North Vietnamese — contained some sort of cache. Landmines and RPGs. 556 ammunition. In one tunnel, a fully equipped triage room. But never a belligerent.

There had been two days of air strikes before they had moved onto the Whale, and it was assumed the fighters had fled. Or been killed in the strikes and all that remained of them were the bone and scorched-skin fragments you found sometimes on the trails running between caves. Yakabuski was less than a hundred yards from the peak of the Whale when he found the entrance to one more tunnel.

Fifty yards east of him was a Special Forces platoon getting ready to clear a cave, two Browning .50 Cal machine guns already in position on the wings of the cave entrance, the company sergeant lying on the ground and about to fire a stun grenade through the opening. There would be no one inside. As there had been no one inside for three days. After firing the grenade and waiting a few seconds, the soldiers would march into the cave to see what supplies they would find this time. About as routine as it gets for a Special Forces platoon.

Yakabuski waved to a soldier holding one of the gun clips for the .50 Cal, and the soldier waved back. Yakabuski pointed to the hole, and the soldier nodded. The platoon would know a light infantry soldier was in the tunnel. Yakabuski turned on his flashlight and walked inside. He saw boxes of medical supplies right away. Plastic gloves and IV bags, gauze and bandages, penicillin and cortisone, boxes stacked six high and running down the tunnel farther than he could see. He started walking, counting boxes at the same time — four, five, six . . . eighteen, nineteen, twenty — was counting and walking like that when he rounded a corner and found himself staring at a dozen Taliban fighters.

It happened so quickly he never had the chance to yell. Never had the chance to raise his gun. Strong hands grabbed his wrists and pinned them beside his body, another hand placed the muzzle of a Beretta M9 against his left temple. He stared at the rag-tag soldiers at the other side of the tunnel, an old man in the centre. The man slowly brought a finger to his lips and blew upon it.

Quiet. Yes, let's everyone be quiet. That's a good idea. The two men who had pinned him took his rifle and sidearm and pushed him to the ground. A rope came out and his hands were tied. His rifle was given to the old fighter, who examined it, took the clip in and out a few times, the sort of things Yakabuski would have done if he had just been handed a gun.

Another fighter came to stand beside the old man. This man took a curved knife from a scabbard and flicked his head in Yakabuski's direction. The old man finished examining the gun and put it down. He shook his head. Took a scarf from his neck and gave it to the man holding the scabbard.

The man walked over and shoved the scarf into Yakabuski's mouth. Then he motioned for the two men who had tied him to leave, and he stood with the muzzle of his Beretta pushed against Yakabuski's head.

Maybe an hour. That's how long they would have stayed like that, no one in the tunnel moving or talking or breathing any more than was necessary. They could hear the Special Forces soldiers moving on the other side of the rock, as though they were buried in stone, their muffled chatter and laughter coming from some other dimension. As Yakabuski's eyes adjusted to the dark, he could see the tunnel they were in ran portside, away from the cave next door. They did not connect. This was a different tunnel from what they had been finding the past three days.

Was it more than an hour? Maybe. Certainly enough time to memorize every line of every face staring at him. Eye color, the shape of noses, the way the youngest was probably no more than thirteen, although he seemed the most alert. Enough time to see there was no anger on any face staring

back at him. No fear. No curiosity. Just a weary sort of purpose, a grudging acceptance of tough work that probably lay
ahead of them. It could have been half the town of High
River staring at him right then, thinking it was time to start
getting ready for winter.

Then the voices in the rock began to drift away. The old
man held up his hand and everyone tensed. Waited for the
voices to start coming down the tunnel. But the voices bled
away and never returned. As Yakabuski knew they would. He
had signalled the tunnel was his. No one would be coming.

When the old man finally brought down his hand, he
jerked his head and the fighter next to him bent to a crouch,
turned, and scuttled his way down the tunnel. When he was
out of sight, another fighter crouched and made the same
retreat. Then another, another, and so on down the line of
fighters. A perfect retreat without a word being spoken.

When it was down to the company commander and the
man holding the Beretta against Yakabuski's head, there was
a pause in the rhythm. There needed to be a different move
here. Yakabuski had seen it coming and had already run
some rough geometry through his mind. He had decided at
the first sign of his captor tensing in any sort of way that he
would catapult himself toward the man. His best chance of
survival would be a bullet deflecting the wrong way. There
was no chance of a bullet missing him if he ran.

Yakabuski tensed his body. Shifted as much weight as possible to his knees. Got ready to lunge.

And the man walked away.

Slid his gun into its holster, crouched, and darted as
fast as he could down the tunnel. The old commander gave

Yakabuski one last look, waved a gun clip in his hand to show him the rifle was useless, then bowed and disappeared down the tunnel.

Yakabuski freed himself within seconds and ran down the tunnel in pursuit, calling in his position as he ran, but the fighters were never found. The tunnel went on for three miles, with other tunnels branching off, and no one could say later where the fighters had exited. Or who they had been. The best-trained light infantry company Yakabuski had ever seen.

The other time he had been on his knees with a gun pushed against his head was during the Biker Wars. An enemy of Papa caught him when he was leaving the Vandome night club one night. But he had been a sloppy man, not frisking Yakabuski properly, and so there was little challenge to escaping, nothing more complicated than slipping a .22 Derringer from his groin and shooting the man's ear off when he bent to whisper something threatening.

So he had seen the best and worst when it came to forcible confinement. He looked around the bar of the Mattamy, wondering how this would compare.

CHAPTER
THIRTY-ONE

They sat around one of the tables in the restaurant: the wait-ress, the tree-marker, Yakabuski, and the man who had been calling himself Tobias O'Keefe. Their hands were cuffed to the high backs of their chairs, tavern chairs being per-fectly designed for such a thing. They had not been beaten, and Yakabuski took that as a good sign. The man who had come with Bangles, who had been positioned in a window the past two hours with a Remington sniper rifle, keeping watch for anyone trying to move on the lodge, was Bobby O'Shaughnessy. Or Bobby Chance, as everyone called him, a cousin of Bangles.

"How you doin', Bobby?" asked Yakabuski.

"Doing well, Yak. You?"

"Just hangin'."

"Better be careful what you say. Don't want to be giving Tommy any ideas."

They laughed. A good-natured, long-day-in-the-bush sort of laugh. Yakabuski had arrested O'Shaughnessy five years ago, right outside the Silver Dollar, after a black street dealer was found burned, castrated, and trussed to the chain-link fence surrounding the Nosoto Projects. Yakabuski had found O'Shaughnessy with gas cans in the back seat of the car he was driving, the dealer's wallet open on the passenger seat, and the dealer's girlfriend bound and gagged in the trunk. Bobby's lawyer got him off after he had all the evidence from the car tossed. Even the dealer's girlfriend. Car didn't belong to Bobby. His client had no idea there was someone in the trunk. Bobby Chance. It was a good nickname.

These men were part of a serious crew working on tight deadlines, so it was possible they would have no time for the gratuitous stuff. Good news for Yakabuski. Good news for the waitress. Wouldn't mean much of anything in a few hours, but a good break to have right then.

"That lab must have been supplying meth and ecstasy to cities all the way up and down the seaboard," said Yakabuski. "You and Sean taken on new partners, Tommy?"

"People come, people go; you know how it is, Yak. Always somebody new kicking around. Some of the new boys would spin your bohunk head."

"Takes a lot to spin my bohunk head. Why you say a thing like that?"

"'Cause they're whacked. Just fuckin' whacked. There's this one dude, he travels around in a mobile home he's got all tricked out. Cutting tables, meat hooks, Sawzalls. You never want to take a ride with that dude."

"He from around here?"

Bangles laughed and pushed strands of hair away from his

face. Then he ran his fingers through his hair and pinched out a piece of ice trapped there. He threw it across the bar so it landed in the service sink, making a sound that reminded Yakabuski of sleigh bells.

"It's hard to say where anyone comes from these days, Yak, don't you think? Not like when we were boys. You had the bohunks from High River, the French on the other side of the river, the Irish in Cork's Town, the Cree and the Algonquin up here. Now everyone moves around too much, don't you think?"

"I think you're full of crap."

Bangles laughed, found some more trapped ice, and threw it into the sink.

"So, what happened to that squatter family?" asked Yakabuski. "They found out about the lab and so you had to kill them?"

"Don't know 'bout that one. Bit of a mystery, actually. I'm just here to do a scrub."

"So you're denying it. I guess that poor family got itself killed by one of those boogeymen you're talking about."

"Ain't boogeymen, darliiin. It's true gen. How many times I got to tell you that? By the way, if it were up to me, I'd just shoot you in the head and be done with it. The boogeymen want something more. It ain't personal with me."

"I don't even know them."

"Bad luck then."

· · ·

Bangles and Chance had a couple of shots at the bar, then zippered their parkas and headed outside, leaving Holly to guard the prisoners. The guide sat at the bar with Yakabuski's Sig Sauer in his lap. No trouble holding anyone's stare. Not an ounce of shame to him.

Yakabuski heard two snowmobile engines turning over in the cold. Bangles and Chance were on their way to scrub the lab. Yakabuski knew commercial grade bleach would be in the cargo bins of the snowmobiles. Ready to burn away fingerprints if the fire hadn't already done the job. Some jaws and lower clefts were about to be smashed in as well.

He listened carefully to the sound of the engines. Revving high in the cold, neither driver bothering to ease up on the gas. Not caring about the machines. He listened as the sound of the engines began to blend and became one high-pitched, single note, growing fainter and fainter before finally fading away. Listened until he was sure.

Just the one sound. They were travelling together. Gone to check and scrub just one location.

Yakabuski didn't bother smiling. Or feel much of anything at all. About a dozen other things still needed to go right.

. . .

"You don't understand?" John Holly spoke from where he sat at the bar, a rock glass with two fingers of Canadian Club in front of him. "I'm surprised it would confuse you, Detective Yakabuski," he continued. "You don't have to stare at me all afternoon. Go ahead. Ask any question you want."

Yakabuski met his eyes. They had the time. "Why did you do it, Mr. Holly?"

"Ahhh. You're disappointed in me?"

"You murdered a police officer. Disappointed isn't the word I would use."

"Tommy's told me a bit about you. You're from here. So I really don't understand your attitude. Do you read any history?"

Yakabuski stared at him but didn't speak.

"It always amazes me how ignorant people are about their own history. At the top of Mount Royal, you have the heart of a Jesuit priest who was tortured and quartered by the Iroquois. We wiped the Beothuk off the face of the earth. Why should anyone in this country be surprised by violence? I could never figure that one out. Maybe it's common for frontier countries, this denial of what you are, the way you were raised, always trying to tidy up your house, clean your hands. I never looked into the psychology of it, but it wouldn't surprise me any if that were the case."

Holly stopped to take a sip of whisky. Looked at the four people handcuffed to chairs in front of him. A captive audience. He laughed and continued talking. "I tell people sometimes 'bout the first winter Champlain spent in Quebec City. The oldest city in the whole damn continent outside of Mexico City. Tell them how there was this plot to kill Champlain and sell the city to some Portuguese fishermen, which is funny in a way, to think how far we've come, knowin' there was a time when the country was almost sold to a bunch of Portuguese fishermen. But Champlain learned about the plot and arrested the traitors, held a trial acting as judge, and decided the best punishment for the ringleader was to have him killed and quartered and his head put on a pike by the front gates of the city. The head sat there all winter, a hard winter that saw Micmacs starving to death outside the walls of the fortress and carrion birds blackening the sky.

"You tell people that's how this country started, and they just flat out don't want to believe you. What am I doing right now that's any different? I'm just trying to survive. Like we've always done around here."

Yakabuski looked at Holly and before letting too much time pass, he said, "You are one seriously fucked up guide, Mr. Holly."

CHAPTER
THIRTY-TWO

"I'm staring at it now." Tommy Bangles looked at the burned-out bunkhouse, marvelling again at how hot the fire must have been, how anything that was wood was now ash, anything glass turned to what looked like clear toffee, anything plastic a sludge that pockmarked the snow around him.

"Nothing?"

"Nothing but ashes," he said into his cellphone.

"Have you been inside?"

"I'm not going to risk it, Sean. I can see the two other bodies. Everyone is accounted for. I want to be gone in two hours."

"Who do you have detained?"

"I've got the tree-marker who found the bodies. I've got a waitress. Some Sport guy. And you're going to love this, Sean — I've also got one fat bohunk dick from Springfield."

There was silence for a second, and then Sean Morrissey started laughing.

"Who isn't in Ragged Lake today? This is getting odder by the minute, Tommy."

"Isn't it? I phoned our friend, and he said to take a video. We may get some sort of bounty from Papa."

"We might. And that's it?"

"No. The guide is still here. Our friend thinks we should leave him to give the cops a story so they don't drive themselves crazy trying to figure out what happened here."

"He may be right. The police may like a good story. Otherwise this is one big cockup, no?"

"One big motherfuckin' cockup. I don't even know how many bodies are lying around here anymore. I'm losing track."

"So maybe give the police a story. Be kind to them, otherwise they'll search for years — the big mystery of Ragged Lake. Give them a story and be done with it. Can our guide be a hero?"

"He already thinks he is."

"So what do you think?"

"I don't like the guy. I say let the cops work."

"Your call, Tommy."

• • •

Bangles and Chance were back in the bar in ninety minutes. They didn't bother brushing off snow before walking in. Didn't kick off their boots in the lobby. They trudged in with giant balls of snow caked to their feet, poured rock glasses half full of Canadian Club, and stood there drinking, letting the snow melt away to puddles around their feet. They carried a disinfectant smell with them, and the tips of their fingers were blanched and wrinkled.

"Anyone else inside the building?" asked Yakabuski.

"Two you didn't see," answered Bangles. "It was flares, right?"

"It was flares."

"Yep, François should have had someone on the windows. That was a fuck-up."

"It was a fuck-up as soon as that squatter family got killed. How did you expect to keep everything secret after that?"

"Don't know shit 'bout any squatter family. I already told you that. You need to talk to François. Oh, right—"

He laughed. Bobby Chance laughed. Holly laughed. Then Bangles slammed the rock glass on the oak countertop of the bar, hiked up his pants, and walked outside. The people handcuffed at the table saw him walk onto the porch. He came into view with a white bleach bottle in his hand, dragging the body of the cook. He bent over and poured bleach over the cook's hands. Then he ground the hands under his boot heels. Back and forth. Back and forth. Then he poured bleach over the cook's face. Opened the mouth and poured more bleach. With his boots he smashed the jaw, the lower cleft, the teeth. Stomp. Stomp.

He repeated the process for the bartender. The two-thunderbolt enforcer. Chance sat at the bar, drinking and looking out the window along with everyone else.

"You don't help?" asked Yakabuski.

"Nah, Tommy likes doing this part."

Yakabuski nodded but didn't say anything. Stared at Holly, but the guide didn't notice him looking, just kept watching out the bay window at what Bangles was doing, as though mesmerized, as though staring at an act of carnage and savagery he had only had the chance to read about before.

It was time.

. . .

It was a gamble, and Yakabuski was no fan of gambling, but he could not avoid it. The best signal was a gunshot. There was no way you could argue it. Anything else had a good chance of being missed. Or never happening. So it was the ultimate gamble, what he was about to do. A game of Russian roulette played with John Holly. Neither man holding the gun that would kill one of them.

Yakabuski had expected the bikers to leave shortly after he and the others had surrendered. With all belligerents detained and accounted for, they would go to the next phase and scrub the lab. He had estimated two hours. He had noted the time when they were tied to the chairs and when Bangles had returned from the porch, sat between Holly and Chance, and resumed drinking. When the clock had measured off exactly two hours, Yakabuski yawned and said, "Are we going to get on with this, Tommy? I'm starting to get a kink in my back."

"You sore, Yak?"

"Every morning. Wait for it. It's coming for you."

"Not me. I'm never sore."

"You're going to be surprised. So, you're finished with the scrub?"

"Think so."

"You're not forgetting anything?"

"No."

"You're done? That's what you're telling me?"

Yakabuski looked at Holly and laughed. Holly, not knowing how to respond, laughed back at him.

Bangles looked at the guide, shook his head, and said, "Fuck off, Yak. I just poured myself a drink." He turned on his bar stool and stared at Yakabuski. A leer spread across his face. He pushed hair off his face, the teardrop tattoos catching the light from the overhead bulb behind the bar.

"I'm not trying to cause you any problems, Tommy," Yakabuski said. "I'm really not. You tell me you're done, then you're done. You know what you're doing."

"I don't know how Papa put up with you."

"I'm not trying to rush you, Tommy. I'm just checking to see where we are."

"Not trying to rush me? You saw me pour a drink."

"Yeah, I guess I did. You're right about that. So maybe I'm just getting tired of sitting around watching your sad ass perform. Are you done scrubbing or not?"

"You really are an asshole."

With that, Tommy Bangles took a handgun from his parka pocket, put it against Holly's head and pulled the trigger. He was reaching for the bleach bottle on the bar when Yakabuski began his dive.

CHAPTER
THIRTY-THREE

Yakabuski let his body go slack and pitched forward, hoping he would hear another gunshot right then, knowing he would be dead within seconds if he did not.

He heard it. A retort that reverberated through the room with a loud metallic blowback sound that echoed and droned and brought everyone's attention to the front entrance of the restaurant, where Bobby Chance was standing, looking in surprise at the blood mushrooming from the front of his parka. Another gunshot, and he was flying through the air. He landed with a thud, coming to rest against the foot-rail of the bar. A bloody bubble of mucous formed around his mouth. His eyes were vacant and stupid-looking. Bobby Chance. How he looked when the luck ran out.

Yakabuski saw none of it. As he pitched forward, he slid his hands under the legs of his chair and kept rolling, snatching up Chance's AR-15 but never stopping — a continuous somersault that saw him throw off the chair, grab the gun, and keep rolling. It was a move that looked as effortless as it had been the last time he'd done it, nearly thirty years ago, when he was handcuffed and held captive in the back room of a cousin's cottage on Lake Kamiskasing. That time, he'd grabbed a bat to chase the cousin from the room.

Unless you were using military-grade handcuffs fastened to something rooted in poured concrete, Yakabuski always liked his chances of getting free.

Bangles stared at the body of Bobby Chance and then at the front entrance of the restaurant, where Anita Diamond was standing with her shotgun in her small hands. Bangles' mouth moved but no sound came out. Just beginning to realize where he had gone wrong. Where he had been lazy.

• • •

When the tree-marker had stood and surrendered, Anita Diamond had snuck in the back door of the lodge and hid in a closet. Yakabuski had told her to estimate two hours for the signal. Use common sense and manoeuvre as close as possible to the bar. Wait for the signal.

So many things could have gone wrong. They could have been killed the minute they surrendered. Bangles could have shot him instead of Holly. That was perhaps the riskiest part of the plan, but Yakabuski had figured the odds were slightly in his favour. He couldn't imagine Bangles liking John Holly.

Bangles reached now for the handgun he had placed on the bar only seconds earlier, as Diamond pumped the shotgun, ejected the casings, took the two shells she had clenched between her teeth, and started to slide them into the breach.

But she was too slow. The old hands not as quick as they had once been. Bangles' first bullet caught Diamond in the upper chest, and her shotgun fell uselessly to the floor. The next four landed near the first, lifting the old woman in the air as though on puppeteer's strings.

Yakabuski was late as well. He tried to aim at Bangles, but the rifle kept slipping in his manacled hands, slipping, slipping, until he pulled the trigger in frustration, not bothering to aim, sticking the gun over the edge of the table he was hiding behind and firing blind, an unnatural thing for him to do, not expecting good things to happen from being so reckless.

But he got lucky. One of the bullets clipped Bangles's ankle. The biker screamed in pain and fell, his handgun skittering across the floor.

"You motherfuckin' bohunk! You don't get this lucky. No fuckin' way you get this lucky!" Bangles twisted on the floor, reaching for his gun. "You fuckin' piece of shit. You lying, motherfucking—"

And that's when Yakabuski ended it. Rose from behind the table, and when Bangles slid his fingers around the gun, he lay down a line of fire that caught the biker flush in the stomach and slid him backwards on the floor, like a hockey player in one of those old children's games with the slotted tracks. Yakabuski fired until Bangles smashed into the far wall. Offside by a country mile. After that he slumped over and, without bullets to support him, without purpose or future, he slid to the ground, and that was the end of him.

. . .

Yakabuski walked over to Anita Diamond. Bent to look at her wounds. He saw immediately that there was no sense fashioning a tourniquet. He would never be able to staunch this much blood. She would lose consciousness in a couple of minutes. Would bleed out and be dead a few minutes after that. He held the old woman's hands.

She looked up at him and said, "You are alive, Detective Yakabuski. That must be a good sign."

"It is. You have saved our lives, Madame."

"For today at least. I hope you can make good use of the extra time."

Yakabuski smiled. That was it in a nutshell. People born and raised along the Northern Divide or the Upper Springfield Valley, they were never fooled about what was on offer in this world. You hoped to put together more good days than bad. You hoped if you worked hard, you could take care of your family. You accepted that you lived in a country that could kill you for the slightest of missteps, but you looked forward to waking up in that country every morning because that country never deceived you, never subjugated you, never claimed to be more than what it was. A tough country, but if you paid attention, you could find what you needed.

He squeezed her hands and said, "Yes, Madame, we will make good use of the extra time. I promise you."

She didn't say anything more. As life ebbed from her eyes, Yakabuski watched and hoped she had been given enough time herself to travel to the place all old people carry with them, the place they hope to be when the time comes, the memory they hope to leave with. He felt with a certainty that surprised him that Anita Diamond had gone back to Five Mile Camp.

CHAPTER
THIRTY-FOUR

He found the key to the handcuffs in Bangles' parka. The waitress was in shock when she was released, and Yakabuski held her to his chest, almost disappearing the girl.

"Breathe deep, child," he said. "Top to bottom. Move it down your spine." He breathed with her. "You're from Buckham's Bay, right?"

"Yeesss."

"Say the word in your head. *Buckham*. Let it fall apart. The syllables. Buck. Ham. Buck. Ham. Are you doing that?"

Against his chest, she nodded.

"Keep doing it. Keep breathing."

"Buck. Ham. Buck. Ham." Her teeth chattered, but after a few minutes, her speech slowed, the syllables landing further and further apart.

When she was asleep, the tree-marker scooped her into

his arms, turned to Yakabuski, and said, "I'm going to take her to one of the rooms. Get her out of here."

Yakabuski looked around at the bodies of John Holly and Tommy Bangles, Anita Diamond and Bobby Chance.

"Good idea," he said.

• • •

The man who had been calling himself Tobias O'Keefe did nothing to help. As Yakabuski talked down the waitress, as the tree-marker swaddled her in warm towels and took her to a room, he stood and watched them work. Just as often, he stared out the front window, the storm now passed and the sun come to bear late witness to the day.

He was not in shock. Yakabuski knew that. He was assessing. Not moving yet because he was not sure what his next move should be. Yakabuski went and stood beside him.

"You have the same name as your father?" he asked.

"No. Same as my grandfather. Thomas. I'm the third."

"Thomas O'Hearn the Third?"

"That's right. The waitress will be fine, by the way. I suspect you know that."

"I suspect. She's in good hands at the moment. I know that."

"I've seen plenty of people in shock. At one of the mills in Springfield, I once saw a man lose an arm. He stood there swearing at anyone who tried to approach him, telling them to back off, they were full of shit, nothing was wrong with him. He stood there swearing and throwing blood all over the place. He was lucky he didn't bleed out right on the floor."

"People react different when they're in shock. It depends

on what you're scared of in this world. Sounds like that fellow was scared of losing his job."

O'Hearn laughed. "I hadn't thought of that. I just thought he was crazy. What do you think the waitress was scared of?"

"Don't know if the girl needs much more than the last twenty minutes."

O'Hearn laughed again. He seemed to think nothing of it — being amused at life while the expanse of all possible things dimmed from the eyes of people dying around him; while they became finite and dead, with specimen-jar eyes where there had been living eyes only moments ago. Thought nothing of it.

The two men began to step carefully around the broken glass and busted furniture, making their way to the fireplace without conversation or question. As though it had been agreed upon earlier.

"So, what happens next?" asked O'Hearn, when they were standing by the hearth.

"The storm is over. Police will be coming on tomorrow's train. I suspect we'll have most of the force out here by the end of the day."

"They'll use planes?"

"They'll use anything that moves."

"Do we need to do anything before they get here?"

"No."

"The bodies?"

"They need to stay right where they are."

"So we are at rather loose ends until the police arrive?"

"No. We're waiting."

Yakabuski went to the timber box, rummaged around, and

took out the three largest pieces of pine he could find. He placed two on the embers, the third at his feet. Flames licked the wood almost immediately. Grew and ran in shifting patterns over the thick grain while sap began to bubble and ooze. The fire bloomed from yellow to orange to vermillion, and when there was a soft, shimmering cap of blue to the flames, Yakabuski added the third chunk of wood.

He sat down and examined his work. After a minute, he turned to O'Hearn and said, "Did you know Lucy Whiteduck was here when you came up, or did that come as a surprise?"

· · ·

It was as though the room changed when Yakabuski said it. A physical thing, not imagined. The walls contracted. The air grew thin. O'Hearn did not turn to look at him, and so Yakabuski kept talking.

"I'm inclined to think it was a surprise. That story you're telling about the mill reopening, it's true, isn't it? Otherwise, why would you have brought Garrett? I figure you saw her when they came in to cash that cheque last week. She saw Tommy Bangles, but she never saw you. That's a funny thing."

O'Hearn's face appeared tired when he finally turned to look at Yakabuski. When he spoke, his voice was flat and distant, like some radio signal you pull in late at night.

"What are you talking about, Detective?"

"How long had it been since you last saw her? Twelve years, right? Twelve years at least. Did you recognize her right away? I figure you must have. I don't think you could forget a face like that."

The room continued to change, the sounds of the Mattamy gathering around the two men like congregants summoned to a late-night service. The bass tick of a stand-up clock. The hum of a fluorescent light. The gurgle of water running in a pipe. It seemed the soft murmur of an orchestra pit before a performance.

"Life's strange, isn't it, Mr. O'Hearn?" continued Yakabuski. "Everything goes away but nothing really goes away, does it? Not in any true way. My dad thinks stuff goes away. He used to fish this lake. He told me once, when something is gone, it's gone. I think he was wrong about that. I think everything comes back. You can go years thinking you're free and clear of something, something bad from your past, maybe even convince yourself it never happened, then one day it just walks right in, sits down beside you, and says, 'Hey, remember me?'"

"Detective, I'm going to have to insist you start making some sense here, or I'll—"

"When did you know you were going to kill her?"

The last of the air whooshed out of the room. O'Hearn tried to rise from his chair but only stood a second before sitting back down, the sequence seeming feigned somehow. As though anger was an emotion from long ago that O'Hearn was having trouble recalling. He sat there moving his lips, but no sound came out.

"Did you know you were going to kill her as soon as you saw her? I'd like to know the answer to that one. It's one of only two questions I have left for you. So this shouldn't take long."

O'Hearn tried again to look angry. Then confused. Then he let a benevolent and slightly aggrieved expression settle upon his face before saying, "Detective Yakabuski, why don't you tell me what you think you have?"

And so he did.

. . .

Yakabuski began by saying he wasn't sure if Johnny Whiteduck knew from the start that O'Hearn was raping his daughter. He didn't think it mattered much. So that wasn't one of his two questions. Whiteduck certainly knew by the end, and sometimes that's all that matters. Foreknowledge, intent, things like that, are almost irrelevant when you're talking about raping little girls.

Yakabuski had done the math and come up with ten years. The age Lucy Whiteduck would have been when the young O'Hearn had first taken her to bed. It would have gone on the next three years, was the reason he came back to Ragged Lake every summer and one full year after graduation. That had nothing to do with his father. Nothing to do with love of the people who lived here. Everything to do with a beautiful, onyx-haired Indian girl and the way her body must have looked in shadows and dim light.

She didn't have much in the way of family, just her daddy, and her daddy wasn't stupid or a drunkard, so he must have known what was going on well enough. He must have been all right with it, too, so long as there was a mill around where he could be foreman. That's another funny thing about life. How often people build everything they have on lousy footings. Bad land. Stupid dreams.

Yakabuski doubted, given O'Hearn's age at the time, that

he wanted to kill Johnny Whiteduck. The decision was probably forced upon him. It was not learned behaviour yet, the way being nasty and brutish would become for men like him. He figured Whiteduck had tried to blackmail him.

"But he didn't know what kind of man he was dealing with, did he, Mr. O'Hearn?"

O'Hearn didn't say anything and Yakabuski didn't wait for an answer. "Your mistake was that you didn't kill her at the same time. You were young and stupid, so you did the murder, cleaned up, covered your tracks, went into hiding for a while, laying low. You would have done all that before it occurred to you that one murder wasn't going to solve your problem. You needed two.

"But by then she was gone. And you've spent a dozen years wondering if she might one day come back. So tell me, Mr. O'Hearn, did you know you were going to kill Lucy Whiteduck as soon as you saw her?"

Again, O'Hearn seemed slow to rise. Like some fat fish coming lazily off the shoals. He gave a long, languid roll of his head.

"For argument's sake, Detective — just to indulge you and only because I am extremely tired — what possible difference would that make? You are not asking if I killed the girl, only when I had decided to kill her. Do I have that right?"

"You do. And you're right; it won't make much difference. You'd be a murdering, narcissistic pedophile either way. It would just help me with the psychopath part."

The two men stared at each other a long time. Eventually, a small smile came to each face, first to O'Hearn's, then to Yakabuski's, and after that a tip of the head, almost in unison, an unspoken acknowledgement of work well done.

"You're wrong about Johnny," O'Hearn said, his voice sounding a little stronger. "You need to do a rethink on that one. It's always been a bit of mystery to me, what happened to Johnny Whiteduck. As for his daughter," and here O'Hearn stopped to make a lazy roll of his shoulders, working out some kinks in his neck, "I suppose I knew right away that I needed to kill her."

CHAPTER
THIRTY-FIVE

The gathered sounds of the Mattamy seemed to run up and down a sad minor scale. The bass tick of time. The mid-range of light. The high keen of water.

"The little girl was a surprise, then?"

"A complete surprise," said O'Hearn. "I had no idea there was a child in that cabin. I didn't see her when they came into the lodge."

"Did you kill her right away, too?"

"I don't think . . . you're doing people a favour when you're indecisive about certain things. You probably know that."

"How did you manage to get the jump on a man like Guillaume Roy?"

"Wasn't that hard, really. He struck me as a bit naïve. He invited me into the cabin. I got the impression he was worried about bikers, not someone like me."

"You used his shotgun."

"Yes."

"She wasn't there."

"That's right."

"What did you make her do when she got home?"

O'Hearn smiled again. But it was a sad sort of smile. Something distant and joyless. "Have you seen photos of Lucy? I have some that would quite amaze you."

"You're a sick bastard."

"Maybe. I'm not sure. But a question for you now, Detective Yakabuski. Do you really think any of this matters?"

Yakabuski leaned back in his chair, put his hands under his chin, and struck the pose of a man preparing to listen.

"You know what I'm going to say?" said O'Hearn.

"I suspect."

"Well, it's true. I will deny everything I've just said. If it ever came to court, it would be your word against mine. My lawyer will say you snapped under the pressure. Everyone at Ragged Lake was killed by bikers. That's a much more believable story than what you will be peddling."

Yakabuski looked at O'Hearn, then at his watch, wondering if he should take the time to argue. Go through the details with him. The various testimonies. The various witnesses. They had the time for it. But he decided he was too tired.

"You may be right about that, Mr. O'Hearn. But I'm still going to arrest you. There will be a trial. I will testify at the trial. Maybe you'll get off like you say, I'm not sure, but it won't happen until everyone in Springfield knows you like to sleep with little girls."

"But I'll be acquitted."

"Maybe. Won't stop people from knowing."

O'Hearn sat there, and the first honest emotion Yakabuski

had seen from the man seemed to come over him. His eyes registered quick surprise. His hands gripped the arm of the chair with enough force to turn his knuckles pinch-white. His brow furrowed, sculpting deep recesses in his forehead, lines that Yakabuski had not seen until then.

"I'm going to stop talking now," he said.

"Was Lucy the only one?"

"Detective, I must insist that—"

"Of course not. It never is. You look tired, Mr. O'Hearn. Tired and spent. You know that?"

"Where are you going with this?"

"Maybe you're tired of having a secret life. Maybe the best thing to do right now would be to not fight this. You're caught. Accept it."

O'Hearn laughed and rolled his eyes. His mannerisms again seemed feigned. "You have a gift for drama, Mr. Yakabuski. I thought that was an Irish failing, not a Polish one. Just to humour me, and only because we have the time, what was your second question?"

"Are you really going to reopen the mill? Is that the reason you're up here?"

"Why in the world would you care about something like that?"

"I'm curious to know if people are going back to work."

"What an odd man you are. Well, yes, if you're that curious, we are planning on reopening the mill. It is the reason I am here. The only reason I came here."

"Japanese magazines? That's what's going to get people back to work?"

"Yes."

"So what's going to happen when I arrest you for murder and rape? What's going to happen to those plans?"

Again, O'Hearn seemed caught off guard. He stammered at first and had to start over. "It would probably end them."

"O'Hearn is a publicly traded company. How do you think that will play out?"

"I'm not sure."

"I figure you're bankrupt. I figure the company is going to shut down. I figure your family is ruined. What do you figure, Mr. O'Hearn? You're big on figuring."

O'Hearn didn't say anything.

. . .

Yakabuski had accused the man of being tired, but he was probably more tired. Tired of living in a world where people who played by the rules always came out the losers, while people like Thomas O'Hearn III always came out the winners, and for no better or different reason than that people like O'Hearn were ruthless sociopaths with a piece missing inside them. A void that ensured they never cared about people and never lost sleep about anything they did to people, a missing piece that made them inhuman, successful, and rich.

Men like Thomas O'Hearn III not only destroyed people, they destroyed history and shared achievement, towns and communities, everything people had spent centuries building and treasuring. Yakabuski remembered a time when work, the survival and comfort of every working family, that was assured. You could shake hands on it. Now he looked around and saw people so frightened, so kicked around and debased, so worried about their futures, they might as well be foraging beasts. Meanwhile, people like O'Hearn kept buying ever-larger summer homes and sailing ships.

He had a chance to bring down O'Hearn and show him for the monster he was. Show everyone the fallacy in how people were behaving these days, trying to get ahead on whatever back was laid out in front of them. Like it was normal. Like it had to be done that way.

But by doing this, he would hurt the people he was trying to help, his family and neighbours, the ones he had sworn to protect and serve. *He* would be the one hurting them. Yakabuski was suddenly overcome with fatigue, a wet, soggy, two-thousand-pound sort of tired.

. . .

"You have a family, Mr. O'Hearn?"

"Two boys and a girl. You?"

"No children. Lots of everything else. They tell me it changes you, having children."

"It does."

"You love those children?"

"I do."

"You loved your father?"

"I did."

"You may have another option here."

"Would we be talking about a bribe?"

"No."

"I didn't think so."

"Are you interested?"

"Do I have a choice?"

"You have two of them."

Yakabuski took his service revolver from his parka pocket, ejected some shells, and put the gun on the table in front of them. Both men stared at it for a minute. The fire was now burning brightly, the shadows it cast broad and vibrant upon the wall.

"There's one bullet in the breach," said Yakabuski.

"What will your story be?"

"Bikers."

"But the tree-marker, the waitress . . ."

"The waitress won't recall anything. Leave the tree-marker to me."

O'Hearn stared at the gun.

After a few seconds, Yakabuski said, "Unless you have that gun pushed to the back of my head and I'm sitting here not doing anything about it, I wouldn't try it."

"I figured that. It makes sense what you're saying. I'm not sure I can do it."

"You must have considered it. With what you've been doing all these years. You must have considered your worst-case scenario."

"Many times. Never thought it would come today. You'll say it was bikers?"

"I'll say it was Tommy Bangles."

"He's the . . ."

"Teardrop tattoos."

O'Hearn stared over at Bangles' body and nodded.

"It seems so unnatural. Like nothing I would ever do."

"Do you need help?"

"You really don't think the tree-marker or the waitress—"

"I don't."

"It's a pity I won't be able to pass along any last words to my family."

"That can happen."

Yakabuski picked up the handgun, asked O'Hearn to turn his head. Before firing he said, "If it makes you feel any better, Mr. O'Hearn, this may be the only decent thing you've ever done."

FIREFLIES IN THE SNOW III

Yakabuski found the photos tucked inside the endpapers of
the journal, along with a sprig of dried flowers, although
it was hard to tell what type of flowers they may once
have been. Not roses.

He laid the photos on the bar. It was 4 a.m. The tree-
marker and the waitress were somewhere in the east wing.
Bodies lay where they had fallen, waiting for the Ident
cops that would be arriving in the morning. There would
be no sleep that night. He had not even tried.

The first photo was a group of people standing and
hoisting quarts of beer, surrounded by the wooden walls,
round tables, and *Pas des Drug* signs of a tavern in the
French Line. The old Claude Tavern perhaps. Or the
Richelieu. It looked vaguely familiar to Yakabuski. All
the people in the photo were Indian and their clothing

was dated. Stone-washed jeans. Gap T-shirts. All had Christmas garlands around their necks.

Yakabuski took his time scanning the photo — there were eleven people — although it was easy to spot him. He stood a couple of inches taller than everyone else. Dressed not in a T-shirt but what looked like a button-down oxford and a tie with a flying duck pattern on it. Johnny Whiteduck. Smiling, laughing, and getting ready to lead his band of late-night revellers on some Christmas folly, his eyes blazing like a cook fire, the strongest pigmentation left in the old photo, the maniacal eyes of the handsome man in the foreground.

He had his left arm thrown around a woman a good head and a half shorter. She had sleek black hair that she wore long. Not one but two Christmas garlands wrapped around her neck. She wore a tight red sweater. There was no date on the photo. No names. It was creased and worn and almost like newsprint.

The next photo was that of a teenage girl. This photo had a date on the back — August 2, 2004 — along with a man's name and a stamp from Family Support Services, the child welfare agency in Springfield.

The girl was beautiful. More than that. She possessed a beauty that was extraordinary, a face so perfect it stopped you from breathing for a second, left you searching for the right word to describe her, so inadequate would language suddenly seem in comparison to what was right there in front of you.

Lucy Whiteduck. At the age of sixteen.

There was a smile on her face but only slight. She stared straight ahead. No tilt to the head or slouch to

the spine. A confident girl. Yet not the confidence you
often see in attractive children who have found the world
pleasant and welcoming, every journey an easy stroll on
level ground, every door wide open. Something different.
Something earned and claimed. Yakabuski stared at the
photo a long time, wondering what a girl like that could
do with a full life.

The next photo was of Guillaume Roy. His hair
was clipped short and he wore the maroon beret of the
Special Forces Regiment. Yakabuski went down the
line of medals on his chest — Bosnia Service Medal,
Meritorious Conduct Medal, the disbandment medal
given to members of the old Airborne Regiment. Just like
Lucy Whiteduck, Roy stared straight ahead, unflinching,
no slackness to his posture, no give to his face. You could
see in the line of the jaw, and the eyes perhaps — a dark
denim blue that had not faded over the years — a hint of
the man Yakabuski had found in the squatters' cabin. But
only a hint. And only when you stared long and hard at
the photo and used your imagination.

Two government-issue photos. Yakabuski looked from
one to the other and wondered if there had been more, if
these two had been chosen for safekeeping because she'd
liked them best. It took him only a few seconds to decide
that, no, they probably wouldn't have had more.

The fourth photo had another date on the back —
May 9, 2013 — although there was something old-looking
about it. It had been taken in a photo booth, the kind
you used to see in drugstores and bus stations. Yakabuski
figured he knew the location of every photo booth in
Springfield — there were only three left — so he was

pretty sure the photo had been taken at the Stedman's in Sandy Hill. A store close to where Lucy Whiteduck had lived.

Her beauty had not diminished from the teenage photo taken years earlier by some bureaucrat at Family Support Services. Her hair was still the hue of a northern lake when summer had gone but winter not yet come, the way deep dark water looks when lit at night by stars and a low moon. Her skin was the colour of white sand after a light rain. Her eyes were almond coloured, if you were pressed to use only one word, a shade of light brown he had rarely seen before.

Guillaume sat next to her. His hair had grown out and he looked a bit like Kurt Cobain, a handsome man, though his face was heavily lined and he looked older than what Yakabuski knew him to be. He seemed happy. His arm was thrown around Lucy and he was looking at her, not the camera, leaning in so as to suggest the next photo would be him kissing her cheek. But there was only the one picture, not the strip you always get at a photo booth. Yakabuski wondered what they might have done with the other photos, but no answer seemed right to him.

In the middle of the photo, sitting on Lucy's lap, was the girl. A newborn that you could tell was going to look like her mother. Her hair was black. The eyes soft brown. Whiteduck was holding the child in a way that kept her head erect, her small, unfocused eyes turned to the flash, making it seem the girl knew what was happening, was posing for the camera, cognizant and curious, ready for her grand adventure.

It was a difficult photo to look at, knowing the family's fate, but Yakabuski kept staring at it, looking for signs they might have known what was coming. Or that one of them knew, perhaps even the child. Yakabuski believed such a thing might be possible, that knowledge could migrate by way of genes, synapse, and blood, not only by experience and knowledge; that there was such a thing as primeval intuition in this world and he had known and believed in such things ever since he'd learned that song-birds returned to the same Mexican river every winter. Would a child knowing its fate be any stranger than that? Would it seem unnatural by comparison?

But he never found a clue. Never found himself looking at anything more than a bus station photo of a happy couple with a newborn baby.

Shortly before sunrise, much to his later surprise, Frank Yakabuski fell asleep.

CHAPTER
THIRTY-SIX

Yakabuski never doubted the tree-marker, what the boy would say when police arrived. The first ones came on the 11 a.m. train from High River, and by dusk, Ragged Lake resembled Springfield on a Saturday night. Red and blue flashing lights. The low rumble of cold engines. The whir of metal. The shouts of people in a panic.

Twenty-one dead. That was the final tally, confirmed only five days later when an Ident team could safely get into the basement of the meth lab and found the body of a woman, never identified. It was a crime scene none of the cops had seen or contemplated before, a majestic, soaring, incomprehensible cockup that filled most of them with awe despite their best efforts to be repulsed. They simply could not help themselves. There was something about Ragged Lake that gave their work an import and grandeur they had never experienced before. As though they had just landed in one of the bad days of history.

No cop asked as much as a follow-up question when the tree-marker said he didn't know how Thomas O'Hearn III had died. He'd just showed up dead. Like everyone else.

. . .

The story was front-page news across the country, international news for many days, the police not the only ones left incredulous by the scale of what had happened in Ragged Lake. The funeral for O'Hearn was covered by media outlets as far away as Japan, each one going with a narrative of O'Hearn being a folk hero for coming to the Northern Divide in the dead of winter to personally oversee the reopening of a shuttered pulp and paper mill. A rich scion who had loved this blue-collar town. Who had once worked at the mill. O'Hearn was cast as a corporate do-gooder tragically caught in the wrong place at the wrong time, a victim of quirky fate, as though he had died in an airplane crash while delivering medical supplies to a remote African village.

The funeral was lavish, the reception the social event of the season, and the opening of the Ragged Lake mill became a thing ordained. It happened that July, after a $15 million retrofit. Within a month it was running two shifts. O'Hearn had been overly cautious in his estimations.

. . .

Police officers from four different agencies stayed in Ragged Lake until spring to finish the forensic work. The last ones left the weekend after pickerel season opened. The owners of the Mattamy had planned to tear down the main wing of the lodge and build something new, so there would be no reminders of what had happened, but before they could get started and right after the S and P was firm enough to allow for automobile traffic, the town was overrun with visitors. Late-to-the-story journalists. Bike-gang cultists. Tourists attracted by the brutality of what had happened, who would be visiting the OK Corral next summer. People who came to stay at the Mattamy because of what everyone agreed after a few weeks should be called "The Battle of Ragged Lake" outnumbered fishermen for several years. The owners kept the bar and restaurant. Added rooms to the east and west wings.

• • •

Tommy Bangles' cellphone was encrypted, and so it was sent to a lab in Toronto for analysis. In mid-April, Yakabuski got a phone call from an investigator who said they had managed to lift a couple of numbers from the phone. One traced back to Sean Morrissey. The other was a mystery. It seemed to be a working number. No way of knowing where it was located, and they had been working on it for weeks. They figured they had one chance to call the number before it disappeared for all time. They had a meeting the day before to decide who might be the best person to place the call. Yakabuski won the vote.

"I'm sure it's all academic, Detective," the investigator said. "There is no way we're getting a physical location from this number. We rarely get that lucky, and this is one mother-protected number. Some people down here are in awe of it. At the same time, we shouldn't assume failure, right? We should at least have someone place a call, someone who might stand a chance of keeping the other person talking. You got picked."

"Why?"

The investigator shrugged. "We're pissing in the dark. But you killed Tommy Bangles. Maybe someone is angry enough about that to cuss you out a bit."

"A full meeting for that?"

"Lunch too. But aren't you a little curious, Detective? I understand Bangles may have talked to you about some new partners he and Morrissey had taken on. Before he died."

"He did."

"Well, this could be one of those people. What do you say? We're all set up on our end. We can place the call right now. You just have to stay on the line with me."

"All right."

There were some clicking sounds, and then the phone started ringing. It rang a long time and then stopped. Yakabuski thought the call had failed, but then he heard a man sigh and say, "Detective Yakabuski. I was about to give up on you."

"You were expecting my call?"

"Yes. It would have given me great happiness to have thrown away this phone. To have misjudged you. But I knew I had not. So, the thing I have been waiting to tell you: Move on, my friend. Consider Ragged Lake your lucky break."

"Don't know if I can do that."

"Why not? I hear you are a smart man."

"Two dead cops."

"You wish to make it three?"

"I'll find you."

"I don't think so. And why should you bother? You came out a winner in Ragged Lake. Why tempt fate?"

"Lots of dead people. I figure there should be some sort of accounting for a thing like that."

"Why? Lots of dead people everywhere. Sometimes lots of dead people because of you, my friend."

"Quit calling me your friend. Tommy said you were some new sort of whacked-out freak. Something truly fuckin' evil. Now that I'm talking to you, I think you're a pussy. Sitting miles from the action and talking big. Like some pussy general."

Yakabuski heard a longer sigh this time. The man sounded older when he spoke again, although Yakabuski had trouble deciding how old.

"I have been to Springfield. Do you know that? Many times. I am not a ghost on the phone. You have a good city. A good country. A great big country where a man can disappear, forget about his sins. It is a country made for absolution. Go away, Detective. Forget this ever happened."

"I have a better plan. Why don't I track you down and piss in your fuckin' mouth."

Again there was a long pause before the man spoke. But no sigh this time. No tired voice. "Come after me, and you are a dead man," he said. "You and everyone you hold dear. Your sister. Your crippled father. That is a promise I make to you, my friend."

Nothing more was said. A moment later, the investigator from Toronto was back, breathless and excited.

"My man, did you hear that? Did you flipping hear that?"

"I heard that."

"That was flipping gangster shit. Right out of the movies."

"Were you able to trace the call?"

"What? Oh, no. Fuck no. Worth a shot, though, right?"

Yakabuski didn't bother answering.

. . .

That June, when no one came forward to claim the bodies of Guillaume Roy, Lucy Whiteduck, or their daughter, Yakabuski made arrangements with the coroner to have the bodies cremated. He picked up the cardboard urns at a crematory company in an industrial park near the Nosoto Projects one Saturday morning and drove to Strathconna Park. He took ash from each urn and tossed it into the Springfield River. By a kayak course. Yakabuski took a minute to look at the kayakers bob down the strong current of the river, twisting and turning, their colourful rain gear flashing through the mist and spray.

He spoke to a city worker and borrowed a spade. Took what was left of the ashes and combined them in one urn, and this he buried beneath a crabapple tree in late bloom. The city worker was going to say something about the burial, but Yakabuski showed him his badge, and so the boy stood silent until the job was finished.

"That looks like a good, healthy tree," said Yakabuski, when he returned the spade.

"It is. 'Bout ten years old. They have great roots, those apple trees."

"How long do they live?"

"They bear fruit for forty, fifty years, live a long time after that. There's apple trees just like it on the other side of the river that have probably been there since before the Shiners."

Yakabuski thanked the boy for the use of the spade and left the park.

· · ·

Later that summer O'Hearn also reopened one of its shut-down Springfield mills. A few months after, the tree-marker began working there, a decision that surprised Yakabuski when he first heard of it but made sense when he met the boy for drinks two weeks before Christmas. The tree-marker brought the waitress. She looked to be in her third trimester.

"When is the baby due?" he asked.

"End of January," Marie answered.

"Do you know yet if it's a boy or a girl?"

"No, we want to be surprised."

"I would think you'd had your fill of surprises this year, Marie. I'd like to know what colour to paint the nursery."

They laughed, and Yakabuski turned to the tree-marker. "So how's the mill treating you?"

"Treating me well. It's steady work. Pays well. I like it enough."

"Miss the bush?"

"Every day. Never cared for the city much. Some days, things don't seem quite right down here."

"I know what you're saying. Feels broken some days, doesn't it? I remember when everything seemed to work in Springfield. People had jobs. People paid their bills. I don't know when that stopped working. It still surprises me that it did. The thing we had, you'd have thought we would have looked after it a bit better."

They ate what the waiter called gourmet burgers, which were beef patties covered in sauces you didn't need, and sweet potato fries instead of regular potato fries, another change Yakabuski didn't think was an improvement. But the coffee was good and strong, and the tree-marker insisted on paying the bill, so he considered it a pleasant enough evening.

He drank his coffee and waited. As soon as he had seen the waitress, he knew why the tree-marker had called. He knew what the boy needed to say. But it wasn't until they were out on the street that it happened. They had already said their goodbyes, and Marie was walking a few paces ahead, heading toward the boy's truck, when he suddenly grabbed Yakabuski's hand one last time and shook it.

"We'll always be grateful for what you did in Ragged Lake, Mr. Yakabuski. I want you to know that."

"Don't need to mention it."

"I never will. You have my word on that." The boy leaned in to whisper, "We're good, right?"

"We're good, son."

The boy was positively beaming when he ran to his truck. Yakabuski tried not to smile. It was what a tree-marker would do before he started a family.

• • •

On his way home, Yakabuski stopped at the hospital. His father had been at St. Michael's more than a month, a bad infection in his hips that had gone internal. At its worst, he was incubated for three days. That was two weeks ago, and he was much improved. But he would still be staying at the hospital over Christmas.

It was past visiting hours but the nurse at the charge station buzzed him in, and Yakabuski found his dad sitting in his wheelchair, looking out the window of his room. A paperback copy of *Cape Fear* lay open on his lap.

"Late for you to be dropping by," he said.

"Went out for dinner. Thought I'd come see you on my way home."

"Who did you have dinner with?"

"The tree-marker and the waitress from Ragged Lake."

"How are they doing?"

"All right. She's pregnant. They'll be parents in about two months."

"Good parents?"

"I suspect."

"So maybe something good came out of all this."

"That would be a charitable way of looking at things."

"Yes," his father said, still staring out the window, the moon two days past full, the city beneath it. "I suppose you're right about that. How are *you* doing?"

"I'm all right. I spread the ashes a few months back. Don't know if I told you that. The family that got killed. She pretty much said in her journal where she wanted to go."

"Strathconna Park."

"That's right."

When Yakabuski signed for the bodies, he had been given a bag of personal effects. The journal was in it. His father asked if he could read it, and Yakabuski had given it to him. An old cop wanting to read a case file. Yakabuski had not seen any harm in it.

"That's a lovely park," said his dad, still staring at the moon. "She lived nearby, right?"

"Sandy Hill. It would have been just a few blocks away."

His father nodded but didn't say anything. They sat in silence until Yakabuski said, "Tommy Bangles said there was some new sort of evil out there. Something I'd never seen before. Said it was coming. I wonder sometimes if he was right. If good people are doomed and we just don't know it yet."

"I wouldn't spend a lot of time thinking about anything Tommy Bangles said. The guy was a fuckin' creep."

"But did you ever see anything like Ragged Lake? In all your years?"

"No, can't say I ever did."

"So maybe something new is coming. Maybe he was right."

"I don't know, Frankie. I think you're tired. And you're thinking too much. You look tired to me."

"I am tired. Doesn't make me wrong."

"No, but it doesn't do you any good, either. I don't think good people are doomed. You just told me the tree-marker is a stand-up guy. About to start a family. You just told me that, right?"

"I did."

"Well, things aren't as hopeless as you think."

They fell quiet again until his father, turning finally from the window to look at his son, said, "And stop beating yourself up about that girl. There's nothing you could have done to save her."

"What makes you so sure?"

"I've read the journal, Frankie. You missed something."

321

EPILOGUE

The following spring, Yakabuski returned to Ragged Lake.

Bernard O'Toole had trouble believing it when Yakabuski said their investigation wasn't finished. But he said nothing. Yakabuski had a wide berth in the police department now; he was looked upon as a folk hero by many and with open mistrust by many others, the older ones mostly, who were suspicious of any multiple-homicide crime scene that wrapped up so neatly no one was left standing to bring to court. To the chief, his senior detective had become a mystery. He found himself choosing his words carefully around him.

"You'll drive up?" O'Toole asked.

"Thinking 'bout this weekend. I'll need a couple bodies."

"I can arrange that. Do you want them to meet you there?" The question was an assumption. That Yakabuski would prefer going up alone. That the other cops would prefer that arrangement, too.

"That works. Tell them to meet me at Cap Lake, noon, Saturday."

• • •

When the two cops arrived with the backhoe, Yakabuski got them to start digging around the cabin. Any raised patch of ground. The backhoe moved from spot to spot like some ungainly animal. The lake in the background was still ringed by ice.

Why here? Yakabuski had been asking himself that question for more than a year. He had spent a long time wondering if Guillaume Roy had simply miscalculated, misread the terrain somehow, only to reach the conclusion he reached the day he read the man's service file. No, he would not have made that mistake.

So why build your cabin on the lowest, darkest point of an otherwise beautiful lake? Yakabuski had considered various possibilities, right up to Roy going mad, becoming coco, as some in Ragged Lake believed. But he couldn't accept it. The answer did not have the completeness you feel when things are right and proper, when they're running true.

Then he reread the journal, as his father had suggested, and it came to him. The obvious answer. It wasn't Roy who had chosen the spot. It had been her.

• • •

When the backhoe was finished with the high ground, Yakabuski got the cops to dig every six feet in a circular pattern starting fifty yards from the cabin and working inwards.

They dug the rest of the day, stopping only when the sun had dipped below the treeline, forcing them to drive down the rail line to Ragged Lake in darkness. They booked into the Mattamy and, after saying he was tired, Yakabuski went straight to his room.

That night he had a dream, a first-time dream, which was rare for his age. He saw his father the morning after they had camped by the abandoned bush camp on Ragged Lake, hooking a muskie on his second pass, a huge fish, a serpent the boy thought when it was brought aboard, his father laughing and hoisting the muskie above his head like a trophy, splashing water all over himself, the boat, his son. The boy finally laughing along with his father because surely this was a good thing. Even as the fish snapped and lunged at him.

He dreamed of Five Mile Camp the way it must have looked in the '80s and '90s, with hundreds of people living on the banks of the Old Duck, fish being smoked in pits scattered in the mud along the shoreline, brightly coloured cottages seen among the spruce. No fences anywhere. Then he saw the mill, men in dark-green factory clothes smoking by a gate. Hundreds of smoking men. Shortly before dawn his dream turned to scenes of bad weather. A late afternoon thunderstorm in High River. The Clyde River swelling its banks and washing away the village of Snow Lake, which actually did happen back in '32, killing more than forty people. Then came a snowstorm, a bad one, first at Snow Lake but then the land changed, the dream shifted, and he was back in Ragged Lake.

The dead were marching past him. Lucy Whiteduck, Guillaume Roy, Cassandra Roy, Roselyn and Gaetan Tremblay,

Donnie Buckham, Matt Downey, John Holly, Tommy Bangles, Bobby Chance. Twenty-three ghosts marching through the snowstorm with heads turned down and eyes fixed to a point six inches in front of their feet. Turning for only the briefest of seconds when they were parallel to Yakabuski to look into his face, then turning their heads away and continuing their slow march through the storm.

When they were gone, the dream shifted one last time, and Yakabuski found himself standing in front of the squatters' cabin. He saw a flash of light inside. Then two more flashes, and suddenly light was exploding around him, skittering dots of light flying around his head, his legs, his arms. The dots faded one by one until only a handful were left, and these final dots did not fade like the others but flew in ever-higher circles until Yakabuski lost sight of them.

It took a long time. He counted them twice. To make sure he was not mistaken about the number of dots that had flown away. Four.

When he awoke the next morning, the answer was right there in his head, waiting for him.

• • •

Yakabuski sipped his coffee and watched the cabin come down. The backhoe made clumsy, spirited runs into the walls until the beer-tin roof started to sag, then collapsed with a noise so loud it scared grey jays from their nests on the other side of the lake.

Who are we to judge, he thought. We each have complicated relationships with the ones we love. Offer remembrance and pay homage in different ways. Maybe it was possible for a heinous crime to be the foundation for love and family. The actual physical foundation.

"Where do you want us to start digging?" one of the cops shouted after the cabin had been pushed to the shoreline.

"Dead centre," he yelled back.

They found the body less than five minutes later. Even from the lip of the freshly dug hole, Yakabuski could see the faded duck pattern on the tie around the skeleton's neck.

He could never say with certainty if Roy knew what he had done. If he had been part of the secret. For a long time, he sought an answer to that question, believing it would reveal some grand truth about love and place, some arcane secret about family and home and secret deeds done on abandoned frontiers long ago. A sort of Book of Deeds for the country.

But it never came. In time, Yakabuski accepted what had happened at Ragged Lake, deciding in a way that seemed silly and illogical to him — although the conclusion always seemed right — that what was meant to happen had simply happened.

He came to feel much the same about the murder of Johnny Whiteduck, deciding after he had thought it through some, that the girl had good reason.

© Julie Oliver

Ron Corbett is an author, journalist, and broadcaster. He is the author of seven non-fiction books, including the Canadian bestseller *The Last Guide* and the critically praised *First Soldiers Down* about Canada's deployment to Afghanistan. A father of four, he is married to award-winning photojournalist Julie Oliver. This is his first novel.